SCREAM OF SILENCE

BRYAN CASSIDAY

Bryan Cassiday
Los Angeles
ISBN 9798988189527
Published in the United States of America
First Edition: June 11, 2024

BOOKS BY BRYAN CASSIDAY

Burn Hot Burn Long (Apocalypse City Book 2)
Hotbed (Apocalypse City Book 1)
Zombie Apocalypse: The Chad Halverson Series 1–7
Cutthroat Express (Zombie Apocalypse: The Chad Halverson
Series Book 7)
Knot of Fear (Scott Brody Thriller 5)
Threads (Scott Brody Thriller 4)
Electric Green Mambas (Scott Brody Thriller 3)
Horde (Zombie Apocalypse: The Chad Halverson Series Book 6)
Ice in the Blood
Crime Blotter USA
Murder LLC (Scott Brody Thriller 2)
Bolt (Scott Brody Thriller 1)
Riptide of Fear
The Payout
Force of Impact (Ethan Carr Thriller 3)
Dying to Breathe (Ethan Carr Thriller 2)
Countdown to Death (Ethan Carr Thriller 1)
The Bus Stops Here—and Other Zombie Tales
Two Moons Rising
Alien Assault
Comes a Chopper
Zombie Apocalypse: The Chad Halverson Series 1–5
Helter Skelter
The Anaconda Complex
The Kill Option
Blood Moon: Thrillers and Tales of Terror
Fete of Death

BRYAN CASSIDAY

"When she saw what she had done
She gave her father forty-one."—Children's rhyme

Chapter 1

He wouldn't wish this job on his worst enemy, decided Gordon, sitting in his nondescript black rental Toyota Camry, staking out his victim's house, gripping a silenced SIG P224 in one hand and a half-empty box of McDonald's fries in the other. An empty, grease-mottled Big Mac wrapper lay crumpled in the passenger's-side footwell beside a waxed cup of leftover Coke losing its fizz.

People thought being a hit man was glamorous on account of the movies. Some chiseled-jawed assassin flying all over the world in private jets, knocking back champagne, and driving the latest-model Ferrari as he collects millions from his contract to kill and stashes the dough in a numbered Swiss bank account.

Gordon, who looked rather ordinary, owned neither a private jet nor a Swiss bank account and ate at McDonald's and Burger King. Movies . . .

In reality most of the time the job was boring, watching your target and planning when to strike.

Gordon had been sitting in his rental for over two hours, waiting for Childress to return home. Gordon had found out from a tap on Childress's phone that Childress should have returned an hour ago from his business meeting in New York.

No sign of Childress outside his Craftsman house in Brentwood, California, as Gordon watched the house from his rental, which he had parked across the street.

Gordon's legs were getting stiff from so much sitting. He needed to get out and take a walk. But he didn't want to be seen in this tony neighborhood, the site of his hit. The first thing the cops would look for after the hit would be a stranger spotted in the neighborhood.

He wished he had the ability and the talent to work at a different profession. But wishing changed nothing. *If wishes were horses, beggars would ride*, his mother used to say. He had to work with what he had to make a living. He was able to whack people and get away with it—so far anyway. It was a talent not everybody had. Not everyone could kill another human being. Very few would want to.

Gordon didn't want to kill anyone, but he needed a paycheck. He had to pay bills. He had to pay the mortgage. He didn't want to think about it. He was late with the first payment on his new house in the Hollywood Hills. Karen would never forgive him if the bank foreclosed on the house.

They had just moved in, and Karen loved the flamingo pink Spanish-styled stucco bungalow with its red pantile roof and black grilled windows perched on the side of a hill overlooking Hollywood and Los Angeles. On a clear day they could see the Pacific Ocean to the west. His ten-year-old son Brady loved it too.

Gordon needed the paycheck on this latest assignment to whack Childress to pay the mortgage. He only wished the paycheck was bigger. It wasn't like in the movies where the contract killer got at least a million bucks for a hit.

Gordon didn't make anywhere near that much. Enough to pay this month's mortgage—if Childress ever showed up.

Gordon scoped out the neighborhood of Spanish-styled bungalows, Craftsman houses, and ramblers set among arching palms, waxy-leafed magnolias, and drooping eucalyptuses. Childress lived a mere half mile from Marilyn Monroe's house at the cul-de-sac on Fifth Helena Drive.

Gordon had been sitting here too long. The neighbors were bound to get suspicious. This was the kind of exclusive neighborhood that hired private security to keep an eye on things.

Gordon didn't know what was keeping Childress.

Gordon heaved a sigh. He would have to leave. He couldn't risk being braced by rent-a-cops. If they made him here, he wouldn't be able to go through with the hit without implicating himself as a prime suspect.

He didn't want to leave. He wanted to get this over with. No hit meant no paycheck. But he had been here too long.

He scoped out the quiet street one more time. No sign of Childress.

He shouldn't make the hit here anyway, he realized. What was he thinking? It was never a good idea to whack out someone at their own house. Neighbors would remember any strangers in the hood.

It was a better idea to target a victim in a public area teeming with strangers who didn't know each other. He could blend in with the strangers, blow away Childress, and flee without getting caught.

This was a mistake. He hadn't thought it out clearly because he was in too much of a rush to claim his paycheck and avoid foreclosure. He had to plan his hit better. *Festina lente.* Make haste slowly, the motto of Augustus. Sage advice.

Gordon had to beat it.

Sweat beading on his face, he fired the ignition and peeled out.

This was madness coming here. Was he losing it? It was the pressure of his overdue mortgage that had made him act rashly. Of course, that was it. He had dealt with pressure before. Why had he screwed up this time?

He wasn't himself lately. Maybe moving to a new house had tired him out.

Driving away from the neighborhood he breathed easier. He wasn't losing it. The point was he *hadn't* screwed up. He hadn't gone through with the hit. He had realized his mistake in the nick of time and had cut and run.

It was all good.

Chapter 2

Childress was a corrupt judge pushing fifty, Gordon knew.

The enraged Zetas cartel wanted him dead because he was taking graft from the Jalisco New Generation cartel and showing them favoritism in his rulings. On the other hand, Childress refused to take bribes from the Zetas and doled out stiff sentences to them.

It was the Zetas who had hired Gordon to take out Childress.

Gordon couldn't blame the Zetas. They had a legitimate beef. Since Childress was corrupt, why wouldn't he accept the Zeta bribes? Not that it was any of Gordon's business. The reason a client was hiring him didn't matter to him. What mattered was the target deserved to be punished.

Gordon didn't take contracts on the innocent. In actuality it was rare that any target was innocent. Clients had no reason to whack the innocent. It was the corrupt, the ones with money and power, that his clients wanted dead, because it was the corrupt that caused clients problems.

The innocent were broke and minded their own business. Nobody was going to put out a contract on them, Gordon knew.

Rumor had it that Childress was supporting a high-maintenance mistress in West Hollywood, which explained his greased palms.

The guy was a crook, even if he served as a judge. Gordon had no problem whacking crooks. He also had no problem accepting the cartel's money. Money was money. It belonged to anyone who could get it, including contract killers, no matter where it came from.

Not that Gordon liked wasting people. He didn't. It was a job. Someone had to do it. Why not him? He could kill people without regrets, just like a plumber could replace a faucet without regrets. Not a whole lot of people could bring themselves to pull the trigger on a fellow human being. Gordon was one of the few who possessed that talent.

Besides, Childress was guilty of corruption. A good reason not to feel regrets about whacking him.

Gordon drove back to his bungalow in the Hollywood Hills. He hoped nobody had made him parked in Childress's neighborhood.

What had he been thinking? How could he have made such a blunder as planning to whack a target at home?

Maybe he had been lucky Childress was late. Otherwise, Gordon might have gone through with his hit—which would have been disastrous thanks to poor planning.

He drove east on the winding Sunset Boulevard to Hollywood then north on Highland Avenue into the hills, negotiating switchbacks and hairpin turns.

He drove up the pebbled driveway to his home, killed the engine, clambered out of the rental, plodded through the white pebbles, and entered the living room.

Karen greeted him. "I thought I heard you drive up."

"How do you like our new house?"

Clad in jeans and an oyster button-down blouse, she was all of five six. She was thirty-two years old with grey eyes and shoulder-length blond hair.

They hugged.

"Could I show you something?" she said mysteriously.

"Sure."

She led him to the front of a closet in the hallway near the center of the house.

"Do you feel it?" she said, shivering.

"Feel what?"

"It's freezing here."

It did feel cold, he realized.

"Probably a draft from an open window somewhere," he said, looking around.

"There isn't a draft here." She stuck her hand in front of her. "It's right here where it's coldest."

He followed her example.

"Maybe it's coming up from the floor," he said. "There could be cracks in the floorboards."

He scrutinized the hardwood floor, searching for cracks.

"It's a nice day outside," she said. "Why's it so cold in this spot? The rest of the house is nice and comfy."

"I wouldn't worry about it. I'm sure there's a logical explanation. The ground's probably cold. The cold is rising—"

"Cold air doesn't rise. Hot air rises."

Gordon looked at the ceiling. "Then maybe it's coming from the next floor."

"Our bedroom. It's not cold up there."

He grinned. "So is it a deal-breaker?"

"No, no. I love this house. The view by itself is worth the price. It's breathtaking," she said, walking to the picture window, taking in LA lying at their feet.

"I know," he said, following her.

"You're back early from work today."

She thought he worked as a security consultant. He had never told her his real profession as a contract killer. He didn't think it would go over well. He had to live a double life.

"It was a slow day," he said. "The boss said we could go home early."

"Did he pay you the mortgage?"

"Not yet."

She pouted. "I'd hate to have to move out of here."

"We're not moving," he said, hoping it was true, hoping he could pay the mortgage as soon as he got paid for his next hit.

"What's that noise? It sounds like humming."

Karen padded down the hallway in her sneakers and halted in front of the bathroom doorway, her face screwed up with curiosity. She entered the bathroom.

Gordon started when he heard her scream.

Chapter 3

She stumbled out of the bathroom into the hall, her face blanketed with flies. She swatted at the flies to keep them off her face. Her eyes watered as flies flew into them. The buzzing of the flies created an uproar. She swatted bluebottles out of her hair. They corkscrewed around her head.

Gordon couldn't discern her face on account of all the flies swarming over it.

Karen choked. She coughed a cloud of flies out of her mouth. She was forced to breathe through her mouth because her nostrils were stuffed with flies. She coughed out scores of flies. She hunched forward and retched.

Gordon's son, Brady, sprinted toward her from the other end of the hall.

"What's wrong, Mom?" he said. "What's happening?"

Gordon pelted to Karen. He helped her swat the buzzing flies away from her face. She coughed another cloud of flies out of her mouth as she tried to speak. She couldn't talk. The flies were jamming her throat. She gasped for breath, allowing more flies to fly into her mouth.

"Why are they targeting only you?" said Gordon.

Karen shook her head, baffled.

"We need to get you out of here," said Gordon, grabbing her waist and hustling her down the hallway toward the front door.

Hundreds of flies kept hovering around her head, following her.

Gordon feared she would suffocate if she didn't get air soon.

He burst out the front door with her into the front yard. He hoped the breeze would disperse the bluebottles that kept caroming off her face and trying to enter her nostrils and mouth.

Karen dropped to her knees and threw up.

Gordon swatted at the flies around her head, shooing them away. He didn't know what else to do. He couldn't very well spray her face with insecticide without poisoning her. He had to think fast. He had to get the flies off her before they suffocated her. Why were they attacking her anyway? Flies didn't attack humans.

He would have to figure it out later. He had to save her life first.

"Get the hose, Brady," he said.

"Hose?" said Brady, confused.

"You heard me. Hurry."

"Where is it?"

That was right, decided Gordon. Brady was new to the house. He didn't know where everything was.

"On the side of the house," said Gordon, pointing.

Brady ran to the outdoor faucet, which had a green plastic hose coiled beneath it.

Hunkered over, Karen vomited again on the front lawn. A mixture of her stomach contents and flies gushed out of her mouth. She was trying to clear her throat of the flies so she could breathe.

In an attempt to disperse them Gordon swatted at the flies swarming around her head.

Brady hauled the unwinding hose to him.

"Here, Dad."

Gordon snagged the nozzle. "Go back and turn on the faucet."

Brady scampered back to the brass faucet and turned it on.

Gordon sprayed cold water on Karen's head, trying to wash the flies away from her face. The water pressure wasn't strong enough.

"Turn it on all the way," he told Brady.

"I did," said Brady, struggling to turn the handle farther without success.

Gordon covered half of the nozzle aperture with his thumb to increase the water pressure as he sprayed Karen's fly-blanketed face. The gushing water forced the flies away from her head. She threw up another cluster of flies combined with half-digested food and suffered a coughing jag.

Gordon brought the nozzle within inches of her face and sprayed the remaining flies from her eyes and nose.

Coughing, Karen gasped for breath, her mouth clear of the invading flies.

Straggler flies circling her head broke off and flew in pursuit of the rest of the horde which was in full retreat, repelled by the constant onslaught of water.

"What the hell happened?" Karen managed to say through a tense throat, her face flushed.

"You tell me," said Gordon.

He signaled to Brady to cut the water.

"I walked into the bathroom, and ten thousand flies attacked me," she said. "They were all over the place."

"Maybe there's a hole in the screen in the bathroom window. We'll have to put in a new screen."

"Why were there so many of them? And why did they attack me?"

Gordon chewed it over. "Maybe the smell of your shampoo attracted them."

"The smell of coconut drives them into a frenzy?" she said, incredulous.

"I guess."

"It felt like they were trying to kill me. They were flying in my nose and mouth, trying to smother me."

"I doubt it was deliberate. The scent of your shampoo attracted them."

"They sounded angry. The way they were buzzing. It was so loud. They were furious with me."

"I never heard of flies attacking anyone."

Karen rubbed water off her forehead and wiped dead flies from her eyes.

"It's lucky they weren't hornets," said Brady, wide-eyed.

"Then I'd be dead from stings," said Karen, and laughed at the absurdity of being killed by flies. "I can see my obit in the newspaper now. Cause of death of thirty-two-year-old Karen. A thousand flies attacked and killed her."

Brady giggled.

Gordon felt the tension ease from his body. He smiled with amusement.

"The first recorded death by flies," he announced like a pompous newscaster.

Sopping wet, Karen wrung her hands and blew water from her face.

The three of them headed back to the house.

"I need a shower," said Karen, "but I'm not going back into that bathroom."

"I'll spray it with insecticide," said Gordon, draping his arm around her sodden shoulders.

"I'll use the bathroom upstairs."

"Good idea."

"It seems funny now, but I have to admit I was scared to death. I couldn't breathe or see, the flies were so thick around my face. It was like having my head stuck inside a beehive with all that deafening buzzing the flies were making."

"I never saw so many damn flies."

"It was like a horror movie," said Brady.

"Remember *The Fly* with David Hedison?" said Gordon, rubbing the top of Brady's head.

Brady shook his head no. "I remember the one with Jeff Goldblum. Who's David Hedison?"

Gordon sighed. "You saw the remake. You need to see the original too."

"I don't want to see either one of them," said Karen, shivering. "If I never see another fly, I will die happy." She looked at Gordon and Brady with admiration. "I don't know what I would have done without the help of you two."

Chapter 4

When Gordon and Karen entered the house, the flies were gone.

"It looks like they left," said Gordon, casting around the living room for stray flies.

"Maybe we should hire an exterminator to go through the house to make sure it's clean," said Karen, starting to get her strength back.

Gordon hesitated. "After I get my paycheck. The mortgage comes first."

"Of course."

"In the meantime I can spray Raid around the house if you want."

"I hate the smell of that stuff. Maybe hit the bathroom. They might have a nest in there."

Gordon made a beeline for the bathroom. He noticed Karen wasn't following him. Stopping in his tracks he turned around and eyed her with curiosity.

"I'm not going near that bathroom till you fumigate it," she said. "Bad memories."

"No problem."

Gordon entered the bathroom, not without a little apprehension. Flies weren't his favorite insects. Any insect that hung around garbage dumps couldn't be good, as far as he was concerned. Born in filth and attracted to rotting meat and feces, they spread diseases. He hoped Karen wasn't going to come down with something thanks to the unsanitary flies that had gorged her mouth and all but suffocated her. Maybe she needed a tetanus shot.

He inspected the bathroom. He didn't see any flies. They had left the house.

Puzzled, he noticed the screen in the open window above the bathtub looked intact. He didn't see how the flies could have gotten into the bathroom. He could believe one might have gotten in somehow but not thousands of them.

If the flies hadn't flown in from outside, they must have a nest inside the bathroom. Maybe there was a dead rodent in the bathroom. Flies bred in corpses. If something was dead in here, he should be able to smell it.

He sniffed. He smelled an odor he couldn't identify. It wasn't pleasant. There was something off about it.

He inspected the linoleum floor, searching for anything dead. No soap.

He flung open the medicine cabinet door.

He didn't see any rodent corpses, or insect corpses for that matter, lying on the metal shelves occupied by various tubes and bottles of antibiotics, boxes of bandages, deodorant aerosols, Vaseline, mouthwash, and orange plastic bottles containing Karen's prescription pills for manic depression and insomnia.

He shut the medicine cabinet door.

Where had the flies come from? Spontaneous generation, he thought with amusement.

He opened the door to the particleboard cabinet beneath the sink. He clapped eyes on a red canister of Raid, latched onto it, snapped off the plastic cap, and sprayed the insecticide in the corners of the bathroom.

He left the bathroom window open for ventilation.

Crouching, he sprayed around the drainpipe in the particleboard cabinet, replaced the cap on the Raid, returned the canister under the sink, and shut the cabinet door.

He stood up. He didn't know what else he could do about the flies.

The hell with them. He had more important things to do. He had to make a living so he could pay for this house.

Chapter 5

Gordon emerged from the bathroom.

Karen sniffed the air with displeasure. "You used the spray."

"I left the window wide open. There's plenty of ventilation."

"I hate that smell. It's sickening."

"As long as the room's ventilated, we'll be fine."

"Do you know who lived here before us?"

"No. Why?"

"They might know what caused the fly infestation."

"It could have happened after they moved out."

Karen nodded yes. "Possible." She paused a beat. "It's strange, though."

"What is?"

"I asked a couple of neighbors who the previous owner of this house was, and they clammed up."

Gordon shrugged. "Maybe they didn't know the owner."

"A recluse, huh?"

"Why not?"

"It piques my curiosity. You know me. I don't like mysteries. I always want to know the answers."

"Maybe the realtor knows."

"I already asked her. She sidestepped the question by changing the subject."

"She probably didn't know the answer and didn't want to sound stupid by admitting it."

"The more roadblocks I run into, the more I want to know about the identity of the previous owner."

"Probably a harmless old coot who kept to himself."

"If that was true, why wouldn't the neighbors tell me?"

"Why does it matter so much to you who the previous owner was?"

"If they're still living in this city, I could ask them about that cold space in the middle of the house. It makes no sense why that area is so cold while the rest of the house isn't."

"Why would the previous owner know?"

"She might have some sort of explanation. And maybe she knows why there were so many damn flies in the bathroom."

Gordon yawned. "I'm not gonna lose any sleep over it."

"This is a beautiful house." Karen took in the house interior with approval. Then she crossed her arms over her chest and shivered. "But there's something strange about it. Something . . . foreboding."

"Ah, it's just a house. I'm not getting any evil vibes from it."

"You're not paying attention, is all."

"Or you're letting your imagination run wild."

Karen laughed. "That happens when a thousand flies try to kill you."

Brady ran up to them. "Where'd all the flies go?"

"To another continent, I hope."

"They were spooky."

"Don't worry," said Gordon. "I sprayed Raid in the bathroom. They're not gonna come back."

"I have a sixth sense that something happened in this house," said Karen. "Something unspeakable."

"You've been watching too many horror movies. I saw you watching *The Haunting* and *The Legend of Hell House* on TV the other day."

"I like *The Shining*," said Brady. "Jack Nicholson was scary when he went nuts in that giant haunted hotel in the winter and chopped up Scatman with an ax. I had nightmares after I saw that movie."

"There's no such thing as haunted houses," said Gordon. "This is a real house. Not a movie set."

"I don't like being near that bathroom," said Karen.

She strode into the living room and gazed through the picture window at the prospect of Los Angeles that spread below the bungalow under a cloud of yellowish grey smog.

Gordon followed her. "If you hate it so much here, do you want to move?"

"Who said I hated it? I just want to know more about the place. What's so wrong about that?" she said, slewing around to confront him. "I bet this house has a history. And I bet it's fascinating."

"I don't care who used to live here. All I care about is it's ours now."

"Every house has a history. I bet this one's is a doozy."

"The former owners are gone. What difference does it make who they were?"

"Something happened here, and I'm not gonna rest till I know what it was. Doesn't it pique your curiosity that the neighbors don't want to talk about the former owners?"

"It's no big mystery. There's probably nothing to talk about. That's all."

Gordon felt his cell phone vibrate in his trouser pocket. He fished out his cell and checked the screen.

It was a text from the Zetas cartel.

He's still alive, it said. What happened?

"I have to take this," he said, and ducked outside.

He never discussed business in front of Karen. He didn't want her to find out he wasn't a security consultant. He doubted their marriage would stand the strain of the revelation of his true profession.

Chapter 6

In the front yard, far enough away from the house to be out of earshot of Karen, Gordon phoned Diego, his cutout with the Zetas.

Gordon could see Diego now with his buzz-cut black hair and the tattoo of a raven on the side of his neck. The guy loved tattoos. He had another one of a diamondback on the back of his wrist.

"He was late," said Gordon.

"You said he'd be taken care of by now. If he's dead, how come he answered his phone at his house when I called him."

"Change in plans."

"I don't like you changing plans on your own without consulting us."

"It won't happen again."

"We need this taken care of. That means now. No fucking around."

"Like I said, he was late."

"Our trial is tomorrow. He has to be gone before then. You're running out of time."

"He has a trial this afternoon. I'll take care of it at the courthouse."

"See to it, or you don't get your paycheck."

Diego hung up.

Gordon drove his rental Toyota to the courthouse in downtown LA.

He didn't like making hits on such short notice. He liked to scout the site of the hit before he whacked his victim, making sure he could execute his escape afterwards.

In this case, he could see the courthouse in his mind, since he had been there several times tailing Childress and knew its layout. It was a white moderne-style high-rise that used to be a post office.

He knew enough about Childress that he knew where Childress parked at the *Los Angeles Times* parking structure on Spring Street when he went to court. Childress had his own parking space.

Gordon drove his rental into the parking structure. He parked as near to the exit as he could get.

He clambered out of the rental and walked up the stairs to the level where Childress parked. Gordon didn't want anyone to see him drive away after he hit Childress. Gordon would whack Childress then run down the steps to his rental and drive away. Nobody would see a car peel away near Childress after Gordon executed the hit.

The concrete staircase was deserted. Most people used the elevator. The fewer people that saw him in the parking structure, the better. He sniffed and avoided a drying puddle of urine on the second-level landing.

Wearing a black blazer and black jeans, Gordon carried a brown leather briefcase, wanting to look like a lawyer assigned to a trial at the courthouse. Inside the briefcase was his SIG P224 and a sound suppressor.

When he reached the judge's level, he remained inside the stairwell and opened his briefcase on the deserted landing. He fished out the SIG P224 and its sound suppressor. He screwed the sound suppressor onto the muzzle.

He racked the slide, chambering a round in the spout.

He pulled open the steel fire door and strode onto the concrete parking level, making for the judge's parking space. Gordon concealed his piece behind his briefcase in case anyone saw him.

As Gordon suspected, the judge's parking space was empty.

Childress should be here soon. He was a maniac for punctuality when it came to attending trials. Which was what made his tardiness returning home so untoward. But late flights from New York couldn't be helped, Gordon knew.

As it turned out, it was a good thing Childress had been late. Otherwise, Gordon would have made a terrible blunder by whacking the guy in his own neighborhood. Gordon still couldn't get his head around his piss-poor planning of the hit. What had he been thinking? Blowing away the guy at his own house. He had never done it in his profession before. It was way too risky.

Maybe he was losing it. Only luck had saved him from pulling off the hit at Childress's house. A successful hit there would have led to Gordon's inevitable arrest by cops.

Gun in hand, he waited behind a silver Land Rover for Childress to arrive. He glanced at his wristwatch. Childress should arrive soon. The Land Rover was thirty-odd feet from the judge's parking slot.

Gordon didn't see anyone else on the parking level, just rows of parked cars.

He heard a car door shut. He saw a fortyish suit getting out of his white Audi.

Not wishing to be seen, Gordon slipped behind the Land Rover at his side. He hoped Childress didn't arrive at this moment. Better for Gordon if Childress arrived after the suit left the parking structure. In the best of all possible worlds, nobody would be on this level when Childress arrived. Except this wasn't the best of all possible worlds, Gordon well knew. Not by a long shot.

He listened to the suit's footsteps fade as they approached the elevator, which was on the opposite wall of the stairwell. He heard a car drive up the ramp to this level. It was about time for Childress to arrive.

From behind the Land Rover Gordon caught sight of Childress's black Mercedes G-Wagen tooling up the ramp. The G-Wagen headed straight to Childress's parking slot.

Gordon scoped out the surroundings. He didn't see anyone. Feeling his heartbeat accelerate he prepared to take out Childress. Gordon willed his heartbeat to slow down. He took a deep breath.

He didn't know why he was nervous. This should be second nature to him. It wasn't like he was an amateur. Still, he wished he had had more time to prepare the hit. He usually spent more time planning. *Measure twice, cut once.*

He saw the five-nine, middle-aged Childress climb out of his vehicle in a navy blue suit, a grey watered silk necktie around his neck. Childress sported a short salt-and-pepper beard. Lugging a black leather briefcase he shut the driver's-side door behind him.

Gordon stepped out from behind the Land Rover, assumed the Weaver stance, drew a bead on Childress, and squeezed off a round. At the last moment, Childress dropped his briefcase and leaned over to pick it up.

Gordon saw Childress spin around as if struck by a bullet. He also saw a white SUV pulling up the ramp and driving onto their level.

Gordon had to beat it. He couldn't risk taking another shot with the SUV driver as a witness. Gordon thought he had hit Childress, but he couldn't tell where. Childress had leaned over to retrieve his briefcase and spoiled Gordon's shot as Gordon had fired.

Out of the corner of his eye he saw Childress crumple on the concrete.

To make sure the guy was dead Gordon should finish him off with another shot.

But it was too risky with a witness present.

Gordon ducked behind the Land Rover as the white SUV drove toward Childress. Gordon felt sure the driver must have seen Childress by now.

Gordon took a powder.

He didn't think Childress was dead, but he couldn't stick around to find out. Yet another car pulled up the ramp. A metallic red Jeep Rubicon.

Hunched over, Gordon stole along the parking structure's four-foot-high concrete wall between it and a row of parked cars. He didn't think anybody saw him.

He shoved the crash bar on the fire door and burst into the stairwell. He raced down the stairs, his footfalls echoing in the concrete and steel stairwell.

Had he botched another hit? What the hell was happening to him? This wasn't like him.

When he reached the level his rental was parked on, he slowed down as he descended the steps. Composed, he opened the fire door and angled toward his car. He saw a family of four returning to their car. He ignored them.

It didn't matter if they saw him here. Childress had taken a bullet on an upper level. As long as they didn't see his SIG, which

Gordon concealed behind his briefcase, no one would suspect him of being the shooter.

He slid into his rental, fired the engine, reversed out of his parking space, and peeled away.

Chapter 7

When Gordon finished brooding in an Irish pub on Sunset Boulevard about his missed hit, it was dark.

He drove up the dim-lit switchbacks in the hills to his house.

Karen and Brady were already asleep, he saw as he wandered around the dark house flicking on lights so he didn't trip and break his neck. He had lost track of the time. He hadn't realized it was bedtime.

He killed the lights downstairs and climbed the steps to the bedrooms on the second floor. He entered the en suite master bedroom, which had a nightlight plugged into one of the wall sockets.

He used the bathroom, changed into his pajamas, and slid into bed next to Karen, careful not to make too much movement and wake her.

He fell asleep in minutes.

He awoke with a start.

He heard loud banging against the bedroom wall. It sounded like it was coming from the wall facing the front yard. Which made no sense. They were on the second floor, and there was no room abutting that wall.

The pounding continued.

He glanced at Karen. He couldn't believe the noise hadn't woken her. She was dead to the world.

Mystified by the racket, he climbed out of bed and padded in his bare feet to the wall in question. He peered out the window.

Rattled by the commotion, he half expected to see an intruder on a ladder pounding against the wall.

There was no ladder or intruder. A eucalyptus tree stood in the front yard, but the branches didn't reach the house. There was hardly any wind at the moment.

Could the wind have blown a branch against the house? He gazed at the tree. It was too far away for one of its branches to hit the house even if blown by a strong gust of wind.

Then what had been pounding against the wall?

Whatever it was had stopped making the ruckus.

It had sounded like a human fist pounding against the wall. Which was impossible. The guy would have to be well over ten feet tall to reach the second floor.

Gordon scoped out the front lawn. Nobody was on it.

Had he been dreaming? That would explain why Karen hadn't woken up. If he had imagined the pounding, she wouldn't have heard anything.

He retreated to the bathroom, turned on the light, and filled a plastic cup with water from the tap.

He started as the pounding resumed.

He placed his cup of water on the sink and belted to the bedroom window, seeking the source of the sound. He peeked out the window. The pounding stopped. He saw no one outside. The eucalyptus branch wasn't striking the wall either.

Puzzled, he craned around and eyed Karen. She was sound asleep.

How could the deafening pounding fail to wake her? Was he dreaming?

He didn't hear the noise.

He returned to the bathroom to drink his cup of water. He halted in astonishment in the doorway. His cup of water wasn't on the sink.

How could that be? He distinctly remembered filling the cup with water and placing the cup on the sink.

He looked around the bathroom.

The cup of water was standing on the dirty clothes hamper lid.

How could the cup have moved to the hamper? Had Karen woken up and moved it?

He wheeled around to look for her.

She was lying asleep in bed.

How could she have not woken when she heard the deafening banging? Was she playing a trick on him by moving his water and pretending to be asleep?

He walked over to her.

"Karen," he said.

She didn't respond.

"Karen," he said louder.

Nothing.

He snagged her arm and shook it. "Karen, wake up."

She remained limp and asleep.

Was she dead? he wondered in a panic, breaking into a sweat.

He leaned down toward her and listened for her breathing. He relaxed. She was breathing.

He stared at her motionless face. She wasn't faking sleep. Why would she?

Hell, he might be asleep too and dreaming. He didn't know what was going on.

He returned to the bathroom and stopped dead in his tracks before he reached the doorway. The cup of water was back on the sink. How had it moved from the clothes hamper lid to the sink?

Either he was dreaming or going nuts. Or there was somebody in the bathroom.

He bolted into the bathroom and inspected it. He didn't see anyone. The shower curtain was closed. Adrenaline shooting through his body, he grabbed the curtain with his left hand and flung it open, balling a fist with his right, preparing to confront an intruder and clout him in the face.

Nobody stood in the bathtub.

All Gordon saw was the rubber suction mat lying on the bottom of the porcelain tub.

The cup couldn't move by itself.

Then he was either dreaming or going nuts.

He grabbed the cup of water and drank it.

He felt a draft on his back. He entered the bedroom and eyed the window. It was shut. Maybe the draft was coming from the stairs and the hall, except he didn't feel it anymore.

He was botching his job and imagining things. Maybe he needed to see his shrink.

He slid back into bed beside Karen.

He checked her out. She was still sleeping.

His body tense, he lay in bed for a while, waiting edgily for the knocking on the wall to resume. It didn't. He drifted off. The last thing he saw before he fell asleep was Karen's blank face. For some reason, it bothered him. How could she sleep through such a racket?

Chapter 8

Gordon, Karen, and Brady sat at the walnut table in the dining room, eating breakfast. Karen and Brady were eating pink grapefruit halves.

Gordon liked grapefruit, but it interacted with his blood pressure meds, which he had begun taking in his late thirties. He ate his Cheerios instead.

"Did you hear anything last night?" he said.

Karen looked up from her grapefruit. "No. Why?"

Gordon wondered if he should tell her. She might think he was going nuts.

"I heard what sounded like someone banging on our bedroom wall," he said.

"That's impossible."

"I know. We're on the second story. Somebody would need a ladder—"

"You must have been dreaming." Karen turned to Brady. "What about you, Brady? Did you hear a noise last night?"

"No," he said, without looking up from his grapefruit.

"His bedroom's on the other side of the house," said Gordon. "He probably couldn't hear it over there. I don't understand how you could sleep through it. I even tried to wake you up, but you kept sleeping."

Karen cleared her throat. "I felt wired last night because of those flies attacking me. I took a couple of Halcions so I could sleep."

Gordon nodded. "That explains it. You were out like a light."

"I sleep eight hours straight when I take those things."

"Then I'm the only one who heard the loud pounding?" said Gordon, cutting his eyes back and forth between Karen and Brady.

"It had to've been a nightmare you were having," said Karen. "On the other hand, it might be this house. I get weird vibrations from it. And what about that cold zone and those flies? I've never been attacked by a bunch of flies in my life."

"Are you saying the house is haunted?"

"I don't know what I'm saying. I'm saying this house is creepy, is what I'm saying."

"I guess pipes in the wall could've made those pounding sounds I heard last night. This house is pretty old. Old water pipes make loud sounds sometimes. But . . ."

"But what?"

"I don't know why water pipes would be in *that* wall. It's on the opposite side of the bathroom. There's no running water on the outer side of the bedroom."

"You'd have to ask a plumber. We don't have a blueprint of the house."

Gordon hesitated about telling her about the cup of water. He decided to go ahead.

"There was something else," he said.

"Huh?"

"Last night. I put a cup of water on the sink and left the bathroom. When I returned, the cup had moved to the clothes hamper lid."

"You must've been dreaming."

"You didn't wake up and move it?"

"No way."

"Could you have done it in your sleep? I read somewhere that some people who take Halcion walk in their sleep."

"I don't know why I would move a cup of water off the sink."

"Are you sure you weren't sleepwalking last night?"

"How can I be sure? People who sleepwalk don't know they're doing it." She searched his face. "Why is this bothering you so much?"

Gordon rubbed the back of his neck. "It was a bad day yesterday."

"Those flies didn't help any." She considered him. "Maybe you should see your psychiatrist. You seem stressed out lately."

"I was thinking the same thing."

"Are you getting paid this week?"

"Your guess is as good as mine."

"The mortgage is already late. The bank isn't gonna wait forever."

He threw down his spoon and bolted to his feet. "Don't you think I know that?"

"I'm not blaming you—"

"It sounds like it."

"I'm blaming your boss."

"It's feast or famine in this business."

Brady looked up at him with concern.

"It's OK, Brady," said Gordon, smiling. "We'll work it out. We always do."

Chapter 9

Gordon wondered if Childress was dead. Gordon hadn't got off a clean shot, because he was interrupted.

He hadn't heard from Diego yet. Diego wasn't going to pay him until Childress was dead.

Driving his rental to his shrink Gordon turned on the news on the car radio. He wanted to know the judge's condition.

No word so far.

It would have to be on the news sooner or later. A wounded or dead judge. How could that not be news?

"Judge Childress's condition remains stable," said the newscaster as if on cue, "after he was shot in the shoulder yesterday afternoon in the *LA Times* parking structure."

Childress wouldn't die from a shoulder wound, Gordon knew. It was only a matter of time before Diego heard the news.

Gordon drove west on Sunset till he reached his shrink's office in Brentwood. He parked in her office building's underground parking lot. He was fortunate she took appointments on such short notice. He supposed she did it because she didn't want any of her patients to commit suicide thanks to psychological problems.

He parked his rental, got out, locked it, and rode the elevator to her floor. He entered her office and greeted her secretary.

"Dr. Goldwyn will see you now," said the secretary, a blonde pushing thirty, who wore her hair cropped.

Gordon entered Goldwyn's office and sat down on the black leather recliner opposite her chair. A middle-aged black woman with a degree in psychology from UCLA, Goldwyn had shoulder-length chestnut hair and wore glasses with powder blue plastic frames with blue tinted lenses. She was wearing a knee-length auburn dress, her legs crossed with an open notebook on her lap.

"How are you today, Gordon?" she said.

"I dunno."

"Do you have issues?"

He didn't beat around the bush. "How do I know if I'm going bonkers?"

Goldwyn smiled. "That's a difficult question to answer. Let me ask you, why would you think you're going insane?"

Gordon massaged his forehead. "I couldn't sleep last night because I heard someone pounding on the other side of my bedroom wall. But there was nobody there. My bedroom's on the second story, and the wall faces the front yard."

"How do you know you weren't dreaming?"

"I believe I was awake."

"Dreams can be very believable."

"There was something else. I put a cup of water on the bathroom sink and left the bathroom. When I returned to drink the water, the cup had moved to the clothes hamper lid."

"Maybe someone moved it—like your wife."

"My wife was fast asleep. She denies she moved it."

"Did this happen after you heard the pounding on the wall?"

"Yeah."

"Again, you could have been dreaming. You can't assume you're going insane because of this one thing."

"I'm convinced I wasn't dreaming."

"Are you having problems at work that would cause you to have trouble sleeping?"

He had never told her he was a contract killer. He confided in her only to a certain degree. He didn't know what doctor-patient confidentiality included. Was a psychiatrist professionally prohibited from telling the cops one of their patients was a hit man?

Gordon wasn't going to take the chance of telling her.

"Work isn't going so well," was all he said.

"Which could be disturbing your sleeping pattern. You're under stress. You need to relax."

"You don't think I'm going nuts?"

"The legal definition of *insanity* is being unable to distinguish between right and wrong when committing a crime. Did the perpetrator know what they were doing was wrong at the time of the criminal act?"

Had she figured out he was a hit man? How could she?

"I'm not talking about crimes," he said, feeling tense. "Who's talking about crimes?"

"The definition of *insanity* is tricky," she said as if she was used to this question and prepared to give a lengthy explanation. "I gave you the legal definition. Now, according to Merriam-Webster's dictionary, *insanity* is a severely disordered state of mind—"

"You're the shrink. I'm asking you. What's your professional opinion?"

"It sounds to me like you had a nightmare. Is there something else that's disrupting your sleep?"

"Hmm. Well, we just moved into a new house. I'm not used to sleeping there."

Goldwyn nodded yes. "That could be a factor. New surroundings make people nervous. Your new house could be giving you nightmares."

"It wasn't a nightmare. Somebody moved that cup of water in the bathroom last night. I'm sure of it."

"What about your son? Could he have moved it?"

"I never saw him in my room. He could only get into the bathroom by going through the master bedroom."

"I doubt it's anything to be concerned about." She grabbed her prescription pad from her desktop. "I'm gonna prescribe the sleeping aid Halcion to help you sleep."

She scribbled on her pad.

"My wife takes that," he said.

"A lot of people who take it have told me they don't dream when they take it, and you'll stay asleep for eight solid hours."

"Karen didn't wake up when I heard the pounding last night. I guess the stuff must work."

"You need to unwind, is all. Don't worry about 'going nuts,' as you put it. Worrying causes more stress."

She handed him the prescription.

"You're the doctor," he said, accepting it and getting to his feet.

He wasn't sure he was going to take the sleeping pills. If he was out cold like Karen last night, what would happen if an intruder entered their bedroom? The same intruder who had moved his cup of water in the bathroom. There was no telling what the guy might do to them.

Could somebody else be living in the house with them? he wondered, cringing. But how? How could the guy go unnoticed? What kind of nutbag would live inside someone else's house while the owners were there? Of course, this was Hollywood. Anything was possible in Hollywood.

Chapter 10

As Karen inspected the birds of paradise in the garden on the front lawn, she saw the mail carrier drive up to her mailbox at the end of the driveway.

Getting an idea, Karen ran down the driveway to meet her.

"Hello," said Karen, smiling. "I'm the new owner."

"Hi," said the mail carrier, a black woman in her late twenties who enjoyed eating. She was wearing her hair in dreadlocks, her Persol sunglasses perched on her forehead. "How are you?"

"Fine. My name's Karen. What's yours?"

"Debbie."

"Nice to meet you, Debbie. I'm trying to find out about the previous owner of this house."

Debbie bridled. "I don't give out information about previous owners. We have strict rules at the post office."

Debbie stabbed Karen's mail into the mailbox, withdrew her hand, and seized the steering wheel.

The Grumman LLV peeled away from the curb.

Baffled, Karen watched the mail truck speed away.

Why had the mail carrier become rude after acting genial? There was something about the previous owners that had triggered her reaction. Yet another person who didn't want to talk about them. Debbie the mail carrier was no different than the close-mouthed neighbors.

What was the big secret? The more that people refused to talk about it, the more she wanted to know.

Karen fished out her cell phone from her purse and called the realtor who had sold them the house.

"Hi, Shelley. This is Karen Carney."

"Hi, Karen. I hope you're enjoying your new house. What can I do for you?"

"We had a bunch of flies in the bathroom yesterday."

"Oh, I'm sorry. I can have an exterminator take care of it."

"That's OK. We got rid of them. Could you tell me a little about the previous owners? This is such a nice house, I'm wondering who they were."

Shelley terminated the call.

Karen startled. She couldn't believe it.

She just wanted to know the owner's name. What was the big deal? Did everyone sign a pact not to talk about the previous owner? Why?

How could she find out who the previous owner was?

She returned to the house and got out her laptop in the study to see if she could find the owner's name on the Internet. She accessed the Los Angeles County Assessor portal and found the house's assessor ID number, which she needed to ask for the owner's name at the help desk at assessor.lacounty.gov. She shot them an e-mail.

She had no idea how long it would take them to answer—if they ever answered.

There had to be a faster way to find out the previous owner's name.

Asking the neighbors seemed like the best way, but the neighbors she had already asked had clammed up. She would just have to find another neighbor, one who wanted to talk about it.

Which begged the question, why didn't the neighbors want to talk? Were they scared? Why would they be scared to talk about the previous owner? It didn't make sense.

Her e-mail chimed.

The assessor help desk replied that they provided only the name of the current owner, which in this case was her husband, Gordon Carney. No help.

Somehow she would have to find a neighbor who wanted to talk about the erstwhile owner.

There was something off about this house, and Karen wanted to know what it was. The previous owners must know the answer. If anyone knew, it had to be them.

Sitting at her desk she came to attention. She thought she heard flies buzzing in the direction of the bathroom.

She stood up and cut across the study to the bathroom, her pulse accelerating. She dreaded coming in contact with more flies. She edged toward the open bathroom door.

The flies sounded like they were flying in the bathroom.

She stood in the bathroom doorway, scoping out the interior, casting around for flies. She didn't see any. She could smell the insecticide Gordon had sprayed yesterday. She didn't see how the flies could survive it. The Raid shouldn't lose its toxic strength in one day. It should remain poisonous for at least a couple of weeks.

Yet she could hear flies buzzing. Where were they? There was no sign of them in the bathroom.

She must be imagining them.

"What's wrong?" said a voice behind her.

She nearly jumped out of her skin. Her heart skipped a beat. She slewed around to see who was behind her.

It was Brady.

Karen exhaled a sigh of relief. "You startled me."

"What were you doing?"

"I could hear more flies. Do you hear them?"

Brady listened. "No."

She didn't hear them now either. "They must have left."

She must have flies on the mind. It was no surprise, since they had almost killed her yesterday.

"I'm going to find a neighbor to tell me about this house," she said. "Will you be all right here?"

"Sure."

"I'm taking my bike."

Chapter 11

Karen retrieved her bicycle from the carport and rode it down the street through the neighborhood, wondering which neighbor she should ask about the house owners this time. She had already asked her nearest neighbors with no luck.

She rode a pink Schwinn bike with a wicker basket braced to the front of the handlebars. The breeze felt nice against her face as she peddled.

She needed the exercise anyway, and it was a beautiful day with perfect blue skies overhead.

As she was riding her bike, she saw a homeless man trudging down the street, carrying a large, stuffed, military-like olive drab knapsack on his back.

She had seen him in the neighborhood the other day. Maybe he was a regular in the neighborhood. He might know something about the former owners of her house.

Part of her warned her not to approach him. The guy could be dangerous for all she knew. It was no secret a lot of the homeless were winos or drug addicts. However, she noticed he had friendly brown eyes. He didn't look like a maniac who would whip out a shiv and slash her throat. Though you could never tell in Hollywood.

If he became hostile, she would ride away. She had her bicycle. There was no way he could catch up to her on his feet.

She pulled over to the side of the road and stood, straddling her bike, ready to push off at a moment's notice.

"Hello," she said, smiling.

"Could you spare a dollar?" he said, his big moist eyes pleading with her.

In his early thirties, dressed in jeans and a T, he looked more or less clean for a vagabond, she decided, not wishing to scrutinize him too closely.

She reached into her purse, withdrew a dollar, and handed it to him.

Paying him might loosen his lips, though she hadn't intended to give him any money. What she wanted was answers. She wasn't here on a mercy mission.

"Thanks," he said, accepting the dollar.

"I've seen you around here before, haven't I?"

"I dunno. Maybe."

"Do you know any of the neighbors who live in this neck of the woods?"

"I see people around," he said, not sure what she was angling for.

She gave him her address. "Do you know anything about the people who used to live at my address?"

"Oh, that house. That's a nice house."

"Do you remember the former owners?"

"Maybe."

"Were they nice?"

He put his finger to his jaw. "Let's see. That house. Hmm. Now I remember. There was a young woman there. A blonde. She had two little girls."

"Why don't the neighbors want to talk about her? Even the mail carrier ran away when I asked about her."

"Let me see. She had two little girls with the nicest blonde hair I ever saw."

"Do you know her name?"

"Nobody tells me their names. I doubt they want me here."

"Do you know what she did for a living?"

He shook his head no. "She never even said hello to me."

"Why did she move away?"

"I dunno." He paused a beat. "Let me see. Something happened there."

"What do you mean?" said Karen, pricking up her ears.

"Could you spare a twenty?" he said, holding out his empty hand.

She dug into her purse for a twenty-dollar bill and paid him.

"Much obliged," he said, rubbing the twenty between his grimy fingers as if feeling it to make sure it was real.

He wasn't as clean as she had first thought.

"You were saying?" she said.

His words came out slow, like he was giving them a great deal of thought.

"I saw cops over there once," he said. "A lot of black-and-whites were parked in her driveway and along the side of the street."

"Do you know why?"

"Nobody tells me nothing. Nobody wants me around. I can tell you one thing, though."

"What?"

"I never saw her again after the day the cops swarmed over her house like vampire bats around a naked throat."

"You have no idea what happened?"

"None."

"When did this happen?"

"Let me see," he said, furrowing his brow in thought. "About a year ago, I'd say."

That sounded right, she decided. The house had been on the market for a year when she and Gordon had first clapped eyes on it.

"Did you see her kids again?" she said.

"Uh-uh. Neither one of 'em."

"Are you sure you can't remember the mother's name?"

"I never knew her name. I just saw her drive by a couple of times in her green Jaguar. A good-looking woman as I recall."

"Do you know what she did for a living?"

"I overheard someone say she was an actress, but I never saw her in anything."

Chapter 12

Brady was streaming *Final Destination* on Tubi, trying to find out who would be the next character to fail to cheat death, when he heard a noise coming from the bathroom. It sounded like running water.

There was nobody here but him. How could water be running? He hadn't turned it on.

He got up from the couch and angled toward the bathroom. The sound of running water was getting louder.

He padded in his sneakers across the carpet to the bathroom doorway. He heard water gushing out.

He peeked inside the bathroom.

Water was gushing out of the bathtub faucet, but nobody was in the bathroom.

Had Mom returned without telling him she was home? He hadn't heard her come back from her bike ride. Of course, he had been watching the movie on TV. It was possible he was so engrossed with the movie that he hadn't heard her return.

He called out her name.

"Mom, the water's running in the bathroom."

Nobody answered.

The bathtub was becoming full. The water level was only an inch from the top. He didn't want the water to overflow. He crossed the linoleum tiles to the tub and reached to turn off the cold water cock.

He felt someone grab his neck from behind and shove his head into the tub full of water.

Terrified, down on his knees, he struggled to pull his submerged head free. His pulse racing, he held his breath underwater. Why would Mom shove his head underwater? Was she trying to drown him?

He wanted to scream for help, but he couldn't with his head underwater.

He thrashed his arms behind him, trying to push his assailant away from him. It did no good. He couldn't hold his breath much longer. The strong hands kept throttling him, holding his head underwater. He struggled to stand up and throw the guy off him, but the guy was too heavy.

Water was pouring over the edge of the bathtub and sloshing onto the floor as it kept gushing out of the faucet.

The attacker yanked Brady's head out of the water and stood him up.

It was Mom, her face twisted with rage.

Desperate to breathe, he coughed out water he had inhaled.

"What are you trying to do?" she said. "You could've drowned."

She turned off the water cocks.

His face dripping wet, he tried to speak, but his coughing jag prevented it.

"Look what you did," she said. "You flooded the bathroom."

"I didn't do it," he spluttered, terrified of her. "I heard the water running and came here. Somebody left the water running in the tub."

"You're the only one at home. How could it get turned on if you didn't do it?"

"I thought you turned it on."

"I just got back."

"Why were you trying to drown me?"

"I saved you," she said, gobsmacked. "You were leaning over the tub, holding your head underwater when I saw you. I pulled you out."

"You were the one trying to drown me."

"What are you talking about? I would never do such a thing."

"You snuck up behind me and shoved my head underwater."

"Stop making up things. I did no such thing. I found you holding your head underwater. I didn't know what you were trying to do."

"Somebody was holding me down. I thought it was you. You're the only one here."

"That's crazy. It wasn't me. When I came into the bathroom, you were here alone, running the water all over the floor, submerging your head—"

"Why would I try to drown myself?" he said, breaking into tears.

"I saved you. Calm down."

He coughed up water from his burning lungs.

"Can you breathe?" she said.

"Yeah. I inhaled water. I thought I was gonna die."

She grabbed a lavender bath towel from the rack and dried off his head.

"You have to understand," she said. "I would never try to harm you. You're everything I have in life."

He remained scared of her.

"I don't know what happened," she said, "but I saw nobody here when I found you holding your head underwater."

"I felt someone shoving my head underwater. I couldn't break away."

"You scared me to death," she said, holding her chest. "Let's get something to eat."

She leaned over the bathtub, removed the stopper, and drained the water.

Chapter 13

After Karen and Brady had grilled cheese sandwiches for lunch, Karen returned to the study, sat at her desk, and awoke her laptop from Sleep mode.

A crime had been committed in this house when the previous owner lived here, according to the transient. Otherwise, why would so many cops have descended on the house when the transient saw them?

She googled "actors involved in crimes last year in the Hollywood Hills."

It would help if she knew the woman's name.

She scrolled down the list that appeared on the laptop screen. A website called Hollywood Life caught her eye. She clicked on it.

They had a list of twenty-five celebrities who had committed crimes last year. She inspected the names. Some of them she knew, but most she didn't.

The name Deirdre Turner caught her eye.

She was a thirty-six-year-old blonde actor with very few credits to her name. She drowned her two young girls and overdosed on drugs in the Hollywood Hills, Karen read in stunned disbelief.

The website didn't give Deirdre's exact address, but Karen figured Deirdre must have been the former owner of her new house.

No wonder nobody wanted to talk about her. Deirdre had led a tragic life and had murdered her own children. It was horrible just thinking about it. She couldn't imagine killing Brady. What kind of woman would even consider committing such a heinous act? What had driven her to do it?

At the end of the article, Karen read the name of the homicide detective who was in charge of the murder investigation. A lieutenant named Wolfgang Gaetz.

Obsessed with the heinousness of the crime, Karen wanted to pick the lieutenant's mind concerning the mass murder and the psychology of the killer.

Leaning back in her chair, Karen produced her cell phone, called the Hollywood Police Department, and reached the watch commander. She asked to speak to Lieutenant Gaetz.

"Is this an emergency?" said the watch commander named Bill Forester. "If you are in danger, call 911."

"It's not an emergency," said Karen.

She had to think of a reason to speak to Gaetz. Cops were notoriously close-mouthed around noncops, she knew.

"What is the nature of your call?" said Bill.

Karen figured Gaetz wasn't going to tell her anything unless she could come up with a good reason to be asking about Deirdre. Being the new owner of Deirdre's house probably wouldn't qualify. Karen cooked up a story she thought would loosen Bill's lips.

"I'm writing a freelance article on the Deirdre Turner suicide in the Hollywood Hills," she said. "I understand Lieutenant Gaetz was in charge of the investigation, and I would like to ask him a few questions."

"Oh, yeah. The press, huh? All right, I'll patch you through."

"Gaetz here."

"Hello, Lieutenant. This is Karen Carney. I'm doing a freelance article on the Deirdre Turner suicide. Could we meet and discuss this?"

"Ah, yeah. I remember that one. An interesting case. Who did you say you work for?"

Karen thought fast. She had to come up with a convincing answer.

"I'm a stringer for *Vanity Fair*," she lied, her palms sweaty.

"OK."

They agreed to meet at the In-N-Out Burger on Sunset Boulevard in West Hollywood.

Chapter 14

Karen drove her 2019 powder blue VDub to the burger joint to meet Gaetz, who arrived in his black-and-white Dodge Charger.

They sat outside on the patio at a round table under an umbrella.

Five eleven with freshly trimmed sideburns, the fortyish Gaetz had white hair and a clean-shaven face pitted with acne scars. His alert slate blue eyes took in the surroundings without focusing on anyone in particular.

Karen ordered a hamburger and fries, even though she had just eaten a grilled cheese sandwich an hour ago with Brady. Gaetz ordered a cheeseburger and fries.

"What can you tell me about the tragic death of Deirdre Turner, Lieutenant?" said Karen, an open notebook on the tabletop, a pen in her hand.

"What exactly do you want to know?" he said in a gruff, whiskey voice.

"Do you believe she killed herself?"

"She OD'd on pentobarbital and chloral hydrate, according to toxicology reports."

"I thought you can't get pentobarbital and chloral hydrate anymore," said Karen, baffled.

Gaetz shrugged. "Maybe she got them in Mexico."

"That's a strange combination of drugs these days."

Gaetz fetched a sigh. "Not so strange if you're familiar with Deirdre Turner."

"What do you mean?"

"She idolized Marilyn Monroe. She wanted to be the next Marilyn. Monroe OD'd on pentobarbital and chloral hydrate."

"Are you saying Deirdre killed herself because Marilyn Monroe did?"

Gaetz shifted in his chair. "It's complicated. Deirdre was having a tough time getting acting gigs in Hollywood. She wasn't popular like Marilyn. Hardly anybody knew Deirdre, but that

47

didn't stop her from trying to get roles. Deirdre read all the books on Marilyn. She had a lot of them in her house. She knew everything about Marilyn. She would drive frequently to the house where Marilyn died at 12305 Fifth Helena in Brentwood, park in front of it, and just sit there for hours like she was on a vigil, even though you can hardly see it from the street on account of a wall around it."

"Did Deirdre have psychological problems like Marilyn?"

"I don't know if their psychological problems were the same, but Deirdre had a few screws loose. After all, she drowned her two girls before she OD'd."

"How do you know she drowned them? Maybe they drowned accidentally while taking a bath."

"We thought of that, but when we found their bodies floating in the full bathtub, we found ligature marks around their necks. Someone had held their heads underwater."

Gaetz took a bite of his cheeseburger.

"Why would she kill her own children?" said Karen.

"Like I said, she had psychological problems, and she was out of work most of the time. She was a single mother. She couldn't pay her bills."

"How tragic."

"What struck me was her overwhelming desire to be like Marilyn Monroe—even the way she died. We found Deirdre's corpse in her bedroom, clutching a phone as she lay in bed. Which was how Marilyn died."

"Maybe she was trying to call for help when she lay dying."

"Like Marilyn. Marilyn used to deliberately overdose on drugs and then call one of her friends, like Peter Lawford, to come and save her. But on the night of her death, she took so much Nembutal and chloral hydrate that she passed out before she could place her call."

Karen chewed it over. "But Marilyn didn't kill her children. She didn't have any. Why did Deirdre kill her girls?"

"We asked Deirdre's shrink about that. He said Deirdre blamed her girls for her failure to make it as an actor in Hollywood."

Gaetz's chair creaked as he shifted in his seat again. The way he held himself, she thought he was getting ready to fart.

"So sad," said Karen. "I guess she wanted attention, but she was never able to get it. What happened to her husband?"

"They were divorced. He didn't live at the house. Deirdre was using alimony checks to pay for it, but they didn't cover the whole cost."

"Does he live around here?"

"He got a job in Silicon Valley and never spoke to her again." Gaetz stared at her. "Aren't you writing any of this down for your article?"

"Oh, I—uh—I have a good memory."

She scribbled in her notebook.

"Remember to spell my name right. Gaetz is G-a-e-t-z. And Wolfgang is just like it sounds."

"Of course," said Karen, and printed his name in her notebook. "I can see why none of the neighbors want to talk about Deirdre."

"I'm surprised you're writing an article about her. Not many people have heard of her. Her death didn't get much play in the papers. Just another Hollywood wannabe who didn't make the grade. This city's full of them."

"They end up waiting tables or driving for Uber for the rest of their lives. Or hooking or dealing drugs. Or they end up junkies living in the gutter, dying for their next fix, rolling in their own puke."

"Is it that bad?"

"I'm a cop. I see the dirty end of the stick in my job. Hollywood dreams are pretty—full of fame and riches. Reality isn't. Deirdre couldn't accept the fact she was a failure who wasn't going to make it in showbiz. So she put an end to her misery."

Chapter 15

"Maybe if she hadn't given up, she would have made it in Hollywood," said Karen.

"We'll never know," said Gaetz. "But how long can you wait till you become successful? Especially with women actors. It's no secret Hollywood likes 'em young. If it takes too long to make it, they're never gonna make it. That was the way she felt. She must've figured it was over for her, because she was too old."

"How old was she? You make her sound like an old lady."

"Thirty-six. I remember because she was the same age as Marilyn Monroe when she died."

"Another similarity between them."

"Deirdre could relate to Marilyn's failures but not to her successes. Deirdre didn't have any."

"How sad."

"It's a tough business. Most of the women who make a career of it are tough as nails—like Bette Davis and Joan Crawford."

"They weren't rejected for roles their whole life like Deirdre."

Gaetz conceded the point. "True. I can still remember her case, because it was so strange."

"How so?" said Karen, intrigued.

"I mean, beyond the fact that it was so grisly—a mother killing her own children."

"She must have been deeply disturbed."

"That she was. She also got it into her head that her bedroom was bugged."

"Bugged?" said Karen, startled.

"Yeah. Bugged with electronic eavesdropping equipment like Marilyn Monroe's bedroom."

"Monroe's bedroom was bugged? I didn't know that."

"People thought she was paranoid when she said it, but owners who moved into her house after she died said they found electronic bugs in her bedroom walls, in the light fixtures, and under her carpets. Several different types of bugs, in fact, planted by different people."

"Who was bugging her?"

"There are different theories. They say Jimmy Hoffa planted one of the bugs because he wanted to get dirt on Marilyn's romantic relationship with Bobby Kennedy. Hoffa hated the attorney general with a vengeance for targeting him in Kennedy's well-publicized investigations of the Mafia when Kennedy was chief counsel on the McClellan Committee."

"The McClellan Committee?"

"It was a Senate committee investigating Hoffa's connection to the Mafia. The committee knew Hoffa had met with the mobster Johnny Dio to rig the Teamster election so Hoffa would become the president of the Teamsters. Kennedy got into several shouting matches with Hoffa."

"Oh," said Karen, looking studious and scribbling on her notepad.

"Hoffa also hated JFK's guts. He knew the president was involved with Monroe." Gaetz gestured with his hands. "More dirt to be collected. Others say the CIA and the FBI bugged her, because they were worried she would spill presidential secrets she got from JFK when he was schlonging her. The CIA also knew she was having an affair with the communist playboy film director José Bolaños in Mexico."

"I had no idea."

"Some conspiracy theorists believe the CIA killed her because she knew too much and was threatening to tell all to the media about her affair with JFK—something neither of the Kennedy brothers wanted to become public."

"How did the CIA kill her?"

"They gave her an enema of Nembutal," he deadpanned.

"That sounds off the wall," said Karen, frowning.

Gaetz popped three French fries into his mouth. "Anyway, getting back to Deirdre. She believed a lot of this conspiracy stuff. She was convinced someone was spying on her. One night she tore apart her bedroom wall, searching for bugs."

Karen widened her eyes. "Did she find any?"

"Of course not. But you can see why I remember this case. It was the most bizarre case I ever had."

"She was a very disturbed woman," said Karen, nodding.

She sipped her Diet Coke through a straw. As an afterthought, she remembered to scribble on her notepad when she caught Gaetz staring at her again.

"Did she leave behind a suicide note?" she asked.

"No. Marilyn didn't either, by the way."

"I can see why people think Marilyn was murdered."

"Suicides don't always leave notes."

"Is there any suspicion that Deirdre was murdered a la Marilyn?"

"Deirdre was paranoid."

"So your answer is no?"

"She *thought* people were trying to kill her, because she suffered a lot of rejection as an actor. That doesn't mean they actually were. Nobody had motivation to kill her. She would audition and never get the part. It affected her emotional well-being, her self-esteem. She became unstable."

"You talk like a shrink."

"I did consult our LAPD shrink about Deirdre, because I wanted to understand what would drive a woman to murder her own children."

"Then you don't think she had any real enemies?"

Gaetz dipped two French fries into catsup and tossed them into his mouth.

"I talked to some of the Hollywood casting directors who auditioned her for parts," he said. "They said she wasn't the type they were looking for to play the role. It wasn't anything personal."

"Maybe she didn't know the right people. It's all about knowing the right people in Hollywood as I understand it. Not that I'm an expert."

"What if she knew the right people, and they didn't like her? Knowing the right people isn't enough to make it in Hollywood. The right people need to *like* you for you to get anywhere in that business." Gaetz yucked. "Listen to us. A cop and a housewife and we act like we're experts on Tinsel Town."

Karen thought about it. "A woman with a fragile ego like Deirdre. She shouldn't have tried to break into showbiz. It's a cutthroat business from everything I hear about it. You have to deal with a lot of rejection."

"Unless you're what they're looking for."

"I guess Deirdre wasn't the one. With her sensitivity, I can understand why she would think people were out to get her after she got rejected constantly at auditions."

Gaetz grunted his approval. "Rejection and paranoid schizophrenia ain't a good mix."

Karen remembered to scribble on her notepad to convince Gaetz she was a genuine reporter.

"Why do you think she killed her kids?" she asked.

"One of her friends said she blamed her kids for her failure in her career, because she spent so much time bringing them up that she couldn't go to all the auditions she wanted to attend."

"She sounds like she was in sore need of a psychiatrist."

Gaetz glanced at his wristwatch. "Ugh. I didn't know it was so late. I gotta get going."

He wolfed down the last of his cheeseburger and knocked back the remainder of his Coke. He stood up and strutted away.

"Thank you, Lieutenant," she called after him.

Two murders and a suicide had taken place in her house, she now knew, feeling queasy at the thought. Maybe she would have been better off not knowing. No wonder none of the neighbors wanted to talk about Deirdre.

Chapter 16

Karen didn't finish her hamburger. She had had enough to eat with her griddled cheese sandwich at lunch with Brady.

She drove her Beetle back to the hills.

Gaetz had given her a lot to think about. A murderer had been the former owner of their new house. Not good news. It explained the heebie-jeebies she felt when she was in the house. The walls oozed with creepiness.

When she had told Gaetz she wrote articles, she had lied. However, she *was* a writer. A writer of fiction. She wrote short stories and dutifully sent them to magazines like *Ellery Queen Magazine* and *Alfred Hitchcock Magazine*. The editors dutifully rejected them. Her stories had been rejected so many times she couldn't remember the exact number. She had given up keeping count when it was over a thousand.

In many ways she felt like Deirdre with her thwarted career of acting. Constant rejection was discouraging.

She didn't know if she wanted to stay in Deirdre's house. She was convinced it gave off bad vibrations.

She pulled into the driveway, parked the Bug, killed the ignition, and slid out of the driver's seat. She stood in front of the house and looked at it.

From the outside it didn't seem creepy. In fact, it was a downright attractive house. It reminded her of a miniature version of Marilyn Monroe's Spanish-styled mansion in Brentwood.

Inside was another story. She felt reluctant to go inside. She dreaded another attack by flies.

The flies had been in the bathroom, which was where Deirdre had drowned her two girls. The thought gave Karen goose bumps and sent shivers down her spine.

What was she so afraid of? She didn't believe in ghosts or spirits. And haunted houses were horror stories for little kids. Her apprehension was childlike. She knew better.

As she entered the house, she felt disoriented. She felt the strong sensation that it was spinning. She became dizzy. She walked to the nearest wall and braced herself against it to prevent herself from collapsing.

Brady saw her in the living room and looked nervous.

"Are you OK?" she said, recovering her equilibrium on seeing him.

He rubbed his neck.

"Have you been playing in the bathroom again?" she said, becoming angry.

"No."

"Don't play in the bathroom again. You could have died in there."

He stared at her with fright.

"What's wrong?" she said.

"Nothing," he said, and scurried away.

Did he still think she had tried to drown him? She couldn't imagine drowning Brady. It was unthinkable. She didn't know what she would do if she lost him. She couldn't bear to think about it.

Up until now she had been writing mystery short stories. Maybe she should try her hand at horror. Deirdre's life read like a horror story. Karen might be able to turn it into a story recalling Shirley Jackson.

Karen heard a car pull into the driveway.

She peered out the picture window and saw Gordon walking up the driveway.

He opened the front door and entered the living room. Brady appeared in the hall and pelted toward Gordon. Scared, he grabbed Gordon's hand.

"Mom tried to kill me," he said.

"What are you talking about?" said Gordon, taken aback.

"She held my head underwater in the bathtub."

Dumbfounded, Karen stared at Brady.

"What's he talking about?" Gordon asked her with concern.

Karen found herself speechless, bowled over by Brady's accusation.

At last she collected herself.

"I'm the one who saved his life," she said. "I found him holding his head underwater in the bathtub. I pulled him out of the water."

"She held me underwater by my neck," said Brady.

"Tell him the truth, Brady."

"I am."

"If this is a joke, it's not funny," said Gordon.

"It's not a joke," said Brady. "I thought I was gonna die."

"You can't go around, making serious accusations like this," said Karen. "Go to your room and pull yourself together. Your lying is not acceptable."

Brady looked with pleading eyes at Gordon then tore out of the living room and upstairs to his room.

Chapter 17

"What's going on?" asked Gordon.

"I dunno," answered Karen. "He's been acting strange ever since we moved in."

"Why would he hold his head underwater in the bathtub?"

"I have no idea. It scared the living daylights out of me when I found him trying to kill himself."

Gordon didn't know what to make of it.

"We can't allow him to make false accusations against people," said Karen.

"Of course not. But he did look terrified of you."

"I was mad at him. How would you feel if he lied and said you tried to kill him?"

Brooding, Gordon paced around the room.

"Let's just settle down," he said, coming to a halt.

"It's this house."

"What?" he said, not understanding.

"This house is stressing us out. It has bad vibes. Can't you feel them?"

"Houses don't stress people out."

"You might want to change your mind when I tell you what I found out about the previous owner."

"Who told you about them?"

"A Hollywood cop who investigated the murders that took place here."

Gordon widened his eyes. "Murders?"

"The previous owner murdered her two girls then killed herself."

Gordon paused, taking it in. "I didn't know. The realtor never told us."

"She knew it would sink the sale if she told us."

"Even if a murder *did* take place here, it doesn't mean the place is haunted. I'm surprised you would believe such bullshit."

"The murderer was a very disturbed actress."

"You think her tormented spirit is haunting this house. Is that it?" he said, his lips dripping with sarcasm.

"All I'm saying is this house gives off bad vibes."

"I can't believe you're saying this. You of all people. You're the last one I would suspect of being superstitious. You're so levelheaded. That's one reason I was attracted to you."

Feeling cold she crossed her arms on her chest. "I know, but this house . . . and those flies that attacked me."

"It's a house. That's all. A house is just a house. A bunch of flies in a house means nothing."

"A house where a murder took place last year."

"It has nothing to do with us."

"What about the pounding you heard on the wall last night?"

"It must've been pipes knocking."

"And the cup of water that moved in the bathroom?"

"I—there must be a logical explanation," he said, frowning because the incident continued to nag at him.

Karen made up her mind.

"It's time we have a psychic medium inspect the house," she said.

He gazed at her in astonishment. "Mediums are a bunch of quacks. Don't tell me you believe in all that supernatural mumbo jumbo." He made a face and wiggled his fingers at her. "We're coming to haunt you, Karen," he said in a spooky voice.

"You're not funny."

"Come on."

Karen rubbed her eyebrow. "What harm would it do?"

"It would harm our checkbook. I still haven't paid the mortgage. You know what I think it is?"

"What?"

"We're all stressed out, because we just moved into a new house."

Karen pouted in disagreement. She scoped out the house.

"This house has a history," she said. "It's not gonna let us forget it."

"There you go again, talking like the house is a living thing."

"Terrible things happened here. Pretending they didn't won't change anything."

"I'm not pretending anything. The past is dead. Dead is dead. We're alive. Let's live out our lives and forget what happened here last year."

She took in the house. "Will the house let us forget, though?"

"What's it gonna do to us, Karen? Eat us up?"

"Maybe it'll send more flies after us," she said ominously.

"Then we'll get more Raid and send them to hell."

"This is nothing to joke about."

"Who's joking? If you want to kill flies, use insecticide."

Karen put her foot down. "I refuse to stay here unless a medium checks out this house."

"All right," said Gordon, weary of arguing. "They'll have to accept credit cards though, because we can't pay them. In any case, it's all moot if I can't pay the mortgage, since we'll have to move out whether we want to or not."

"You always look at the dark side of everything."

"It's called facing reality. Somebody in this family has to do it. Anyway, *you're* the one who thinks evil spirits are haunting this house."

"Pretending evil doesn't exist won't make it go away."

A loud noise made them both start.

They looked in the direction of the bang.

A book had fallen off the bookshelf on the wall and hit the floor.

Brady ran into the room.

"*Final Destination 3* is on TV tonight," he said eagerly.

"That's a good flick," said Gordon. "Which one in the series do you like the best?"

"Hmm. The first one."

Karen's eyes were glued to the book that had fallen.

"It fell off the shelf," said Gordon. "It happens. A gremlin didn't push it."

His cell phone chimed. He answered it.

Chapter 18

"Are you watching the news?" said Diego on the other end of the line, his voice edged.

"No," said Gordon, his cell phone pressed against his ear, his heartbeat accelerating.

He had no desire to talk to Diego, figuring he knew the purpose of Diego's call.

"Turn on the news on CNN," said Diego.

Gordon found the TV remote on the coffee table and turned on the 4K TV mounted on the wall. He switched the channel to CNN.

The newscaster was standing on the sidewalk in front of a hospital.

"Judge Childress was taken to St. Thomas Hospital with a gunshot wound to his arm. Hospital authorities are describing it as a flesh wound. He is in good condition and is expected to be discharged shortly. Police are investigating the shooting that took place in the *Los Angeles Times* parking lot downtown where a shooter ambushed the judge. No suspects have been identified at this time."

The blood drained from Gordon's face.

He had expected as much. He knew he hadn't gotten off a kill shot, because his aim had been thrown off when the judge had stooped to pick up his briefcase at the last minute and a witness had foiled a second shot. The TV news confirmed the worst.

"What the hell happened?" said Diego, irate.

Wanting to be out of earshot of Karen and Brady, Gordon walked outside the house.

"A witness interrupted me," said Gordon.

"You already blew the contract once. And now again. Can't you do your job?"

Gordon was beginning to wonder the same thing. He had never botched a contract as bad as he had this one. He had never botched a contract, period. This one he had botched twice. What was happening to him?

"I'll get it done," he said. "The best laid plans—"

"I don't want excuses. Childress has to be taken out. Do you understand?"

"I do. And I will take care of it."

"If you don't keep up your end of the deal, we're not paying you."

"It's just taking a little longer than expected."

"Let me be clear. We have a trial coming up, and he's the presiding judge. This cannot happen. A flesh wound in his arm isn't gonna stop him from doing his job."

All he needed was the Zeta cartel on his case, decided Gordon. Beautiful.

"The judge will be taken care of," he said.

"That's what you said last time."

"Let me handle it."

"You better be telling the truth this time. I got sicarios who could do this job no sweat."

"Then why hire me?"

"Because you're in the right place at the right time. No fuck-ups this time. Or no *dinero*. Three strikes, you're out. You already got two. *Comprendes*?"

"Childress got lucky. There's one thing I've learned in life. Luck doesn't last forever."

"Your luck is running out. The *patrón* won't be happy if he finds out he hired a *pendejo*."

"Your worries are over," said Gordon, wondering if what he said was true, wondering why this contract was giving him so much trouble.

He was making errors in judgment regarding this job. He shouldn't have tried to take out the judge in the parking garage, because there were too many variables. Too many things could go wrong, such as a stranger driving into the parking lot and approaching the judge at the same time Gordon tried to execute the hit. *Measure twice, cut once.*

Maybe he was losing the killer instinct. No one could succeed in this job without it. Was he subconsciously screwing up this hit because he had lost the killer instinct and couldn't go through with the kill? Was it possible to lose the killer instinct? If it was something you were born with, how could you lose it? But what if it wasn't something you were born with? What if it was something you developed or acquired through working at it?

He was asking too many questions, second-guessing himself. He would never do anything if he thought about it too much. Self-doubt would kneecap him.

He looked at the house façade.

It was the evil house tormenting him that was causing him to make errors in judgment executing his job, he decided with amusement. He laughed at the thought.

But how could the cup of water he had put on the bathroom sink move to the clothes hamper if he hadn't moved it? Somebody else must have moved it. But there was nobody else in the bathroom.

"Hello?" said Diego. "Are you there?"

"Yeah," said Gordon.

"Get it done ASAP, *amigo*. No dicking around. *No trabajo, no dinero.*"

Diego hung up.

Gordon fills the cup with cold water. He puts the cup on the sink and returns to the bedroom. He returns to the bathroom. Nobody is there. But the cup of water has moved to the lid of the dirty clothes hamper.

He could see the scene playing out as clear in his mind as if it had happened two minutes ago.

Impossible. The cup couldn't have moved by itself.

Had Karen pretended to be asleep last night? Had *she* moved the cup?

No. She had been out cold. He had tried to wake her without success. Her sleeping pills had done their job.

Then how did the cup move?

He couldn't waste time thinking about it. He had to whack Childress. The mortgage had to be paid.

Chapter 19

Karen sat at her laptop and tried to write another short story. She knew that successful writers had to suffer much rejection before getting published. The only way to deal with it was to write another story. You could never give up if you wanted to be a writer.

She found it hard to concentrate. Maybe this house was throwing her off stride.

Brady entered the study.

"Mom, I'm hungry," he said.

"Go get something in the kitchen, you spoiled brat. Can't you see I'm busy?"

Terrified, he tore out of the study, his eyes moist.

She could never get any work done if he persisted in bothering her. She couldn't let him monopolize her time if she was going to make it as a writer. A writer had to write. The only way you could do that was by sitting in front of your laptop and grinding out words. Or, to paraphrase Hemingway, to sit in front of your laptop and bleed. Like he had said, it was easy.

The point was, you had to get something down on paper, she knew. A blank piece of paper was anathema to a writer.

She couldn't let herself be distracted by every little thing, including Brady's demands for attention. She understood Deirdre's blaming her failure as an actor on her two girls. You couldn't let your kids destroy your pursuit of your dream job with their constant demands. In that sense, Marilyn Monroe had an advantage over her and Deirdre, because Marilyn didn't have any offspring to get in the way of her career. Was that why Marilyn had been successful in her career? Because she had no children to take up her valuable time?

Brady bolted back into the study.

"I hate you," he said.

Dumbfounded, she couldn't believe her ears. "Don't ever talk to me like that."

"I don't recognize you. You're not my mom."

"How dare you speak to me like that?" she said, steaming. "I'm your mother. I'll wash your mouth out with soap. And then I'll kill you."

Terrified, Brady fled out of the room.

What was wrong with the child? she wondered. Why had he tried to drown himself in the bathtub? Maybe he needed a psychiatrist. They couldn't afford another psychiatrist. Psychiatrists were for rich people. Gordon couldn't pay the mortgage, let alone afford another shrink. He couldn't even afford one for himself the way things were going.

What was Brady's problem? Why would a small boy try to drown himself?

She didn't have time to think about it. She had to keep busy writing or she would never succeed as a professional writer. The world was littered with writers manqué who failed to apply themselves to their difficult craft.

She stared at the blank piece of paper on her laptop screen. How could she write with all these interruptions?

She felt sympathy for the murderess Deirdre who had killed her daughters because they had thwarted her career in the movies.

Karen felt the floor vibrating. What was causing it? It must have been a quake. They happened all the time. Welcome to California.

Where was she? She had lost her train of thought. She needed to get something written down. Anything. Even if it was crap.

She started. She heard pounding on the wall that abutted the living room.

Was Brady doing it to torment her? She didn't think he could make such a racket with his fists. She would tan the brat's hide when she got hold of him.

She sprang out of her seat toward the other side of the wall, her eyes blazing with fury.

The pounding stopped before she reached the living room. She scoped out the room.

Nobody was there.

Then who had pounded on the wall?

Could Brady have done it and run away before she got here? She didn't understand how he could make such a din with his small fists. The entire wall had juddered as he had pounded on it.

She inspected the wall. She didn't see any dents in it. The Sheetrock looked intact. The pounding hadn't damaged it.

She had to get back to work.

A bluebottle buzzed around her head.

Not another fly, she decided, dreading she would be the target of another attack by thousands of flies. She sweated with apprehension.

She was tempted to run outside to escape the flies.

She swatted the fly away from her head. It buzzed off in another direction. She didn't see any others in the room. She could deal with one fly. She thought about hunting it down and killing it with the fly swatter she kept in the kitchen.

The floor vibrated again. It had to be an aftershock. Whenever there was a quake, aftershocks followed. Or was it a quake? Maybe it was this house, she decided, surveying the living room walls with suspicion. A frisson went down her spine as she experienced the feeling of being watched. She wheeled around, expecting to see someone behind her.

She saw no one.

Yet she couldn't shake the feeling of being watched.

What was going on?

This house was driving her nuts. She needed to hire a medium to exorcise it, or whatever they did to haunted houses, if for no other reason than to give her peace of mind.

A weird, noisome odor that she couldn't identify assailed her nostrils.

She felt more alone than she had ever felt. It felt as though the house was crushing her, suffocating her. She gasped for breath. She could hear the walls breathing, sucking the air out of her lungs. She needed to get outside.

Claustrophobia overwhelmed her.

She wasn't in a house. She was nailed in a coffin six feet under, struggling to breathe. The coffin was shrinking around her, she realized, her eyes bugging out of her head.

She tried to scream. The scream died in her throat.

How could she be trapped in a coffin? She was in the living room. She must be hallucinating. She was imagining the coffin. *The house*. The house was making her hallucinate.

The air smelled stale. She pounded on the coffin lid, trying to attract someone's attention.

"Let me out," she cried. "Let me out."

She felt her cell phone vibrate in her trouser pocket. She fished out the phone and took the call.

"This is Lieutenant Gaetz."

"Hello," said Karen, aware that she was standing in her living room instead of lying in a coffin.

His voice had brought her back to reality, she realized with relief.

"I want to make sure you spell my name right," said Gaetz. "My wife is looking forward to reading the article you write. She told me to make sure you get my name right. It's Gaetz. G-a-e-t-z. Not G-a-t-e-s."

"I got it. Thanks."

"Is there anything else you want to know about Deirdre Turner?"

"What were the names of Deirdre's two girls?"

"Let me see. Um—Theresa and, uh—Frieda, I believe. If you have any more questions, give me a call. Bye."

It was time to call a medium, she decided, pacing around the living room, making sure she wasn't trapped in a coffin.

Chapter 20

Gordon saw Brady run into the front yard.

"What's wrong?" said Gordon, seeing that Brady was upset.

Brady scurried across the lawn and hugged him.

"What happened?" said Gordon. He chuckled. "You look like you saw a ghost."

"That's not my mom in the house."

"What are you talking about?"

"She's not Mom."

"Of course, she's Mom."

"She looks like her, but it's not her."

Gordon held him at arm's length and looked him in the eye. "Why would you say such a terrible thing?"

"She said she was gonna kill me," said Brady, fear in his voice.

"What?" said Gordon, taken aback. "She would never threaten you like that."

"Mom wouldn't. But that woman in the house did."

"That's your mother in the house."

"It's like that movie *The Shining*. Remember it?"

"Of course."

"Remember how the father went nuts and tried to kill his son with an ax when they were running around in that maze in the snow?"

"That was just a movie," said Gordon, smiling.

"She's the father. She called me a spoiled brat and said she was gonna kill me."

"You must have misheard her. She would never say that to you."

"She did."

Gordon frowned. "It's not right to tell lies about people."

"I'm not."

"I'm sure this is a misunderstanding."

"I don't feel safe in there with her," said Brady, eyeballing the house with consternation.

"There's nothing to be afraid of. Let's go inside."

Brady balked, his body tense with fear. "No."

"You can't be afraid of a stupid house. Nothing will happen to you. We'll go inside together."

Gordon made for the front door.

He looked behind him and saw Brady standing petrified.

"Come on," said Gordon. "You don't want everyone to call you a scaredy-cat, do you?"

Plagued by misgivings, Brady opted to follow him.

"We'll straighten this out with your mother," said Gordon.

"She's not my mother."

"Then who is she?"

"I dunno."

Gordon entered the house and looked for Karen. He found her in the study sitting at her desk in front of her open laptop.

"What have you been telling Brady?" he said.

"What are you talking about?" she said, looking up from the monitor.

"He said you said you were gonna kill him."

"What?" said Karen in astonishment.

Gordon looked behind him for Brady. Brady wasn't there.

"He said you called him a spoiled brat and threatened to kill him," said Gordon.

"You know me," she said, indignant. "I would never say such a thing."

"Are you saying you didn't say it?"

"I resent your giving me the third degree."

"Why would he make it up?"

"Maybe he's stressed out from moving to a new house."

"It's not like him to make up lies."

"You sound like you believe him," she said, offended.

"He also said something strange." Gordon paused a beat. "He said you're not you."

"Phooey. Crazy talk. I'm not me? Ha. Does that make the slightest bit of sense?"

"Can you at least spend a little more time with him? Maybe he feels lonely. Maybe it explains his making up stuff."

"I'm working on a project. I can't get anything done if I have to pay attention to him 24/7."

"Is your project more important to you than your own son?"

Karen bristled. "Why don't *you* spend more time with him? He's your son too."

"You're making this difficult."

"I found out more about Deirdre Turner. The names of her daughters were Theresa and Frieda."

"Let's forget this Deirdre Turner. She's a complete stranger. We have our own lives to live. Life is gonna pass us by if we don't live our own lives instead of the life of a failed movie actress who murdered her kids."

"Exactly. I'm trying to live out my life by doing my project, but Brady keeps interrupting me and demanding attention."

"What do you want us to do? Send him off to boarding school? I'm sure we can afford it."

"I don't appreciate your sarcasm."

Gordon eyed her with suspicion. "Did you move my cup of water last night?"

"How could I? I was asleep."

"True," he conceded.

"Are we done with your inquisition? I need to get back to work."

He turned to leave.

"Did you feel an earthquake a little while ago?" she said.

"No."

"I did. Maybe you couldn't feel it outside. The house was shaking."

"As long as it doesn't slide down the hill, I guess we're OK."

"I'll take care of Brady for his lying."

"What's that supposed to mean?" said Gordon, unsettled by her tone.

"We can't let him get away with telling lies about people. He needs to be punished."

"I suppose. He seems genuinely scared of you, though. Why would he be so terrified of you if you didn't say you would kill him?"

"He must be scared I'll find out he's telling lies about me."

"I have to go to work now. I better not find Brady dead when I come home," said Gordon with a half-smile as he turned away from her.

His attempt at a joke had bombed. The silence was deafening.

Why wasn't she laughing? Didn't she know he was joking? Her silence chilled him. Was she really considering killing Brady? No way. Brady must have misunderstood her.

Gordon booked.

Chapter 21

Gordon drove his rental south on the Hollywood Freeway to St. Thomas Hospital in downtown LA, where they were treating Childress for a gunshot wound.

He couldn't waste any more time on this hit. He had to get it done to get his paycheck from the cartel.

He might be able to pull off the hit in the hospital. It depended on whether the LAPD had posted a guard in front of Childress's room.

There was only one way to find out.

He managed to find a curbside parking space at a meter. He didn't want to park in the hospital parking garage in case the cops had it under surveillance. If he needed to make a quick getaway, the cops could block the garage exits in no time. They couldn't block curbside parking.

Wearing his SIG P224 in an ankle holster, he made for the hospital. He didn't pick up on a heavy police presence in the area.

He entered the lobby and spotted a uniformed cop standing guard.

Gordon's heart skipped a beat. What did he have to fear? he asked himself. The cops weren't looking for him. The newscaster had said they had no suspects. Unless the cops had lied to the media. Which they were prone to do, he knew.

Gordon needed to find out which room contained Childress. Gordon approached the front desk. A black receptionist in her early thirties was sitting behind it, studying her cell phone screen.

"Hello," he said, smiling. "Could you tell me which room Mr. Childress is in?"

She looked up and searched his face. "The judge?"

"Yeah."

"Are you a family member?"

"Uh, no."

"A reporter?" she said with a scowl.

"No."

"He's not taking visitors at this time," she said, and returned to inspecting her cell phone screen, unsatisfied with his answers.

"I'm sure the judge wants to see me."

"How can you be so sure?" she said, not looking up.

"I found his wallet on the sidewalk outside the lobby. I want to return it to him."

She looked up and extended her hand. "I can take it for him."

"It's not that I don't trust you, but I want to make sure the judge gets his wallet back. I don't want it to fall into the wrong hands."

"I'll see that he gets it."

"This is too important to trust to anyone else. I need to deliver it to him myself."

At that moment, Childress stepped out of the elevator whose door opened at the bank of elevators, his bandaged arm in a sling, a uniform at his side. Childress's gaze fell on Gordon.

"Stop him," he cried, pointing at Gordon.

Adrenaline surging through his body, Gordon cut his eyes back and forth across the lobby, casting around for the best exit. He didn't like the front door. The cop would be right behind him. Gordon opted for the fire door on the opposite side of the building.

He pelted across the lobby floor.

"Stop," cried the cop. "This is the LAPD."

Gordon slammed his elbow into the crash bar on the steel fire door, shoved the door open, and burst into an alley. He sprinted down the alley toward the street where he had parked his rental.

He had no idea Childress had seen him at the site of the hit in the *LA Times* parking garage. If Childress had seen him, he couldn't have gotten a very good look at him. Gordon was surprised Childress could ID him.

He wasn't going to think about it. He had to keep running. He knew the cop had to be behind him and was calling for backup.

"Stop or I'll shoot," cried the cop.

Gordon figured the cop was training his Glock on him even now.

Gordon dashed around the corner of the building at the mouth of the alley and charged toward his parked rental, churning his legs, his face pouring with sweat, his lungs bursting.

He unlocked the rental door with his key fob, flung open the door, ducked into the driver's seat, and fired the ignition. He peeled away from the curb, tires shrieking, executed a three-point turn, and rocketed down the street, hoping the cop wouldn't be able to make out his license plate at this distance.

Gordon hung a right and disappeared from the cop's sight.

Even if the cop had seen the license tag, he couldn't trace the rental back to Gordon, because Gordon had rented the car under an assumed name. It was a matter of escaping this part of town without picking up a black-and-white on his tail. If he could do that, he would be in the clear.

He made it to the northbound ramp of the Hollywood Freeway and accelerated to merge into heavy rush-hour traffic, which forced him to slow down.

Driving on the freeway he hoped the judge wouldn't be able to provide an accurate description of his face to a police sketch artist. How could the judge? Childress had been leaning over, picking up his briefcase when Gordon had winged him. Childress hadn't been looking in Gordon's direction. Childress must have glimpsed him out of the corner of his eye for no longer than a split second, but long enough to ID him in the hospital.

This job was getting harder by the minute, decided Gordon. Everything was going sideways. He had never come this close to getting nailed by the cops.

He needed to get a drink. He would find a pub in Hollywood when he pulled off the freeway.

He was starting to wonder if he could complete the hit. He felt like he was losing it, like he didn't have it in him to get the job done. Maybe it was time to call it quits. Too many failures could eat away like acid at your self-confidence.

For sure, he wasn't going to tell Diego he had tried another hit and blown it. Gordon would keep this latest blunder to himself. The problem was he hadn't had enough time to plan the hit. Ad-libbed hits had the least chance of success.

Chapter 22

When Gordon drove home, it was night. The house was dark.

Karen must have gone to bed, he decided, parking his rental in the driveway and climbing out of the driver's seat.

The house looked gloomy in the dark under a gibbous moon. Like something dead. He shivered. Nothing good had happened to him since he had moved here. He shrugged. Just a run of bad luck. The house had nothing to do with it. He had to live somewhere. Why not here? The hills were a ritzy area. Not everybody could afford to live in them. He couldn't afford it either, now that his professional life was going south.

He entered the living room and tossed his key fob on the sideboard.

He felt woozy from his drinking at the pub on Sunset.

He heard the stairs creaking.

Karen was descending them in the negligee she wore to bed.

"Hi, Karen," he said. "I didn't mean to wake you."

Her hair mussed, she reached the floor and glided past him in her bare feet, ignoring him. She snapped up the key fob on the sideboard and walked outside.

What was she doing? he wondered.

He hurried after her. She padded down the driveway toward the rental.

He was surprised the pebbles in the drive didn't hurt her bare feet. She paid no attention to them as her naked soles crunched over them. Her shadow followed her in the moonlight, skimming along the pebbles.

"Where are you going?" he said, watching her open the rental's door and slide into the driver's seat.

She ignored him.

He hurried over to her.

"It's kind of late to be going out for a drive," he said.

Sitting in the rental, she stared ahead of her like she was in a trance, looking like a doll with an apron of moonlight across her lap.

She fired the engine, backed out of the drive, and tooled down the street.

She looked out of it, he decided. How could she drive in her condition? A helluva time for her to take a joyride. He debated driving after her. He shouldn't be driving himself thanks to his drinking.

He wasn't going to call the cops. He wanted nothing to do with them. There might be a BOLO out for him, for all he knew.

Yawning, he returned inside the house. He needed to rack out.

He decided to leave the front door unlocked, because he didn't think Karen had a house key. She hadn't taken her pocketbook with her. She didn't even have her driver's license. He didn't like the idea of leaving the door unlocked while he was sleeping, but he didn't want to lock her out.

He climbed the steps to his bedroom.

In the hallway he saw Brady shuffling toward him in his PJs.

Brady rubbed his eyes. "What's going on?"

"Your mother went to the drugstore," lied Gordon.

He didn't want to upset the kid by telling him Karen was driving around in the middle of the night in a trance in nothing but her negligee.

"She's not Mom," said Brady. "I don't know who that woman is."

"Are you still harping on that?"

"It's true."

"You need sleep. When you don't get enough sleep, you imagine things."

He ushered Brady down the hallway.

"She scares me," said Brady.

"We'll talk about it tomorrow after you get some sleep. The best thing for you now is sleep."

"What if she tries to kill me in my sleep?"

"Stop talking like that. Nobody's killing anybody."

Including him, decided Gordon. He had botched the hit on Childress once again.

"Is she coming back?" asked Brady, looking up at Gordon with worried eyes.

"She's coming back and she's going straight to bed. I'm not gonna let her hurt you," said Gordon, leaning toward him.

"You have bad breath," said Brady, pulling a face.

It must have been the booze he had been swilling, decided Gordon.

"I'll brush my teeth," he said. "You go on to bed. I won't let her go into your room."

"All right."

Brady returned to his bedroom, consoled after a fashion.

Gordon hated the idea of Karen driving around in a trance. How did she know what she was doing in her condition? She was an accident waiting to happen. It was too late to find her now. She could be anywhere. In any case, he had too much booze in his system to go out driving.

His eyelids heavy, he changed into his pajamas and hit the sack.

No sooner had his head hit the pillow than he jackknifed up in bed, his eyes staring, his head throbbing, when he heard loud pounding against the wall.

Chapter 23

How long had he been asleep? It seemed like he had dozed off for a few seconds. But it could have been much longer. He had lost track of time.

He glanced at the other side of the bed and saw it was empty. Karen hadn't returned. Or, if she had, she hadn't come upstairs.

He sprang out of bed and looked out the window, trying to find what had banged against the outside bedroom wall. The eucalyptus in the front yard was blowing in the wind, rattling its leaves, but none of the branches reached the house.

Had Karen returned, pounded on the bedroom wall, and left? He cast around the room. He saw no evidence she had returned.

Gordon cut across the bedroom floor to the bathroom.

He flicked on the light, turned on the faucet, and filled a plastic cup with cold water. As he was about to drink it, the thumping on the wall resumed. He set his cup on the sink and darted to the bedroom window, trying to catch the culprit in the act.

The pounding stopped.

He peered outside.

Nothing was pounding the wall. Nothing could reach the second floor.

He returned to the bathroom to drink his water.

Once again, his cup had moved to the lid of the clothes hamper.

He looked around for Karen. She wasn't in the bathroom. He didn't see her in the bedroom. Then who had moved his cup? It was a repeat of last night. The hallucination of a drunk?

Was he still in bed dreaming? He pinched his arm. His arm felt the pinch. He must be awake. Or did he dream he pinched his arm?

He was too rattled to go back to sleep. He had to find out what was going on. Who was moving his cup of water? There had to be an answer, and he wanted to know it. The cup of water couldn't move by itself.

He thought he heard a noise downstairs.

He retrieved his SIG from the closet.

Tensing, he flicked on the light over the stairwell. Gun in hand, he descended the steps, alert for any sound, his heartbeat ratcheting up with anticipation. He didn't see anyone moving in the dark living room.

He hoped it was Karen who had entered the house. But he remembered he had left the front door unlocked. It could be anyone prowling around the living room in the dark.

He kept descending the stairs.

He entered the living room.

Karen tossed the key fob on the sideboard, glided past him, and climbed the steps.

"Karen?" he said. "Did you pound on the wall?"

She ignored him and reached the landing.

"Where did you go?" he said, ascending the steps behind her.

She padded into the bedroom.

She looked like she was still in a trance, he decided. At least she hadn't gotten into an accident while driving in the night.

He followed her into the bedroom.

"Did you move my cup of water?" he asked.

She climbed into bed, slipped between the sheets, rested her head on the pillow, and stared at the ceiling without moving. A fly alighted on her eyeball and walked on her cornea with skinny black legs. She didn't even blink. How could she stand the sensation of the fly walking on her eyeball without reacting to it? She was dead to the world like a corpse.

The fly flew away. A minute later Karen closed her eyes.

Her behavior creeped him out. She must be in a sleepwalking trance.

He returned downstairs and checked the front door. Karen had left it wide open. He peered outside. He saw his rental parked in the driveway. It didn't look like there were any new dents in it, though it was difficult to see in the dark. He didn't see any prowlers. He pushed the door shut and locked it.

He went back up the steps, placed his SIG on the top shelf of the closet, and got into bed beside Karen.

A feeling of being watched unnerved him. He stared at the ceiling, expecting to see hundreds of eyes staring back at him. He saw only the ceiling. Maybe he was going nuts. He needed to check in with his shrink.

Karen was acting as crazy as he felt. Shambling in a daze like a zombie in the middle of the night and driving around. What was that all about? And Brady saying Karen wasn't Karen. Was Brady cracking up too? The hell with it. Why worry? Worrying was a waste of time. Life went on.

Too tired to dwell on the night's eldritch events, he fell asleep.

Chapter 24

Karen woke up in the morning and went downstairs to prepare breakfast.

When she passed the bathroom, she heard water running. She ducked her head into the bathroom and saw water pouring out of the bathtub faucet. The bathtub was full. Brady was floating face down in the water.

Karen screamed.

She flew to the tub, grabbed Brady, and pulled his head out of the water.

Gordon ran down the steps and thrust his head into the bathroom. "What happened?"

Looking wretched, Karen stood near the empty tub with a loofah sponge in her hand.

"I could've sworn I saw Brady floating on his stomach in the bathtub," she said.

Gordon examined the bathtub, which was empty. "He's not here."

"I thought this sponge was his head," she said, raising the round flesh-colored sponge in her hand.

"You must be seeing things."

Gasping, she clutched her heart. "I thought I was gonna have a heart attack."

"It must be those sleeping pills you're taking. They're making you hallucinate."

Karen rubbed her face. "I guess."

"You did take pills last night? Right?"

"I had to. I couldn't sleep. This house makes me nervous."

"That explains last night."

"What happened last night?" she said, eying him. "I slept like a log."

"I saw you sleepwalking last night."

"I had no idea," she said, amazed.

"Not only that, you took the car and drove it during the night."

Bemused, Karen tried to wrap her head around it. "Where did I go?"

"I wish I knew. Maybe you should lay off the Halcion. My shrink said it can make people sleepwalk and drive around at night."

"I'm lucky I didn't run over someone. I had no idea I was in a car."

"It must be the pills. Maybe you're taking too many."

"It's not the pills," she said, tossing the sponge into the bathtub and leaving the bathroom. "It's this house. It's taking over our lives."

She entered the kitchen.

"I don't believe in that supernatural nonsense," said Gordon. "Your pills are messing up your head. You're acting so strange your own son doesn't recognize you."

"It's this house, I'm telling you. It's driving us crazy. I'm calling a medium. I don't care what you say."

"How do we afford it?"

"Our credit cards aren't maxed out. I'll hire a medium who takes credit."

"If it'll make you feel any better, OK. We can't go on like this. That's for sure."

Karen drank her orange juice and made her way to the study, where she awoke her laptop from Sleep mode and searched the Internet for mediums in Hollywood. There was no shortage of mediums in this neck of the woods. Showbiz types consulted them on a regular basis, it appeared.

Karen selected Dr. Rudolph Armitage, because he accepted credit cards and had a PhD in parapsychology, whatever that was. It sounded official. She figured he must not be a quack. He had a website and guaranteed cleaning a haunted house of spirits or your money back. He was forty-five years old and claimed he had never failed a job. His website was filled with glowing testimonials from former clients extolling him.

"How do you get a PhD in parapsychology?" said Karen.

Gordon entered the study. "A diploma mill? You can bet it's a scam. Mediums are scammers."

"Not all of them."

"Come on. You don't really believe in that stuff. Ghosts floating around, spooking people? It's ridiculous."

"What if I had gotten in an accident while driving in my sleep? That could easily have happened."

"That's not because you're haunted. It's because you're taking too many sleeping pills."

Karen ignored him. She produced her cell phone and called Armitage.

After listening to a brief explanation of her problem, Armitage agreed to meet her in an hour.

She terminated the call.

"So soon?" said Gordon, overhearing her conversation. "He must be hard up for customers."

"He said we're in great danger. That's why he's coming here so fast."

"We're in great danger of being fleeced."

"Stop complaining."

"I don't like being taken for a chump."

"You'd rather go insane and kill yourself?"

"Huh?"

"Armitage said the owners of haunted houses frequently go insane or commit suicide."

"Not only is he a parapsychologist, he's a psychiatrist too. Is that it?"

"I'm tired of your scoffing. Look, you don't have to be here when he comes if you don't want to."

"I wouldn't miss it for the world."

"You wouldn't be so flip if you were the one who had been almost smothered by flies."

Gordon became sincere. "I know we're having problems here, but it's not a ghost that's causing them."

"It's this house," she muttered.

Chapter 25

An hour later to the minute, Karen heard Dr. Armitage knock on their door.

"He's punctual if nothing else," said Gordon, who let him in.

"Hello," said Armitage, scanning the living room as he entered.

The five-ten Armitage wore a shepherd's check blazer and black jeans. With long sideburns, black hair, and black Ray-Ban sunglasses, he reminded Karen of the paranoid preacher Jim Jones, who committed suicide along with hundreds of members of his cult in Guyana. A Canon digital camera hung from a leather strap draped around Armitage's neck.

"Hello, Doctor," said Karen. "We're pleased to meet you."

"Likewise," he said, continuing to scan the living room as if sensing a vibration.

"Would you like something to drink?"

The tinted lenses of his shades were so black she couldn't see his eyes through them.

"A chilled Coke from a can if you have one," he said.

"You want it in the can?"

"I sense an evil presence in this house. It's best to drink from a secure container."

She stared at him with puzzlement.

"Don't get me wrong," he said. "I don't suspect that *you* would poison me, but there is an entity here. A malignant entity. I wouldn't put anything past it."

Karen saw Gordon roll his eyes.

"Aren't we gonna have a séance first?" said Gordon. "I thought you guys were big on séances."

His expression grave, Armitage eyed him. "Not at this time."

"I'll get the Coke," said Karen, fixing to leave for the kitchen.

"Never mind. I'll have it later. I want to check this room first."

"Check it for what?" said Gordon.

"A presence."

Armitage withdrew a palm-sized plastic device with a gauge on it from his jacket pocket and circled the room with it, watching the activity on its screen.

"What is that?" asked Karen.

"It's an electromagnetic field meter," he answered. "It can sense the presence of spirits."

"We have booze in the kitchen," said Gordon, winking at Karen. "Your machine should get a reaction there."

Karen frowned at him, not appreciating his feeble attempt at humor.

Armitage ignored him and continued walking around the room, studying the readings on his meter.

"Yes," he said to himself, engrossed in the meter readouts, his face grim.

"Do you have any questions for us?" said Karen.

"Uh, yes." Armitage pocketed his meter. "Have you smelled unexplained stenches in your house?"

"Maybe."

"I plead guilty," said Gordon. "Too much beer. I have a lot of gas."

"Will you shut up," said Karen. "Try to act like an adult."

"Unpleasant odors can signify the presence of an evil spirit," said Armitage, his demeanor somber.

"Do ghosts have gas?" said Gordon.

Armitage ignored him. "How about apparitions? Have you been seeing apparitions in this house?"

"I thought I saw our son floating dead in the bathtub," said Karen.

Armitage nodded.

"I must've imagined it was Brady when I saw the loofah sponge in the tub," said Karen.

"There could be a rational explanation for your seeing things," said Armitage. "Carbon monoxide poisoning and mold in a house can cause hallucinations in the tenants."

"Our carport is detached. I doubt we have carbon monoxide in our house."

"Carbon monoxide doesn't come only from cars. It can come from furnaces and kitchen appliances like stoves."

"We have smoke detectors that pick up carbon monoxide," said Gordon. "The detectors haven't sounded."

"Good to know," said Armitage. "What about mold? Have you had your house checked for mold?"

"We inspected the house before we bought it. We didn't see any mold."

"Mold isn't always visible. It could be behind the walls. But in your case I don't believe you're hallucinating."

"Then what's happening to us?" said Karen.

"You're not hallucinating. You're seeing what the spirits want you to see."

"Why would they want me to see my dead son?"

"I would need to know more about them to be able to answer you. I have more questions for you."

"Fine. Shoot."

"Are you doing strange things you don't ordinarily do?"

"She's been sleepwalking," said Gordon. "She never used to do it till she moved here."

"A spirit possessed her," said Armitage, nodding.

"I drove around in my sleep last night," said Karen.

"Where did you go?"

"Who knows? I didn't even know I was driving."

"It gets weirder," said Gordon.

Chapter 26

"I'm listening," said Armitage.

"Our son Brady keeps saying Karen isn't his mother," said Gordon.

"Children are sensitive to spirits. They can sense things adults cannot. Adults have learned to ignore sensations as a part of growing up. They focus their energy on problem solving, because it's the essence of their jobs."

"He's stressed out because of our moving."

"That's what I'm talking about. You're an adult and you're solving the problem with a rational explanation."

"Because that's how you determine the truth."

"There are different kinds of truths. Physical ones, which obey the laws of physics, and metaphysical ones, which go beyond those laws into the realm of the spiritual."

"You learn that in grad school, did you?" said Gordon, cocking an eyebrow, his visage skeptical.

"Do you hear strange noises or see lights flicking on and off for no reason?" said Armitage without skipping a beat.

Gordon stared at him. "A loud pounding on my bedroom wall has woken me up two nights in a row. When I go to the window to see who's doing it, I see nobody outside. Our bedroom's on the second floor. Nobody could reach it without a ladder. And there's no ladder."

"As I suspected," said Armitage, glum-faced. "Inexplicable loud noises and lights that flash on and off by themselves indicate a spirit presence."

"It could be pipes groaning in the wall. Old pipes make a racket."

"Let's move on. Do you have any really cold or hot areas in your house?"

"We do," said Karen, excited. "It's really cold in part of the hall. Follow me."

Armitage did so, keeping his shades on despite the dim lighting in the corridor.

"Feel how cold it is here," she said, shivering.

"Yes. A definite sign," said Armitage, cocking his head like a dog trying to sense something in the air.

"It's a draft," said Gordon. "We just have to figure out where it's coming from, and I can fix it."

"It's coming from the negative energy permeating this house."

"Tell him about the water, honey," Karen told Gordon.

"What?"

"The cup of water in the upstairs bathroom."

"Oh, yeah." Reluctant to speak about it, Gordon faced Armitage. "I placed a cup of water on the sink and left the bathroom. When I came back, the cup had moved to the dirty clothes hamper."

"I'm not surprised."

"I must've been dreaming, but . . . it was so real."

"It wasn't a dream." Armitage cast around the living room. "Have you noticed insect infestations in your house?"

Karen exchanged looks with Gordon.

"How did you know, Doctor?" she said.

Armitage eyed her. "Houses with an active spirit presence tend to have insect infestations. Flies usually."

"Exactly," said Karen, her eyes lighting up. "Thousands of flies attacked me. They blanketed my face and tried to smother me."

"Where?" said Armitage, growing animated.

"In the downstairs bathroom, where I saw Brady floating in the tub."

"Something traumatic must have happened in the bathroom when the previous owner lived here. Where is it? I must see it."

Karen led him to the bathroom.

Armitage stuck his electromagnetic field meter in the bathroom and watched the screen come to life.

"There is a strong presence," he said.

"Two murders took place here."

He whipped his face toward her. "How do you know?"

"I did research on the former owner. She drowned her two girls in the bathtub."

"I see. I was afraid of this. It explains the strong malignant vibrations in your house. There is an angry spirit with evil intentions present."

Karen clenched her jaw, her body tensing. "What can we do?"

Armitage lifted his camera to his face and snapped several photos of the bathroom. He studied them on the camera display monitor.

"As I suspected," he said, his face solemn. "Take a look."

He showed Karen a photo of the bathtub.

Karen examined the photo. "What am I looking for?"

"Do you see that wavy white line on the inner side of the tub?"

"Yeah. What about it?"

"It's an ectoplasmic strand."

"I never heard of it." Karen glanced at the bathtub. "I don't see it on the tub, only in the photo."

"Ectoplasmic strands show up in houses troubled by spirits. You can't see the strands with the naked eye."

Gordon snagged the camera and eyeballed the picture. "That's soap scum on the tub." He looked at the tub. "There," he said, pointing.

"I don't see anything," said Karen, looking where he pointed.

Armitage snatched the camera from Gordon and clicked on a picture in the viewfinder of the grouted, cobalt tiled wall above the tub.

"There's another strand on the tiles," he said.

Gordon seized the camera and scoped the image of a wavy white line on the tiles. Then he scoped the tiles. He reexamined the photo. He looked up at the light mounted over the mirror on the medicine cabinet.

"It's a reflection of the light," he said.

"I wish you were right, but it's an ectoplasmic strand."

Chapter 27

"Do you ever have the feeling you're being watched?" asked Armitage.

"I do," answered Karen.

"You need to exorcise the demon in this house. Otherwise . . ."

"Otherwise what?"

"Your whole family will die horrible deaths in the near future."

"Is that a threat?" said Gordon, taking umbrage.

"It's my expert opinion as a professional medium. You are in great danger in this house."

"Are you saying these evil spirits are gonna kill us?"

"They will cause your deaths."

"Are you trying to get us to move? Does somebody else want to buy this house? Is that it? Are they paying you to get rid of us?"

"I'm a professional medium, a parapsychologist. I don't work for real estate companies or house buyers," said Armitage, in high dudgeon at the idea. "I'm not a moneygrubber. I'm a seeker of the truth. Please . . ."

"Can you prove you're not working for a realtor?"

"I don't have to prove anything."

"He sees scams all over the place," said Karen, indicating Gordon with a reproachful glance.

"Hollywood is the city of scams," said Gordon. "Spiritualists, mind readers, palm readers, fortune-tellers, hypnotists, and sundry purveyors of boogeyman mumbo jumbo."

"Ignore him," Karen told Armitage.

"I've encountered unbelievers before," said Armitage, unfazed. "Quite a few, actually."

"Is there anything you can do to help us?" said Karen, scrunching her face with concern.

"There are ways to exorcise evil spirits."

Gordon nodded, his face cynical. "How much is it gonna cost?"

"This is serious, Gordon," said Karen. "Stop acting smug like you know everything."

"My standard rates will apply," said Armitage.

"Fine. What do we do to exorcise the demons harassing us?"

"There are various methods you can use."

"Like what?"

Armitage sucked in a deep breath and blew out his chest.

"First," he said, "you need to use a floor wash composed of water, lemon, and cinnamon. Boil the water and add the lemon and cinnamon to it. When the water cools, use the solution to wash the floors and door handles."

"Hawaiian punch is supposed to exorcise the evil spirit?" said Gordon.

Armitage did his best to ignore Gordon.

"Sprinkling salt water in the corners of the house and pouring salt over your house's thresholds is another way to get rid of the negative entity," said Armitage. "Demons don't like salt."

"I don't blame them. It causes high blood pressure."

"Even better. 'Smudge' your house with sage."

"I don't understand," said Karen.

"You can buy a sage smudge stick at any voodoo shop. Jean Baptiste's House of Voodoo on Sunset sells it."

"House of Voodoo, huh?" said Gordon. "Are you sure this isn't a scam?"

"I assure you it isn't. Your lives are in grave danger," said Armitage, ticked off by Gordon's flip tone.

"How's some invisible ghost gonna hurt us?"

"You don't want to find out. I can help you exorcise the spirit if you follow my instructions. As I was saying, it's better to get sage at the House of Voodoo than at a grocery store. Baptiste's sage smudge sticks have been blessed."

"And you get a kickback from any sale to a customer you point in his direction no doubt."

"He's trying to help us," said Karen. "Why do you have to go out of your way to be unpleasant?"

"Just saying," said Gordon, amused.

"What do we do with the sage, Dr. Armitage? You said something about smudging it. What is that?"

"You light a sage smudge stick and walk through your house, filling the rooms with smoke. Keep the windows cracked, however, to provide ventilation."

"What does the smoke do?"

"It forces the demon from your house—unless . . ."

"Unless what?"

"It would have to be a very powerful demon to be able to fight the sage and stay in place. A demon that powerful is rare. Let's not consider it at this time. I don't want to alarm you."

"Then how can you get us to fall for your protection racket?" said Gordon.

Armitage cast a baleful glance at Gordon.

"What happens after we smudge the house?" said Karen hurriedly.

"The smudging should exorcise the house," said Armitage.

"How will we know for sure?"

"I can come back and inspect it for you."

"We'll have to pay him again if he comes back," Gordon told Karen.

"This isn't about money," she retorted. "It's about saving our lives."

"Or fattening the doctor's wallet," said Gordon.

He stalked out of the house, unimpressed with Armitage's performance.

"Your husband doesn't understand the extreme danger you're in," said Armitage.

"He doesn't like showing his ignorance of things he doesn't understand," said Karen, looking after Gordon.

Chapter 28

Gordon strode onto the driveway and saw Armitage's silver Mercedes AMG sedan parked behind his rental. Armitage wasn't hurting in the money department, he decided. Exorcising demons raked in hefty paychecks.

Steamed that he had to pay the psychic a fortune, Gordon clambered into his rental and closed the door. He wanted to be alone so he could think.

He noticed the odometer. It had been at 40,000 miles when he had parked it last night. He had remembered it, because the four zeroes in a row had caught his attention. Four of a kind, he had thought at the time, a winning poker hand. The type of hand he rarely got in life. He was lucky to get a measly pair.

In any case, the odometer now said 40,020. Karen had driven twenty miles on her midnight cruise last night. Ten miles away and ten miles back. Or maybe she had driven in a circle all night.

What was ten miles from here? Could she be seeing someone on the sly? Was the sleepwalking escapade an act? A cover-up of a midnight assignation with a lover?

He was starting to think like Brady. Maybe Karen wasn't Karen. Maybe the real Karen was hidden from him, like she was hidden from Brady—hidden so well from Brady that he didn't recognize her. Was the real Karen leading a secret life?

Karen walked out of the house, her face intent. She saw him sitting in his rental and approached him.

He powered down the driver's-side window.

"Why did you walk out like that?" she said. "It was rude to Dr. Armitage."

"He sounds like a quack."

"He has a PhD. Quacks don't have degrees."

"He could be lying about it to inflate himself for customers."

"You're too damned skeptical. Why do you think everything's a scam?"

"Because it usually is."

"I'm gonna do as he says to exorcise the demon from our house."

"Jean Baptiste will thank you for buying sage smudge sticks at his House of Voodoo."

Scowling, Karen held her arms akimbo. "Would you rather die in this house?"

"That's how Armitage gets customers. By scaring them to death, so they'll do whatever he says. It's a protection racket. Pay him and he'll save your life from the demon."

"Then how do you explain your cup of water that moved by itself in the bathroom?"

"I dunno." Gordon glanced at the odometer. "You drove twenty miles last night."

"I can't believe I didn't crash into someone," said Karen, putting her hand on her heart.

"What's ten miles from here?"

Karen thought about it. "Marilyn Monroe's house."

"How would you know that?"

"I was doing research on the previous owner, Deirdre Turner. Like I told you, she was obsessed with Marilyn Monroe, so yesterday afternoon I drove to Monroe's house at 12305 Fifth Helena Drive in Brentwood. It looks a lot like this house, except much bigger, of course. I couldn't see very much, because there's a wall around the house that's on a cul-de-sac."

"And you counted the miles to the house?"

"When I googled the house on my laptop, it gave me the route and the distance from here. About ten miles if I took Sunset."

"You drove all the way there in your sleep?"

"I guess. I have no memory of driving in the middle of the night. You're the one who said I was out driving."

"The odometer proves it. There are twenty miles on it that I didn't put there."

"I wasn't aware what I was doing."

"Why was Deirdre so obsessed with Marilyn Monroe?"

"I'm beginning to believe she felt like she was Marilyn's reincarnated spirit."

"Maybe you should stop researching Deirdre. It's impacting your life, making you drive while asleep and putting you in jeopardy."

"I'm trying to understand her. What would make her commit such a heinous crime like drowning her own children? It's unconscionable."

"Why's it so important to you to know?"

"Because I can't imagine myself committing such a crime. I don't understand how she or anyone, for that matter, could do it."

Armitage exited the front door.

"Thank you for coming, Doctor," said Karen, approaching him.

"My pleasure. I suggest you smudge your house with sage first thing. Smudging is much more powerful than using the floor wash of lemon and cinnamon. Your house has a strong malignant presence. You need to exorcise the demon before it possesses you and your family."

Armitage made a beeline for his car.

Gordon watched him drive away.

"I'm going to the House of Voodoo on Sunset," said Karen. "Want to come?"

"I have to go to my shrink," he said.

He saw Brady standing in the front doorway. Brady looked terrified of Karen.

Chapter 29

Gordon was lying on the sofa in Dr. Goldwyn's office. Dr. Goldwyn sat opposite him in her chair, a notebook in one hand, a pencil in the other.

"My family's falling apart," said Gordon. "I feel like I'm the reason."

"Why do you think so?"

"Karen is sleepwalking at night and driving while she's asleep. She's gonna get killed if she keeps it up."

"Why do you blame yourself?"

"What else could explain it?"

"Maybe she's having psychological issues. You're not the only one who has them."

"I'm not bringing home a paycheck. It's affecting my whole family."

"How can you be sure? There could be another explanation."

"My son is acting strange too. He says Karen isn't his mother."

Goldwyn raised her eyebrows. "Interesting. But it's not that strange. I've heard of other cases of children claiming their parents are someone else."

"Really?" said Gordon.

He had never heard of anything like it.

"You say she's taking sleeping pills," said Goldwyn. "What brand?"

"The same ones you gave me. Halcion."

Goldwyn nodded. "If you take too much triazolam, it can affect you psychologically. Patients have been known to drive their cars while asleep. Could you convince her to lower her dosage?"

"She's pretty set in her ways."

"Do you think she's acting differently?"

"She's sleepwalking. She has never done it before."

"If the drug's affecting her psychologically, it could explain why your son is saying he doesn't recognize her."

"I never thought of that."

What she said made sense, decided Gordon.

"You shouldn't blame everything on yourself," said Goldwyn.

Gordon frowned. "I'm having trouble doing my job."

"Why?"

"Beats me."

He couldn't go into it with her. After all, he was a contract killer. Discussing his profession with her was beyond the pale. Maybe she could legally testify against him in a court of law if he confided in her. Or was he protected by doctor-patient confidentiality? He didn't want to take the chance of telling her his profession.

"Do you think your problems at home are affecting your work performance?" she said.

"It's possible."

"How do you think you should handle it?"

"That's what I want to know." Gordon paused in thought. "That parapsychologist, or medium or whatever he is, didn't help matters."

"Explain."

"He's got Karen thinking our house is haunted by a demon."

"She's blaming her psychological problems on a haunted house?"

"I don't know what's going on. Everything's going to hell. I can't explain it. I don't believe in haunted houses, though. Do you?"

"Of course not. I believe in science. There are scientific explanations for everything."

"How can I get Karen to believe that?"

"I can't tell you how to change your wife's opinions or beliefs."

"Do you think she's dangerous?"

"In what respect?"

"Would she try to harm me or Brady?"

"Why do you ask?"

Gordon wondered if he should tell her. He wasn't sure it was her business. However, he wanted to get it off his chest.

"Brady said she threatened to kill him," he said.

Goldwyn crossed her legs, her nylons scratching against each other.

"She probably lost her temper," she said. "It happens. People say things they don't mean when they're out of sorts."

"Yeah, I guess. He's scared of her, though. I'm convinced of it."

"He'll get over it."

"I hope so. I can't afford to get him a psychiatrist too."

Goldwyn smiled. "Kids are impressionable. That's all. He'll get on with his life."

Gordon glanced at his wristwatch.

"I gotta be going," he said, getting to his feet.

Was he supposed to feel better after a session with his shrink? If so, this session was a bust.

Chapter 30

When Gordon drove away from the high-rise containing Goldwyn's office, he picked up on a black Audi tailing him.

He hoped the cops hadn't seen his license tag after he had split from St. Thomas Hospital. If one had, it could be a plainclothes cop driving the Audi. Most cops couldn't afford Audis. They drove Mustangs or Chargers. If it wasn't a cop, who was it?

Or was he paranoid?

Maybe the Audi wasn't following him. But he knew it was. It was hanging back just so, in order to keep him in sight and to keep out of sight at the same time. He knew how tails operated.

He needed to shake the tail.

He hung a right into a strip mall parking lot, where a CVS drugstore hogged most of the space. Small fast-food restaurants, a hair stylist, and a laundromat took up what was left.

He parked and checked his rearview mirror. He didn't see the Audi behind him. Looking to his right he saw the Audi park two spaces from him.

The guy wasn't going out of his way to avoid being seen, decided Gordon. At least, not now.

The guy jackknifed out of the Audi, swaggered behind it, and headed toward the rear of Gordon's rental. Clad in a black Windbreaker and black jeans, sporting Oakley wraparounds, he maneuvered toward Gordon's driver's-side window, holding his right hand in his jacket pocket.

Pushing thirty, stocky with cropped black hair and a downturned mouth, he looked like he could handle himself. A tattoo of a coiled diamondback decorated the back of his left hand.

Gordon recognized him. It was Diego.

Before Diego reached him, Gordon groped under his trouser leg, withdrew his SIG from its ankle holster, and sandwiched the piece between the bottom of his thigh and the driver's seat.

"Fancy meeting you here, amigo," said Diego, coming from behind the rental's left rear fender into Gordon's line of vision.

"Fate plays strange tricks on people. The ways of fate are inscrutable."

"It's not fate," said Gordon. "You were following me."

"It's lucky I found you."

"Why don't you get to the point?"

"You're giving me a hard time."

"You're *wasting* my time. Maybe I should leave," said Gordon, firing the ignition.

"I wouldn't do that. In my jacket pocket is a Glock 17 aimed at your head."

Gordon glanced at the aforementioned pocket, which had Diego's hand in it and was sticking out toward Gordon.

What Diego said could be true, Gordon decided. He killed the ignition.

"I thought you were just glad to see me," he said.

"I'm not that way. I know a lot of you gringos are *maricones*. That's your problem."

"I have better things to do."

"That's right, amigo. And that's why I'm here. We hired you to take out the judge. You winged him, and he's out of the hospital *ahora*. What's your excuse?"

"He ducked."

"No joke. We hired you to do a number on this *puta*. The *puta* still lives. What's going down?"

"I'll take care of it."

"That' s what you said the last time you blew it. Don't you want the *dinero*?"

Looking at Diego's pocket Gordon broke into a sweat.

He can squeeze that Glock trigger faster than I can whip out the SIG from under my thigh.

"I'll do him," he said. "No problem."

He had no idea if Diego had his finger on the trigger. The guy could be pulling the trigger even now. And the muzzle was aiming straight at his head.

"If you don't get the job done, I will take you out," said Diego. "I don't miss like you. When I say something, I do it. *Comprendes*?"

"Why bother?"

"Because you know too much. You could rat us out to the cops. But if you take out the judge, you're not gonna incriminate yourself."

"What if I don't take him out?"

"*Luego lo mato*. I could do it here."

Diego pushed the piece in his jacket pocket toward Gordon's face.

"He's as good as dead," said Gordon. "Give me more time."

"We need him removed from his current trial. That gives you no time. I'm not gonna go through this again with you. You won't know when the bullet goes through your head the next time we meet."

"I'm not replaceable. Where are you gonna get someone to fill my shoes?"

"You're joking," said Diego, snorting a laugh. "Sicarios are a dime a dozen."

The real reason I can't do this job is because I live in a haunted house and I'm losing my nerve.

"On such short notice?" said Gordon.

"Don't you have bills to pay?"

"I need a little time, is all."

"A little is what I'm giving you." Diego held up his hand and showed a quarter-inch of space between his forefinger and thumb. "*Muy poquito.*" He slewed around to leave. "*Hasta la vista.*"

Diego returned to his Audi.

Chapter 31

In the living room, Karen lit a bundle of sage she had bought from Jean Baptiste's House of Voodoo. The sage had a woodsy, slightly sweet odor.

She strolled through the living room, waving the smoking sage bundle.

"I smell smoke," said Brady, running into the living room. "Is the house burning?"

"Don't interrupt me," said Karen. "This is very important. Now get out of here. If you interrupt me again, I'll kill you."

Brady fled in terror.

Karen cracked the front door, allowing a breeze to ventilate the living room, which was clouding with smoke.

The door flew wide open as a gust of wind propelled it.

She tried to adjust the door so it was open an inch, but the wind kept blowing it wide open. She decided to shut the door. She would have to ventilate the house with the windows.

She kept strolling through the living room, making sure she was smudging every square inch, holding the sage bundle close to the walls, near the carpet, and up toward the ceiling. She coughed on the accumulating smoke.

Satisfied, she entered the study and smudged it. She opened the window a crack for ventilation.

She felt like an idiot, filling the house with smoke, but she believed Armitage knew what he was talking about. She believed the house was possessed by an evil spirit that needed to be exorcised. Her family couldn't go on living here in peaceful coexistence with the entity, which wanted them gone.

She made her way down the hall to the bathroom.

As she stood in the bathroom doorway, she started at an explosion emanating from the living room. She sprang into the living room and felt a strong gust of wind blowing against her face.

She noticed the front door was wide open.

How did it get open? She had shut it. It couldn't blow open. Maybe she hadn't closed it all the way. Then what was that explosion she had heard?

She fought the wind and headed to the door to close it. She couldn't believe how hard the wind was gusting. It was fighting her every inch of the way. It was blowing so hard, in fact, that it blew out her smudge stick. She would relight it later. She had to shut the damn door first. It was like walking through a hurricane. She thought she would blow away any second.

At last she reached the door. She managed to push it shut, but it wouldn't stay shut. She inspected the door latch. It was broken. The hurricane or whatever it was had broken it. That was the explosion she had heard. The brass strike plate had been ripped out of the wooden doorjamb. The latch had nothing to support it.

Was the wind strong enough to tear out a brass strike plate that was screwed into the jamb? She had never heard of such a thing.

She released the door, since it was impossible to secure it.

The door flew open and slammed its knob against the living room wall. Wind rushed into the room, clearing it of sage smoke.

Karen threw up her hands in disgust. The hell with it.

She returned to the bathroom and relit the edge of her smudge bundle. She entered the bathroom. Holding the smoking sage in front of her, she cut across the linoleum floor to open the window a crack.

The window over the bathtub burst, hurling glass shards into the bathtub and across the floor. Shards glanced off Karen's face, cutting it.

She screamed.

The wind howled through the bathroom, whipping the nylon shower curtain into a frenzy and extinguishing the burning sage. The torqued, wind-swept shower curtain slapped her face, blinding her. She backed away from the tub, crunching the fragments of glass underfoot.

Where did all this wind come from? she wondered, brushing blood away from her scratched face as she exited the bathroom. How was she supposed to smudge the house with a gale blowing through it? It was turning into a high velocity wind tunnel.

Juddering, the house creaked and groaned under the punishing barrage of buffeting gusts.

Was the house getting ready to fall apart? She debated whether she should run outside. She would be safer outside if the house was in the process of collapsing.

Was a tornado or hurricane striking the house? Los Angeles didn't get either. This much wind made no sense.

The wind began to ease up.

"What's happening, Mom?" cried Brady from upstairs.

"Hide under your bed," she said.

Brady scurried back to his room.

Should she resume smudging the house now that the wind was dying down?

The house felt like it was settling.

The bathroom was a mess, littered with broken glass on the floor and on the bottom of the bathtub. She needed to clean the bathroom before returning to smudge it. She didn't want to step on any glass fragments. Pulverizing them would make them that much more difficult to clean up.

"What the hell happened?" yelled Gordon at the front door.

Chapter 32

Karen entered the living room.

"Isn't it a mess?" she said.

"Did somebody break in? What happened to your face?" said Gordon, noticing her face was bleeding.

"Broken glass cut it."

Gordon shook his head in confusion. "Begin at the beginning."

"The wind blew the door apart."

"What?" said Gordon in disbelief.

"There was a hurricane or tornado that ripped through the house."

"There's hardly any breeze today. I was just outside. What are you holding in your hand?"

"I was trying to smudge the house with this bundle of sage when the wind stopped me."

"Mom, is that Dad?" cried Brady from the top of the stairs.

"Do what I told you or you know what I'll do."

Terrified, Brady dashed back to his bedroom.

"What will you do?" asked Gordon.

"I told him before," answered Karen.

Gordon searched her face. "Have you been threatening him again? He looked white as a sheet when you answered him."

"I don't know what you're talking about."

"He told me you threatened to kill him."

"You can't believe I would say such a thing to my own son," said Karen, indignant.

And you better do it to him.

"What did you say?" said Karen, dumbfounded.

"I didn't say anything," said Gordon. "I don't understand why Brady would make up such a wild story."

And you have to do it.

Karen stared at him. "Do what?"

"Do what?" said Gordon, puzzled.

"You said I have to do it."

"You're hearing things."

"Don't play tricks on me."

"Are you out to lunch or what? Are you sleepwalking again? Is that it?"

"Do I look like I'm sleepwalking?"

"What you're telling me is incredible. You said the wind broke the door. There's hardly any wind. How could it break open the door?"

"How do you explain it being broken if you have all the answers?"

He didn't answer her question. "Why did you say I'm saying things I didn't say?"

"If you didn't say them, who did?"

"Maybe it was the wind," said Gordon, looking disgusted.

"I don't appreciate your sarcasm. Follow me," she said, becoming angry.

"Is Armitage here?" said Gordon, scoping the house. "Did he sell you that stupid voodoo sage? What did that Baptiste scammer charge you? Hundreds of dollars? You can probably buy that worthless weed for a nickel at Ralphs."

"Don't you realize our very lives are in danger in this house?"

"In danger of getting scammed by a quack spiritualist."

Sick of his complaining, Karen stalked to the bathroom, Gordon in tow.

"Look," she said, pointing into the bathroom at the broken glass scattered on the floor.

"Jesus Christ," said Gordon, his eyes bugging out. "It looks like you exploded a bomb here."

"The wind burst through the window."

Gordon eyed the shattered window. "That shouldn't have happened. The glass must have been flawed. A little wind shouldn't break it."

"Glass shards blew into my face. I'm lucky I didn't lose an eye."

He inspected her face with concern. "Do you want me to take you to the hospital?"

"No. They're nicks. It could have been a lot worse."

"I guess this house is older than I thought. I should have inspected the doors and the windows. They must have been defective from old age."

"I'll sweep up the glass and call a glazier."

"This house is nothing but trouble."

"But first I need to smudge the rest of the house," she said. She relit the bundle of sage.

"Do you really think burning some weed does any good?" he said. "You're just succeeding in stinking up the house."

Listen to him.

There was that voice again, decided Karen. If it wasn't Gordon's, whose was it?

She scanned the house. She didn't see anybody other than Gordon present.

"Did you say something?" she said.

"I said you're stinking up the house with that bundle of weeds in your hand."

Listen to him.

She heard the voice again. There was something androgynous and inhuman about it. A voice devoid of passion, machinelike but oozing with malignance. Maybe hearing voices was an aftereffect of the triazolam. Her doctor had said the drug could cause hallucinations.

She climbed the staircase.

"Where are you going?" said Gordon.

"I need to smudge the upstairs."

The overpowering stench of raw sewage permeated the house. She felt like she was going to throw up.

"Where's that stink coming from?" said Gordon, screwing up his face.

"Sudden horrible, unexplained stenches mean a house is haunted. Remember what Armitage said?"

"We may have a broken sewer pipe near the house," he said, disregarding her.

Feeling queasy Karen ascended the steps to the landing, holding the smoking bundle of sage in front of her. She ambled down the hall to the master bedroom. She commenced smudging the bedroom with her sage wand.

It felt cold here. The temperature kept dropping. She shivered. She didn't want to stay much longer. It was nice outside. Why was it freezing inside the bedroom?

The ceiling lamp flashed on and off.

She figured it needed a new bulb.

She thought about opening the window a crack, but she didn't want to suffer another window exploding in her face, so she made tracks for the bathroom instead, waving her sage wand in front of her.

She crossed the hall to Brady's bedroom.

When he saw her, he fled in horror, dove onto his stomach, and crawled under the bed.

"It's just me," she said.

You should kill him now.

That dreadful voice again, she decided. It made her hair stand on end.

She smudged the room.

He's ruining your career. You'll never make it as a writer with him hanging like an albatross around your neck.

There was truth in those words, unfortunately, she had to admit. But she would never lift her hand against Brady. She needed to calm down. The house was stressing her out. She was hearing voices. She laughed. What a joke. What was supposed to happen next? Was she having a nervous breakdown?

Step on his neck and break it when he crawls out from under the bed.

She refused to listen to the unearthly voice. It was a figment of her imagination.

Kill him. It's the only way you can succeed in life. I know. Believe me, I know.

Chapter 33

Armitage was driving along the tortuous Mulholland Drive, thinking of the Carney house in the Hollywood Hills. The house bothered him. It was a threat. He had never felt such negative vibrations emanating from a spirit in any of his previous exorcisms.

He doubted smudging the house with burning sage would be successful in ridding the house of the demon that haunted it.

He would need to study the previous owner to find out why she had murdered her two daughters.

One hand on the steering wheel of his Benz, with the other he slapped at a fly buzzing around his head. The fly buzzed away. Another fly took its place and another.

He powered down the driver's-side window, hoping the passing wind would suck the flies out of the car. The wind had no effect on them. In fact, more of them circled his head. He negotiated the abrupt curves in Mulholland, swatting at the flies as he steered.

Where did they come from? He remembered that Karen Carney had said a pack of flies had attacked her and tried to smother her. Could one of those flies have hitchhiked on his body as he had left the Carney residence? One was possible. But not this many. There were scores of them corkscrewing around his head.

They were disrupting his vision. He was having trouble keeping the Benz on the winding road.

He powered down the passenger's-side window. Maybe the cross ventilation would blow the flies out of his car.

Nothing doing. The flies kept circling his head, screening his vision. He found himself swerving in the road, crossing the solid double-yellow lines into the opposite lane and back again into his own lane.

The cloud of flies around his head was becoming thicker as more flies joined the frenzy.

He veered across the solid yellow lines. The driver of a stake truck driving in the opposite lane leaned on his horn.

Armitage cut his wheel to the right and reentered his proper lane.

Were the flies telling him something? Were they messengers from the failed actress Deirdre Turner, the murderer of her two children? Was she telling him to get lost? It made sense if she was the evil spirit possessing the house. She was a murderer. What was preventing her spirit from resting in peace? Would she never be satisfied until she committed more murders? But how could she commit murder now that she was dead, had died by her own hand? Could the bloodlust raging inside her never be satisfied?

As he approached a hairpin turn in Mulholland, a swarm of flies enveloped his head, blinding him. No matter where he looked he saw a wall of flies. He tried to swat them away from his eyes, but there were too many of the noisy insects and they kept swarming back.

He felt the powerful Mercedes AMG run over the curb and buck up and down as the front and back tires struck it. Unable to control the steering wheel, he slammed into a sycamore tree and came to a jarring halt. His head whiplashed forward. His seat belt and the inflating airbag prevented his head from smashing into the windshield.

The spirit of the mass murderer Deirdre had tried to kill him by sending the flies after him, he decided, dazed and hanging onto consciousness by the skin of his teeth. Not only was she going after the Carneys, she was targeting him now as well.

The cursed flies were still swarming around his head, blinding him. At least they weren't wasps. Then they would have stung him to death.

His neck throbbing, he passed out from shock.

Chapter 34

Karen knew what she must do. She retrieved a hammer from the closet in the hall and made for the master bedroom.

The problem was here, she decided. It was in the walls.

She pressed her ear to one of the walls and listened. She thought she could hear electric humming or buzzing.

She raised the hammer and slammed it into the drywall, smashing a hole in it.

She peeked inside the hole but couldn't make out anything behind the wall.

She resumed hammering the wall, bashing in the stucco and Sheetrock. Pounding out a large hole, she saw timber studs and an electric cable. She put her ear to the cable. It wasn't making the humming she was hearing. The hum was coming from elsewhere in the wall. It had to be a bug. There should be at least three.

The FBI, the CIA, and Jimmy Hoffa were bugging the bedroom, she knew. Sam Giancana of the Mafia was probably bugging it too. The Mafia wanted dirt on the Kennedy brothers. Her enemies were all spying on her. They wanted dirt on her so they could destroy her. Everybody wanted her to fail as a writer.

She had to find the bugs and remove them.

She raised the hammer and smashed another section of the Sheetrock. The bugs had to be here somewhere. She could hear them. How could she write, knowing everybody was spying on her? Their eavesdropping made her too self-conscious. She couldn't concentrate on her writing with everybody spying on her. She had to remove the bugs.

Even if she managed to write anything, she had no doubts that the CIA, the FBI, and the Mafia would break into her house and delete her work from her laptop.

She bashed in another section of drywall in her search for the electronic bugs. They were here somewhere. She hammered away in frustration, unable to locate any of them.

She would try the other wall. The bugs must be secreted there.

In earnest she strode to the adjoining wall and hammered the plasterboard, smashing through it and inspecting the insides. She would not let them get dirt on her with their bugs. She refused to let them destroy her writing career. The lot of them were in league with Brady, doing everything they could to sabotage her artistic career.

The government wanted dirt so they could accuse her of being a communist and throw her in jail for being a traitor. The Mafia hated her because she wrote crime stories that revealed the truth about their crimes. Hoffa hated her because he was jealous she was going to marry the president . . .

Flummoxed, Karen stopped hammering. Why was she thinking about the president? She didn't know the president and vice versa. And why Jimmy Hoffa? Hoffa was dead. She wasn't thinking straight. The presence of the bugs had her rattled. She told herself to calm down and find them.

She resumed smashing through the wall, sending plaster chunks flying. She coughed on the clouds of plaster dust mushrooming through the bedroom.

Brady stood in the doorway, concern on his face as he watched her.

"What are you doing?" he cried, squinting through the plaster dust at her.

"Are you talking to me?"

"Yes," he said, eyes wide.

"Shut up or I'll crack open your skull with this hammer," she said, glaring at him and brandishing the hammer.

Brady screamed and ran for his life.

Whenever she tried to accomplish anything, he was always there to interrupt her. She couldn't let him continue derailing her projects.

She resumed bashing the drywall with a vengeance. She had to find the bugs, tear them out, and destroy them.

Gordon stormed up the stairs and burst into the bedroom. He halted in astonishment.

"What the hell are you doing?" he cried as she pulverized another section of drywall with her hammer.

"I have to get rid of the bugs in the wall."

"When I walked into the house, I heard Brady scream. What did you do to him?" said Gordon with consternation, casting around the smoky room for Brady.

"Nothing," she said, hammering away. "He left."

Gordon stalked over to her and grabbed her hand, preventing her from wielding the hammer.

"Stop it," he said. "Look what a mess you've made. What's gotten into you?"

"Do you want bugs in the walls?"

"We'll get an exterminator. You don't have to tear down the walls to kill insects."

"Bugs. Electronic bugs. The government's spying on me."

He snatched the hammer from her hand.

"No more of this," he said. "You're wrecking our house."

"The CIA and the Mafia don't want me to write anymore," said Karen, trying to retrieve the hammer from him.

"Listen to yourself," he said, keeping the hammer out of her reach. "You're cracking up."

"That's what they want you to believe so I won't be able to write anymore."

Coughing on the thick clouds of plaster dust, Gordon crossed the floor to open the window and let air into the room.

"I'm beginning to think you're the one who broke the front door. That story about a gust of wind doing it was nonsense."

"I didn't break the door. Why would I do such a stupid thing?"

"Why are you tearing apart the bedroom walls?"

"I told you. The CIA and the Mafia are spying on me."

"We just bought this house, and it's falling apart already. It's a beautiful house, and look what you're doing to it."

"I'm saving us."

"Saving us from what?"

"It has to be done. Do you want them to sabotage my career?"

"I got news for you. Trashing the house won't save your career."

Karen narrowed her eyes. "You don't want me to write either. Is that it? You're in it with them, conspiring against me?"

"In it with who? There aren't any bugs in the wall. Can't you see? You bashed everything to smithereens. Did you find a single bug?"

"Not yet. They're well hidden by professionals," said Karen, scrutinizing the wall. "But I will." She reached toward him. "Give me back the hammer. I haven't finished inspecting the walls."

"No way. If I find out you harmed Brady, I'm calling the cops."

Gordon left the room, hammer in hand, searching for Brady.

Karen fetched a sigh. How could she make anyone understand there were powerful forces aligned against her? She refused to let those forces prevent her from writing.

Writing was hard enough by itself, without all these enemies arrayed against her, not to mention the burden of bringing up a son.

Chapter 35

Before he could find Brady, Gordon heard someone knocking on the front door downstairs. He descended the staircase to find out who it was.

He could see the door from the stairs. It was ajar, because the wind had broken the latch, according to Karen, preventing the door from closing all the way.

By the time Gordon reached the bottom of the steps, he saw the door swinging open.

"Who is it?" he said, clutching the hammer.

A fortyish guy with white hair and a pocked face stood in the doorway.

"Hello," he said. "I'm Lieutenant Wolfgang Gaetz of the LAPD."

Gordon cringed. Had the cops tailed him here after he had tried to take out Childress at the hospital? Gordon hadn't picked up on any cops tailing him on the freeway as he had fled the scene. Sweat pouring out of his armpits and rinsing his palms, he tried to remain calm—at least on the outside.

He cleared his throat. "What can I do for you, Lieutenant?"

"I got a call to come here."

"I didn't call you."

"The emergency dispatcher told me she received a call from this residence from an endangered child. He said his name was Brady."

"Ah, he's our son."

"Didn't he tell you he called the police?" said Gaetz, cocking an eyebrow with suspicion.

He unbuttoned his brown blazer, revealing an FN 509 pistol holstered on his belt.

"No, he didn't," said Gordon, puzzled. "In fact, I was looking for him when I heard you knocking on the door."

"I see. Could I speak to him? I have questions for him. He said he was being threatened with murder, and he was scared of dying."

"Murder?" said Gordon, aghast. "There's obviously a mistake. I'll get him."

Gordon looked up the staircase and called out Brady's name.

Brady scampered to the staircase landing and stood next to the newel.

"Yeah, Dad," he said, glancing furtively toward the debris-strewn master bedroom.

"There's a policeman here who wants to talk to you."

Was it a ruse? wondered Gordon. Was the cop's tale of Brady's call for help a ploy to get Gaetz inside the house so he could bust Gordon? Gordon had misgivings about letting Gaetz into the house.

Brady trotted down the steps and saw with apprehension Gaetz's imposing figure in the living room.

"Don't be concerned, son," said Gaetz. "I'm here to help you. We received your call for help. What exactly happened?"

Brady had trouble speaking.

"What's this about, Brady?" said Gordon. "Why did you call the cops?"

Brady shifted nervously on his feet, not sure whether to talk to Gaetz.

"I—uh—I'm scared," said Brady.

"Are you scared of your father?" said Gaetz, casting a suspicious glance at Gordon. "Is he the one who threatened to kill you? Feel free to talk in front of me. I won't let him hurt you."

"Lieutenant, I resent—"

Gaetz held up his forefinger to silence Gordon.

"Go ahead, son," said Gaetz.

"It wasn't him," said Brady, feeling bolder. "It was her."

"Her?"

"The woman upstairs."

"The woman upstairs is your mother, Brady," said Gordon.

"No, she isn't."

"What exactly did she say to you?" said Gaetz, trying to get Brady to open up.

"She said she was gonna crack open my skull with a hammer and kill me."

Gaetz widened his eyes. He picked up on the hammer Gordon was clutching.

"I was doing home repairs," said Gordon, holding up the hammer and smiling, all innocence. "Our new house needs a little work."

"Hmm," said Gaetz, not convinced. "Son, are you sure it wasn't your father who threatened you with the hammer?"

"I'm sure it wasn't him," said Brady. "It was her."

"Brady," said Gordon, his face somber. "Is this true what you say about your mother, or is this another one of your stories you made up to get attention?"

"It's true."

"Is he in the habit of making up stories?" asked Gaetz.

"He's a kid. You know kids," answered Gordon, trying another smile.

"I know that threatening a child with murder is a serious accusation," said Gaetz.

"My wife is under a lot of stress," said Gordon. "If she said anything like this, I'm sure it was in the heat of the moment and she didn't mean it."

"Do you mind if I talk to her?"

"Uh, well—uh, she's kind of under the weather."

"I'd like to clear this up before I file a report at the Hollywood station."

Gordon didn't think Karen was in any condition to be talking to cops. She had acted like a maniac when she had trashed the bedroom. There was no way he was going to let Gaetz upstairs to talk to her. The demolished state of the bedroom would arouse his suspicions. He would think a horrible act had taken place in it.

"Karen, could you come down here for a second?" called Gordon up the stairs.

He found himself wishing she would refuse and remain upstairs. At least she wasn't clutching the hammer anymore. Had she really threatened to kill Brady? He remembered Brady had said she had threatened him before. And what about her raving about bugs in the wall? It wasn't like her to act paranoid. He was the one who normally acted paranoid—with good reason. He was a contract killer with enemies who wished him dead.

Karen shambled to the landing and peered down the stairs. Her hair was mussed from her strenuous obliteration of the bedroom walls. Her face wore a blank expression—until she spotted Gaetz. She started.

Chapter 36

"It's a small world," said Gaetz, recognizing her.

"I didn't think I would be seeing you so soon after our talk," said Karen, descending the steps.

"You two know each other?" said Gordon, surprised.

"He's the one who told me about the previous owner of this house."

"I remember this house very well indeed," said Gaetz, looking around. "A horrible crime was committed here. It's a beautiful house but . . . sad."

"We love it," said Karen.

Gordon gave her a look, which she didn't return.

"What happened to your front door?" said Gaetz. "I couldn't help but notice the latch was broken. Did you have a break-in here?"

"The wind broke it," said Gordon.

"Wind? That's funny. We haven't had any wind lately."

"The house is showing its age, is all. Things get old, they wear out. One gust of wind was all it took and pfft," said Karen, puffing out her cheeks and pantomiming the blowing wind.

Gaetz hiked his eyebrows. "Strange, all the same."

"It startled me when it happened. I thought it was a burglar."

"Lucky for us, it wasn't," said Gordon.

"To get back to my reason for coming here, your son has made a serious charge against you, Mrs. Carney."

"I'm sure there's a mistake," chimed in Gordon.

"What did he say about me?" asked Karen.

Gordon didn't know what Karen was going to say in her stressed condition, though she seemed to have regained her composure, despite her unkempt appearance. She wasn't as manic as she had been during her hammer frenzy.

"He said you threatened to crack open his skull with a hammer and kill him," said Gaetz.

Anticipating her angry reaction Brady shivered with fear.

Karen cast a cursory chiding glance at Brady then became a concerned parent.

"He was playing with the hammer, Lieutenant, and I thought he might hurt himself," said Karen. "I warned him he might lose his grip on the hammer and it would bash in his skull."

"That's not what he told the emergency dispatcher at the station."

"He tends to exaggerate things in order to get attention. I've warned him to stop doing it. It's not a good character trait to develop as a child."

"Why would he invent such a story and call the police?" said Gaetz.

"He misheard me."

"Couldn't you tell from his reaction to your words that he was terrified of you?"

"I'm trying to understand him. Yesterday he tried to drown himself in the bathtub."

"Drown himself?"

"He claimed I was holding his head underwater."

"Were you?"

"Of course not. Maybe he's watching too many horror movies on TV. He doesn't understand how much he hurts people when he says such things."

"Why would he try to drown himself at his young age?"

"Kids grow up fast these days. It's the Internet, you know. They see all sorts of things on it."

"Is it true you tried to drown yourself, Brady?" said Gaetz.

Fearing Karen, Brady said nothing.

"I wish I could question him alone," said Gaetz, sensing the boy's discomfiture.

"He's a minor, Lieutenant," said Karen. "That would not be a good idea. At his age he doesn't understand how much authority you wield in your position as an agent of the law."

"He looks scared to me."

"People in authority like the police upset him. I'm sure you understand. He's just a child."

"I'm trying to get to the truth of the matter. What would prompt him to call the station and make such a serious accusation?"

"He's in desperate need of attention, because we just moved here and he feels alienated in his new neighborhood."

"Maybe we should let him speak for himself," said Gaetz, and looked at Brady.

Brady gnashed his teeth.

"He's tired out from all your questioning," said Karen. "He needs to rest."

Gaetz kept eying Brady. "Did anyone else hear your mother say she was gonna kill you, son?"

Brady chewed his fingernail. "I don't think so."

"All right, son." Gaetz turned to Karen. "Let me remind you, Mrs. Carney, threats are illegal in the state of California. Child endangerment is also illegal."

"I'm aware of the law, Lieutenant."

Gaetz scoped the house again, his expression grim. "This house has a horrific history. Don't let history repeat itself."

"Are you talking about ghosts?"

"Not per se. I don't believe in the supernatural."

"We're having the house exorcised to prevent anything untoward from happening."

"Why?"

"Why what?"

"Why exorcise the house? What prompted you to make such a decision?"

"We've been hearing loud noises at night," said Gordon, feeling silly for going along with Karen and hiring a medium.

"Probably pipes in the wall. These old houses have loud plumbing issues."

"Maybe Brady is being affected by the evil vibrations this house is giving off," said Karen.

"Ah, I don't believe that stuff. People harm other people. Ghosts don't do it."

"There's no sense in taking chances when it comes to our son's health."

120

"I can't argue with that." Gaetz paused. "Well, I guess I'll be on my way. Your son might have an overactive imagination. I dunno." He turned to Brady. "If someone threatens you again, Brady, don't hesitate to call 911. Try to get verification of the threat with a witness or use a camera to record it."

"Thank you for coming," said Karen.

Gaetz glanced at the bathroom where Deirdre had drowned her two girls.

"This house gives me the creeps," he said.

"I told you, Lieutenant," said Karen. "There's an evil entity here."

"I'll show you to the door, Lieutenant," said Gordon, relieved Gaetz hadn't arrived to bust him for the murder attempt on Childress.

Reaching the doorway Gaetz said, "You need to get that door fixed."

"I have a lot of carpentry to do," said Gordon, thinking of the master bedroom upstairs and looking up toward it.

He wasn't about to tell Gaetz about Karen's hammer rampage in the bedroom. The guy might take Karen to the station for grilling, figuring Brady was telling the truth about her threat to kill him with a hammer.

After watching her demolish the bedroom walls, Gordon suspected Brady *was*, in fact, telling the truth about her threatening him. Brady had looked genuinely terrified of her. Then again, a child's imagination could magnify the most inconsequential things into grotesque, terror-inducing nightmares.

Gordon didn't want to involve the cops in a family matter. He didn't want the cops anywhere near him. He still had a job to do for the cartel.

But was it safe to leave Brady alone with Karen the way she was acting, wreaking havoc on the bedroom walls like a one-woman wrecking crew on a mission?

Chapter 37

Gordon returned to Karen at the foot of the stairs, where she was standing alone.

"We need to talk," he said.

"I don't have time to talk," she said. "I have to go back to writing."

"Writing can wait. What about Brady?"

"Are you part of the conspiracy to keep me from doing my job as a writer?" she said, her dander up.

"What conspiracy?" said Gordon, bemused. "What's gotten into you?"

"Everybody's trying to keep me from writing, especially Brady. He's always blocking me. He's the very definition of writer's block."

"Can you stop talking like a monomaniac and start talking like a parent?"

"Monomaniac?" said Karen, staring at him.

"You're obsessed with this writing jag you're on. You didn't have it till you moved here."

"I'm trying to fulfill myself and reach my full potential in life. I want to be a successful professional writer. The only way I can do that is by writing."

"And what about Brady? Do you want to forget he's our boy and let him fend for himself? He's just a kid."

"You make it sound like I'm kicking him out of the house. I just want some time to myself so I can pursue my craft as a writer."

"You weren't obsessed with it like you are now. I don't understand what changed you."

"I had an epiphany. I realized what I'm supposed to be doing with my life. I'm supposed to be writing."

"So what do we do with Brady? Put him in an orphanage because his mother is disowning him?"

"I'm not disowning him. He can continue to live here."

"You're so sweet. You're allowing him to live with us, even though he's ruining your writing career."

"I've had enough of your sarcasm. I don't have to listen to this, not after having to listen to that cop accuse me of trying to crack Brady's skull with a hammer."

Gordon realized he was still holding the hammer he had seized from her.

"You should stay away from hammers for the time being," he said.

Karen eyeballed the hammer. "Those CIA bugs have to be removed from the bedroom."

"There aren't any CIA bugs, or FBI bugs, or Mafia bugs in the bedroom. Nobody's gonna waste their time bugging you."

"Maybe they read one of my crime short stories, and it was a little too realistic for them, like maybe I know what they're up to in this country with their constant illegal surveillance of us. They want to block me from writing another too-true work of crime fiction."

"You sound like you're leaking secret documents about the CIA's PRISM program like Edward Snowden or writing Philip Agee's exposé of the CIA, *Inside the Company*. Let me remind you, you self-published your stories, because no magazine would publish them. You make up stories from whole cloth. You have no access to secret documents."

"It's obvious my stories are touching a nerve with some very powerful people if they're going to such great lengths to bug my room to find out what I'm writing now."

Gordon chuckled. "Are you serious? You don't have any inside skinny on the CIA or the FBI. Why would they bug you?"

Or even the Mafia and the Mexican drug cartels. Maybe I could help you there.

"You don't understand how the government works," she said. "They're surveilling us. They did the same thing to Marilyn Monroe before they had her assassinated. There were bugs all over her bedroom."

"You're not Marilyn Monroe. She was a famous movie star who was messing around with the president of the United States."

"But I'm a writer who knows the truth. And the truth is the most dangerous weapon to those in power. We have to remove their bugs from the bedroom."

"I'm not letting you tear down another wall," said Gordon, gripping the hammer harder as if preparing for Karen's lunge to grab it.

"You'll be sorry. The bugs are gonna overhear all your secrets."

He started. He couldn't afford to let the government find out about *his* secrets. After all, his profession was illegal. But he didn't believe her. There were no bugs in the wall. Why did she keep going on about Marilyn Monroe? The dead movie star had nothing to do with her. Karen had become obsessed with the woman ever since they had moved here.

Chapter 38

Brady took a shower. He found the warm water pelting his flesh relaxing.

There was a balmy breeze blowing through the window the wind had shattered earlier. Karen had cleaned the shivers of glass off the bathroom floor and out of the bathtub before he had started his shower.

He thought he saw something moving beyond the drawn shut translucent shower curtain that hung from plastic rings looped around the metal curtain rod. The phantom figures he thought he saw appeared as smudges. He hadn't heard anyone enter the bathroom. How could the figures have gotten inside?

He became scared, his pulse picking up speed. He didn't like the idea of strangers in the bathroom while he was taking a shower. He felt vulnerable.

His heartbeat thundered in his ears as he swiped open the curtain to confront the phantoms.

Panic-stricken, he took in the shocking sight that greeted him.

Two little blonde girls drenched with water stood in the bathroom staring at him. Their damp hair hung straight down the sides of their faces. Their scarlet pinafores hung sopping wet over their equally wet yellow dresses. Beads of water stippled their faces.

The girls smiled at him.

Their smiles sent shivers down his spine. They weren't friendly smiles. They were more like death's head grins. The flesh on their grey faces was dissolving or melting due to the water on it.

His teeth set on edge, he shut the shower curtain. He couldn't stand looking at them. Maybe they would go away if he closed the curtain. The door was locked. How could they have gotten into the bathroom in the first place? How could he get them to leave? What did they want, anyway?

He peered through the shower curtain, wondering if they were approaching the bathtub. He didn't see their figures.

He yanked open the curtain, his eyes starting from their sockets with fear.

The bathroom was empty.

He must have imagined the two girls.

Puddles of water were all that remained of the two specters, or had that water splashed from the shower onto the floor when he had opened the shower curtain? He couldn't be sure.

He drew the shower curtain shut. He didn't want the girls to return and watch him taking a shower.

He lathered his arms with soap, the shower impinging on his flesh.

And then the water stopped.

Confused, he looked up at the shower head. He didn't understand why the water had stopped. He hadn't turned off the faucet handles.

He saw something oozing out of the perforations in the metal shower head. It looked like a multitude of blonde hairs snaking toward him. The lengthening hairs reached his face and tickled him. It felt pleasant as if they were caressing him. There were millions of them. They began intertwining, forming a thick braid that snaked around his neck and commenced throttling him.

Terrified, his face flushing, he yanked at the hair and tried to wrench the plaited noose away from his neck. He struggled to breathe. He couldn't scream for help. The hair was too tight. He couldn't pry it away from his throat. He couldn't run away. The hair had too firm a grasp on his throat.

Clutched up, he wondered how he could escape the braid's viselike grip.

Desperate to stay alive, he pounded on the shower stall's ceramic tiles, hoping someone would hear him and come to his aid before he suffocated.

What seemed like hours passed before he heard a voice. He knew it couldn't have been that long or he'd be dead.

"Brady, is that you?" said Karen, outside the bathroom door. "What are you doing in there?"

Brady kept pounding the wall with all his strength, feeling like he would black out any second from lack of oxygen.

"You're gonna break the shower," Karen cried.

Brady pounded again, feeling his consciousness slipping away. He forced himself to hold on a little longer. He needed air.

"Unlock the door," cried Karen.

Brady struggled to answer, but no words came out as he choked on the noose of hair strangling him.

The door flew open under the impetus of Karen's foot. She bolted to the bathtub and flung open the shower curtain to see Brady collaring his red throat with his hands and coughing.

"What are you doing to yourself?" said Karen, aghast.

She pulled his hands away from his throat.

Brady tried to speak but kept coughing.

Gordon stalked into the bathroom. "What happened?"

"He wouldn't let me in," said Karen. "I had to kick open the door. I found him strangling himself in the bathtub."

"What?"

"He was standing here with his hands around his throat. Look how red his neck is."

"Ligature marks. Why the hell would he strangle himself?"

"Remember, I told you he tried to drown himself in the bathtub. I don't know what's got into him."

"Brady, what happened?"

His face red, Brady coughed. He kept grasping at his throat. He wanted to speak, but his body wouldn't cooperate. His vocal cords were too sore to use. He kept trying in futility to form words with his mouth.

"Try to calm down," said Gordon. "Everything's OK. Tell us what happened."

Karen pulled the bath towel off the rack and placed it around Brady, who was shivering.

He looked up at the shower head with terror.

"Hair," he managed to gasp.

"Hair?" said Gordon, confounded.

"It was coming out of the shower head. It wrapped around my neck and strangled me," said Brady between intermittent hacks.

"A strand of hair?" said Karen.

"A lot of strands. Millions of them."

Gordon eyed the shower head. "I don't see any hair."

"Step out of the tub," said Karen.

Brady obeyed.

Gordon turned on the cold water handle. Cold water shot out of the shower head.

"Water's coming out, not hair," said Karen, toweling off Brady. "You must have been daydreaming."

"Then why's his throat all red?" said Gordon.

"Because he was choking himself when I first saw him."

"Choking himself? It makes no sense."

"He thought hair was around his throat, so he tried—"

"To suffocate himself," cut in Gordon, not buying it.

"I admit it sounds crazy, but I saw him try to drown himself before."

"I guess he's not dealing well with moving to a new house."

"I still think he's making up things. Like he made up that story that I threatened to crack his skull with a hammer."

Gordon heaved a sigh. "Maybe you're right."

"Of course, I am. I would never threaten to kill Brady."

"It looks like you're gonna go on living, Brady," said Gordon, smiling at Brady.

Brady massaged his red throat.

"Can we stop with all the disruptions?" said Karen. "I can't write with so many disturbances."

Somebody knocked on the front door.

"Now what?" said Karen, leaving the bathroom.

Chapter 39

When Karen entered the living room, she saw that the broken front door was half open.

Armitage was standing on the threshold, peering inside the house, his neck in a brace.

She approached him. "What happened to you, Doctor?"

"I was in a car accident," said Armitage.

Karen looked through the doorway and saw a carmine Mercedes SL roadster parked in the driveway.

Gordon came up from behind her and stared over her shoulder at the car.

"Where's your other car?" he asked.

"I wrapped it around a sycamore," answered Armitage.

"Is that how could you got the brace?" said Gordon, patting his neck.

Armitage nodded with difficulty in his neck brace. He scoped the house, his face studious.

"Did you smudge the house?" he said.

"I tried to," said Karen. "That's how the front door got broken."

"I don't understand."

"When I smudged the living room, a gust of wind broke open the door."

"I'm not surprised."

"You're not? Well, I sure was."

"Go on."

"The wind burst the window in the bathroom too."

"There is great evil in this house," said Armitage, surveying the house, his face drawn.

"Why do you say that?" said Gordon.

"I told you I was in an accident. I didn't tell you why. The fact is, I crashed into a tree because I couldn't see where I was going because a million flies hovered in front of my face and blinded me."

"Flies?" said Karen, remembering her ordeal with flies with alarm.

"I believe they came from this house. They must have flown into my car when it was parked in your driveway the last time I was here."

"Flies are all over the place," said Gordon. "You can't blame flies in your car on us. They could've come from anywhere."

"They attacked me in the same manner they attacked your wife—by swarming onto my face."

"But they didn't smother you. You said they blinded you so you crashed your car."

"Both assaults were staged by large numbers of flies attacking the face. The flies came from your house."

"Why are you blaming us? They're not our flies."

"I'm not blaming you. I'm blaming your house. The evil spirit that inhabits it. It wants me dead."

"Why?"

"Because it knows I'm here to exorcise it."

"Or it was just an accident," said Gordon. "Accidents happen."

"Not such bizarre ones," said Armitage. "I know my profession. This house must be exorcised. Until it is, your lives are in grave danger."

"You said smudging the house with sage would remove the spirit," said Karen.

"Normally, it does. Unless the possessing demon has extraordinary powers—like the one here."

"Are you saying the smudging didn't work?"

"From what you say, it sounds like the wind blew the sage smoke out of the house before the purging of the spirit could take effect. You needed to open the windows just a crack. Instead, the wind broke through both the door and a window and dissipated the cleansing smoke."

"What can we do?"

"Have you had any untoward occurrences since the smudging?"

"Brady tried to strangle himself in the shower."

"Is he OK?" said Armitage, his face knotted with distress.

"Yes. He said strands of hair from the shower head tried to strangle him. I know that can't be true. He either made it up or was daydreaming."

"I don't think he imagined it. I believe it was a manifestation of the demon possessing your house, and, as I suspected when I came inside, the smudging didn't work. Even now I can sense the demon's presence," said Armitage, looking around the house.

"Where does that leave us?"

"Where is the bathroom?"

Karen led Armitage to the bathroom.

Chapter 40

Armitage's eyes widened as he gazed into the bathroom from the hall.

"The demon's presence is strong," he said. "Didn't you say something horrible happened here before you moved in?"

"I did research and found out that the previous owner Deirdre Turner drowned her two girls in the bathtub and then OD'd on sleeping pills," said Karen.

"An unspeakable crime. A mother murdering her own babies. It doesn't get any more abominable than that. Do you have any smudging sage left?"

"Yes."

Karen retrieved a bundle of sage sticks and handed it to Armitage.

"Where did you buy the sage?" he asked.

"At Jean Baptiste's House of Voodoo, like you told me."

"Good."

Armitage produced a lighter, lit the end of the bundle of sticks, and thrust the bundle into the bathroom before he entered.

"Be gone, demon," he intoned "Leave this house. It's not yours anymore. Leave the new owners alone."

Wind gusted through the broken window, fluttering the shower curtain and extinguishing the smudge. Such was the ferocity of the wind that it compelled Armitage to retreat out the doorway.

"Be gone, demon," repeated Armitage. "You have no power here anymore. Your evil cannot affect the new owners."

The wind blew harder, flapping the vinyl shower curtain and tearing it off the rod, breaking the plastic rings that held it in place. The shower curtain blew out the doorway into Armitage's face.

"Be gone, I say," said Armitage, the curtain plastered to his face and body.

The wind kept thrusting him backward.

"Your evil cannot exist here anymore," he went on, his voice muffled by the curtain adhering to his face. "You are dead. You do not exist."

As he was backing up, Armitage tripped over Karen's foot and fell on his back, the shower curtain shrouding him.

"Doctor, are you all right?" said Karen, crouching over him and trying to pull the curtain off him.

"Jesus Christ," said Gordon, and helped her with the curtain. "Did the wind knock him over? If this fucking wind would stop, we could pull this curtain off him."

"He fell over, is all I know."

"Armitage, are you OK?"

Armitage wasn't moving beneath the curtain.

Gordon snagged the curtain and yanked it with all his might, pulling it off Armitage, who lay supine, his eyes shut.

"Doctor, wake up," said Karen, hunched down beside him.

"He must have hit his head," said Gordon.

Karen shook Armitage's chest. "Wake up."

"Don't tell me he's dead. His relatives will sue our asses off."

"I don't think he's dead," said Karen, shaking Armitage again.

"Feel his pulse."

"I can't. His neck brace is in the way."

"Feel his *wrist*."

Karen jumped in surprise, as the wind gusted through the bathroom window and slammed the bathroom door shut.

"Shit," said Gordon.

Karen pulled herself together and felt Armitage's wrist with her fingers.

"I can feel a pulse," she said. "The fall knocked him out. He must have a concussion."

"Should we call an ambulance?"

"No. He hasn't finished his job yet."

"He could be dying, Karen."

"I don't think so."

"He can't finish anything flat on his back and blacked out. I'll get water."

Gordon retreated to the kitchen, retrieved a cup of cold water, and returned. He flung the water into Armitage's face.

Groaning, Armitage shook his face and blew out his lips, spraying water. "What?"

"You fell," explained Karen.

"I was tripped," he said, trying to gather his wits.

Gordon extended his hand to Armitage to help him up.

Clasping Gordon's hand Armitage sat up and rubbed the back of his head, blinking and grimacing.

"Let me help you stand," said Gordon, extending his hand again.

Armitage took it and rose to his feet. Feeling woozy, he almost fell over.

"Are you sure you're OK, Doctor?" said Karen. "Maybe you better have a seat."

She and Gordon led him to the couch, where he sat down.

Chapter 41

"I need to ask you two a question," said Armitage, rubbing the back of his head and wincing.

"Fire away," said Gordon.

"Are either of you religious? Are you Christians or Jews or do you practice another religion?"

"I can't say that I do."

"No," said Karen. "I'm not religious."

"That's unfortunate," said Armitage. "It would help us exorcise this house if either of you believed in something."

"I don't even believe this house has a demon in it," said Gordon. "I believe the house is falling apart. That's why we're having so many problems."

"It goes beyond that," said Armitage. "You have an evil force here working against you."

"I believe there's an entity here," said Karen, "but I don't know what it wants."

"It wants your family dead, I'm afraid," said Armitage. "It wants you to be scared."

"I'm not scared," said Gordon. "I'm pissed off. I don't know how I got scammed into buying this ramshackle wreck."

"I like this house," said Karen.

"I thought you were itching to move out," said Gordon, bewildered.

"I want to stay. It reminds me of Marilyn Monroe's house in Brentwood."

"Boy, I don't get you, and what's Marilyn Monroe got to do with it? You never said a word about her till we moved here."

"She was a successful movie star. I want to be like her."

"You're not an actor. What's got into you?"

"As a writer, I mean. Actors are creative people like writers. As a creative person, I want to be successful like her."

"The Hollywood gutters are full of people like you who come here thinking they're gonna make it big in the movies and end up as junkies, scammers, and hookers."

"And you're the great expert on art? You can't even pay the mortgage. Give me a break."

"You're gonna end up like that Deirdre what's-her-name if you don't watch out," said Gordon, simmering with resentment.

"If you stay, your whole family is in danger of losing their lives," chimed in Armitage.

Karen and Gordon cooled off their feud at the interruption.

"We hired you to save us, Doctor," said Karen.

"I'm doing my best, but the demon here possesses awesome, terrifying powers that I've never encountered before," said Armitage.

"What's the next step?"

"If you were religious, I would tell you to say your prayers and wear your religious symbols in full display, like a crucifix or a Star of David necklace."

"What about garlic around our necks?" said Gordon.

"Don't be an idiot."

"It works for vampires."

"This is serious," said Karen. "Can't you get it through your head you could be dead in a matter of days if not sooner?" She turned to Armitage. "If we're not religious, does that mean the demon will kill us?"

"Not if I can exorcise it."

"You already tried with those smelly weeds," said Gordon. "They didn't work."

"There are other ways. I suggest in the meantime that you move out of here and check into a motel."

"Not gonna happen. I bought this house, and I'm staying here. I'm not afraid of ghosts and some evil entity nobody can see."

"You will be by the time this is over—if you're still alive."

Armitage stood up. Unsteady on his feet, he reeled out of the house. He managed to reach his car without falling and drove away, weaving down the street.

"He shouldn't be driving with a concussion," said Karen, watching him from the doorway. "He could pass out at the wheel."

"You should talk," said Gordon. "*You* drive around in your sleep."

Chapter 42

Brady was sitting in his room playing the video game *Alan Wake* when he saw Karen standing in his doorway like a mannequin with her head tilted to the right.

She didn't even stand like his mother, he decided, let alone act like her.

"Come with me, Brady," she said with a strained smile.

"Why?"

"You'll see. Come along."

Brady wasn't sure what she wanted with him. Despite misgivings, he followed her.

Karen descended the steps.

"It's ready," she said.

"What is?"

She entered the bathroom. He followed her. He could smell the residual stink of the burning sage Armitage had used to smudge the bathroom.

Karen stood beside the bathtub and pointed at it, her head canted.

"I drew your bath, honey," she said.

The bathtub was filled to the brim and overflowing with water, which was gushing out of the faucet. Water splashed over the sides of the porcelain tub onto the linoleum floor.

"I don't want a bath. I just had a shower."

Brady didn't want to go near that bathtub. Every time he stepped into it something or somebody tried to kill him.

"The doctor's smudging got on all of us," said Karen. "I need to wash it off you. You don't want to smell like sage for the rest of the day, do you?"

"Why is the tub overflowing? You don't need to put so much water in it."

"I want to make sure you get good and clean."

You want to make sure there's enough water in the tub to drown me.

"Why don't you turn the water off?" he said.

"The drain stopper is faulty. It's allowing water to go down the drain. If I turn the water off, the bathtub will become empty."

"You tried to drown me in the tub last time."

"That wasn't me. I'm the one who saved you. Remember?"

"You were the one holding my head underwater. We were the only two in the room."

"You were trying to drown yourself. You'd be dead if it wasn't for me. Now take off your clothes and get into the tub."

Scared, Brady stood rooted to the spot. "You're not my mother."

"What are you talking about? Of course, I am. Stop fooling around and get into the tub."

Adrenaline surging through him, he broke into a fearful sweat.

"No," he managed to say.

"Stop disobeying me," said Karen, becoming furious. "I'm your mother. Do as I say."

Brady took a powder.

"Come back here, young man," cried Karen, hopping mad.

Gordon strode down the hall, approaching the bathroom. "What's going on?"

"I'm trying to give Brady a bath," said Karen. "He disobeyed me and ran away."

Gordon stood in the bathroom doorway. "Why do you keep running the water? The tub's overflowing. Water's pouring on the floor."

"The drain stopper's not working."

Gordon entered the bathroom, cut across the floor, and twisted off the faucet handles.

"He doesn't need a full tub for a bath," he said. "No wonder he ran away. Anyway, he just took a shower."

"The stink of sage is on him. I need to get it off him."

"Why?"

"Uh—it's not good for his health."

"Armitage said the sage will protect us from demons. You're the one that thinks we need protection. So why do you want to wash the sage off Brady?"

"Why do you keep interfering with me? No matter what I do, you try to stop me."

"If Brady wants a bath, he can take one himself. You don't have to baby him."

"I'm trying to do what's best for him. I don't have time to argue with you any longer. I have to get back to writing."

She brushed past him and stalked down the hallway.

Brady had heard everything. He was crouching on the landing and peeking downstairs through the balustrade at Karen and Gordon, when Karen left in a huff.

But she wasn't Karen, he knew. She was someone else, and she scared the bejabbers out of him.

Chapter 43

Brady had trouble falling asleep that night. He kept tossing and turning, his mind churning thoughts. He couldn't stop thinking about Karen trying to drown him in the bathtub and about the hairs wriggling out of the shower head like worms and trying to strangle him.

He felt cold. His teeth chattering, he clutched his blanket around his neck to keep warm. His room was cold as ice. It felt more like winter than summer. Even in winter it didn't get this cold.

He opened his mouth and exhaled. He saw his breath vaporizing. He shivered under the blankets. He couldn't understand why it was so cold.

He was tempted to get out of bed and see if Mom and Dad's bedroom was as cold as his, but if he got out of bed, he would freeze. He didn't want to leave his warm bed.

It must be this house, he decided. There was something wrong with the heating. But it shouldn't be this cold. It was summer. The heating shouldn't even be on. It shouldn't be necessary.

Then why was his room a refrigerator?

He had to stop thinking about it, or he would never fall asleep. How could he sleep when he was shivering? He didn't want to be a wuss and run into his parents' bedroom crying for help. He was too old to cry.

He needed to relax and fall asleep.

He felt like somebody was watching him. Terrified, he opened his eyes and tilted his head up to scope out the dark room. He didn't see anyone. Of course, it was difficult to see much of anything in the dark. He didn't see any movement.

Relaxing after a fashion, he tilted his head back onto the pillow and eyed the ceiling. He couldn't shake the feeling of being watched by a thousand eyeballs.

It must be a nightmare. He would wake up when it was over. He drifted off.

Screaming, he jackknifed into a sitting position when he felt keen pain throbbing in his arm, which was lying outside the covers. He discerned blood on his upper arm. Out of the corner of his eye he picked up on a woman in a chiffon nightgown gliding down the dim-lit hall toward the stairs. His mother. He thought he saw blood dripping from her mouth.

He inspected his arm but couldn't see much in the dark. It felt like something had bit him. He needed to wash the wound. He had heard of people getting tetanus from infected wounds. He sprang out of bed to the bathroom in the master bedroom. It was the only bathroom on the upper floor. He debated whether he should wake up his parents and tell them of the attack.

His fake mother would have a cow if he woke her, he knew. She might threaten to kill him again. However, she wasn't in the bedroom. She was going down the stairs when he last saw her.

He turned on the light in the bathroom, stuck his arm under the sink faucet, and sluiced cold water on his bloody wound. It looked like teeth marks in his arm. His mother must have bitten him and left. Was she a vampire? Only vampires bit people and sucked their blood.

In the wash of light from the bathroom he could see his parents' bed. His father lay alone between the sheets. The other side of the bed had its covers pulled down and was empty.

Fear overwhelmed him. He couldn't help himself. He darted to the bed and tried to shake his father awake. He didn't care if his father thought he was a pussy.

Brady was all alone in the night. He had been attacked and he needed help.

"Dad," he said, shaking his father. "Wake up, wake up."

"What?" muttered Gordon, half awake.

"Mom bit me."

Trying to wake up, Gordon opened and closed his eyes, which were gummy with sleep.

"Look," said Brady, showing Gordon his bloody arm.

It was much warmer in this room than in his, noticed Brady.

Gordon struggled to sit up in bed. "What happened?"

"Mom bit me."

Gordon glanced to his side and saw an empty bed.

"Are you making up stories again?" he said.

"No," said Brady, shaking his head in protest. "I felt pain in my arm when I was asleep. I woke up and saw her walking down the hall."

"Where is she?"

"She went downstairs."

Gordon bounded out of bed, through the hall, and down the stairs. Brady ran after him.

Gordon flicked on the living room light. No sign of Karen.

"Karen," he said. "Where are you?"

No answer.

He angled to the front door, flung it open, and surveyed the front yard.

"Is she outside?" asked Brady, and stood beside him, peering into the moonlit darkness.

"My rental's gone," answered Gordon, disconcerted, noticing the empty driveway. "She must be sleepwalking again."

"Are you gonna go after her?"

"I have no idea where she went. Unless she went to Marilyn Monroe's house again." Gordon yawned. "I can't drive in this condition. I took a sleeping pill myself. I just hope she doesn't get in an accident. She has no idea what she's doing."

Gordon closed the front door and retreated to the living room, yawning again.

"I'm dead on my feet," he said.

"Why did she bite me?"

"Are you sure that's a bite mark? I can't think straight with this drug in my system. We'll talk about it tomorrow."

"It must've been her that did it. I saw her walking away after I felt the bite in my arm."

"Maybe it was a rat."

"Rat?" said Brady, widening his eyes. "Are there rats in this house?"

Gordon rubbed his forehead, barely able to keep his eyes open. "It makes more sense than Karen biting you."

"I thought I saw blood on her lips."

Gordon looked skeptical. "How could you see in the dark? You probably imagined it."

"What if she comes back and attacks me again?" said Brady, trembling with apprehension at the thought.

"Yell for me." Smiling, Gordon rubbed Brady's head. "Let's go back to bed."

"Can I sleep with you tonight?"

Gordon yawned. "You better not. When Karen comes back, she'll get into bed and crush you. She's out of it. She doesn't know what she's doing when she's on that drug. You're not scared, are you? A big boy like you."

"No," said Brady quickly. "Of course not."

"Your arm's still bleeding," said Gordon with concern. "I'll put antibiotic on it and wrap it in gauze. Let's go to my bathroom."

Gordon stood for a moment, listening for the sound of his rental pulling into the driveway. Not a peep.

"Go on," he said, motioning for Brady to mount the steps.

A bead of blood dripped from Brady's wounded arm onto a tread.

Gordon killed the living room light and climbed the staircase after Brady.

Chapter 44

The next morning, Karen and Gordon were eating scrambled eggs and bacon for breakfast in the dining room. Karen spread marmalade on a toasted English muffin.

"Did you sleep well last night?" asked Gordon.

"Fine," she answered.

"Are you sure?"

"I'm well rested. I feel fine today. What's with the third degree?"

Gordon took a deep breath and sipped a cup of coffee. "We gotta talk about Brady."

"He must still be sleeping," said Karen, and took a bite of her English muffin.

"He told me you bit him last night," said Gordon, searching her face.

Karen choked on her muffin.

"What?" she spluttered. "What the hell? You make me sound like a goddamn vampire."

"I know it sounds far-fetched. But he had a bloody wound on his arm last night. I saw it."

"Well, I didn't do it. You really think I did it?" she said, dumbfounded.

"He said he felt pain while he was sleeping. He woke up and saw you walking down the hall outside of his room."

"I wasn't walking around in the middle of the night."

"Actually, you were. You weren't in your bed last night, and my rental was missing from the driveway. You were sleepwalking again and drove it somewhere. Where did you go?"

"I didn't go anywhere."

"You drove my car last night."

Karen shook her head. "I don't remember."

"Did you take triazolam last night?"

"I had to. I'm stressed out. I can't sleep when I'm stressed."

"Maybe you should lay off that stuff. My doctor said it could affect your personality if you take too much of it."

"If I don't get any sleep, it'll affect my personality. I'll feel irritable and grouchy all day."

Gordon ate a slice of crispy bacon.

"I doubt you would bite Brady," he said.

"I did *not* bite Brady. How can you even think such a thing? It must've been some animal that bit him."

"I thought it might be a rat. Have you seen rats in the house?"

"No." She shivered. "I hate rats. Just thinking about them gives me the creeps. Can we talk about something else? I'm trying to eat my breakfast."

"Brady is terrified of you. How do you explain that?"

"I told you he makes up stories about me. That stuff about me trying to drown him. Bullshit. He's a kid with an overactive imagination."

"He didn't imagine that bite on his arm. I saw it with my own eyes."

"Maybe we should hire an exterminator to clean this house of rats or whatever it is that's creeping around biting people at night."

"To be honest, it looked like human teeth bit him when I examined the wound last night. A rat couldn't make a bite that big."

"How do you know he didn't bite himself?"

Gordon didn't answer right away.

"Why would he do that?" he said at last.

"For the same reason he makes up stories. For attention. He's coping with growing up."

"Ever since we moved into this house, we've had nothing but trouble. And the place is falling apart at the seams."

"You can't blame everything on the house. It's a beautiful house. It just needs a little work."

"You need to spend more time with Brady. Maybe then he won't be so scared of you."

"I'm not gonna let him monopolize my valuable time. I need to spend my time resurrecting my career as a writer. I've been putting it off too long by finding excuses not to write and spending too much time with Brady. He has to learn to take care of himself. It's called becoming an adult."

"Can't you think about anyone bur yourself?"

She glared at him. "Are you trying to sabotage my writing career too? You're in it with him, aren't you?"

"In what? Stop talking crazy."

"I will not be stopped from pursuing my writing career. Do you hear me?" said Karen, jabbing her index finger against the tabletop.

"Nobody's stopping you. You're the one with the overactive imagination, thinking everyone is stopping you from writing. You're paranoid and wacked out. Nobody is stopping you but yourself."

"Calling me crazy isn't gonna stop me."

"It's that triazolam you're taking. You're taking too much of it."

"You need to mind your own business."

The dining room lights mounted on the ceiling flashed on and off.

Gordon looked up at them. "This house isn't helping matters. Not only is it disintegrating, it has electrical problems."

"Armitage will exorcise it for us, and we'll be fine."

"How can he exorcise anything? He can't even drive his car without crashing into a tree and nearly killing himself."

"It wasn't an accident. You heard him. He said the flies attacked him."

Gordon stared at her. "Do you believe he was telling the truth about those flies blinding him?"

"I do. They nearly smothered me to death."

"Or he's trying to get us to believe he's telling the truth about this house being haunted so we'll keep ponying up more money to exorcise the demon," said Gordon, making air quotes around the word *demon*. "There are a lot of scammers in the parapsychology racket."

"Not everybody is as cynical as you. He wouldn't be able to stay in business if he was a scammer."

"The problem with ghosts and demons is you can't prove they exist or they don't exist. Which lends itself to fraud exploited by so-called mediums and psychics."

They both started when someone knocked on the front door.

"Are you expecting someone?" said Gordon, finishing his slice of bacon and getting to his feet.

"No."

"I'll get it."

He left the dining room, Karen in tow.

Chapter 45

Gordon opened the front door and let Lieutenant Gaetz in.

"What brings you here so early in the morning, Lieutenant?" said Gordon, wondering if there was a BOLO out on him for the attempted murder of Childress, and Gaetz had found out about it.

Gordon was loath to whack the lieutenant, but he would do anything to stay out of the joint. If whacking Gaetz was the only way to keep his freedom, Gordon would whack him. Gordon was becoming suspicious of Gaetz, because the guy had returned to the house unbidden. Maybe Gaetz had an ulterior motive—like busting him.

"I happened to be in the area," said Gaetz. "I thought I'd check to see if everything is OK with Brady."

"Of course, it is," said Karen brightly, entering the living room. "We were just having breakfast."

"Could I speak to him?"

"He's still in his bedroom."

"Could you ask him to come down?"

"Why do you want him? I can answer any questions you have."

"I'd like to see if he's OK."

"He's fine."

"Do you mind if I ask him myself, Mrs. Carney?" said Gaetz, his voice edged.

"Don't you believe me?"

"I do, but I'd like to make sure by checking with him."

"Fine. I'll get him," said Karen, and retreated to the foot of the staircase. "Brady, we have a guest. He would like to talk to you."

His arm wound swathed in gauze, Brady appeared at the landing, cutting his eyes back and forth with anxiety.

"Come on down," said Karen.

Brady descended with tentative steps.

Gaetz approached him at the foot of the staircase.

"Good morning, Brady. How are you?"

Brady glanced nervously at Karen. "Uh—fine."

"That's good to hear." Gaetz narrowed his eyes. "What happened to your arm?"

"A rat bit him," cut in Karen.

"Is that right, Brady?"

"Uh . . . ," Brady trailed off.

"Yes?"

"Uh—I guess. Uh—it happened in the dark," said Brady, glancing with fearful eyes at Karen, who was leveling a steady gaze at him.

"You should have it examined at the hospital," said Gaetz. "They'll give you a tetanus shot."

Brady nodded yes.

"There you see, Lieutenant," said Karen. "Everything is fine."

"You seem scared, Brady," said Gaetz.

"No," said Brady.

"He's scared of you, Lieutenant," said Karen. "Police make him nervous."

"Has anyone threatened you again, Brady?" said Gaetz.

"Uh—no."

"I'm here to help you. I'm your friend."

Brady said nothing.

"If that'll be all, Lieutenant," said Karen, "I'll show you to the door."

"Actually, I also wanted to talk to you about Deirdre Turner."

"What about?"

Eager to leave, Brady ran back up the stairs.

"Your son strikes me as nervous," said Gaetz, watching Brady bug out.

"He's not used to having guests, especially in this new neighborhood," said Karen. "Surely you can understand that."

"Of course."

Chapter 46

"What did you want to tell me about Deirdre?" said Karen.

The overhead light flicked on and off.

Gaetz looked up at the light. "You need a new bulb, it looks like."

"This house needs a lot of repairs," said Gordon. "I didn't realize it was such a run-down hovel."

"We need to fix a bunch of things," agreed Karen.

"Anywho, I did a little digging into Deirdre's case and found out she was involved in a satanic cult," said Gaetz.

"Satanic cult? Wow. What kind of a life was she living?"

"Why are you resurrecting her case?" said Gordon.

"I had forgotten about it till your wife started asking me about Deirdre during our interview," said Gaetz.

"Interview?"

"For the true crime article I'm writing, honey," said Karen.

"Oh," said Gordon, puzzled.

"Deirdre was into sinister stuff," said Gaetz.

The front door slammed shut with a loud crash.

Everyone started.

"The wind," said Gordon. "I guess I left the door open."

"I suggest you get your door fixed soon to prevent a robbery. There have been break-ins in this area recently," said Gaetz.

"I will."

"Maybe Deirdre learned from the satanists how to haunt a house," said Karen.

"Why would she want to?" said Gordon.

Karen shrugged in ignorance. "Maybe she wanted to become immortal."

"Satanists know how to do that?" said Gaetz.

"Dracula and all that," said Gordon. "Vampires are immortal."

"Except for a stake through their hearts," said Gaetz, grinning with a twinkle in his eye.

Karen smiled. "I'm just saying. I know nothing about satanic cults in Hollywood. The less I know the better. The whole cult scene gives me the willies."

"The most famous cult in these parts"—Gaetz cleared his throat—"actually it was down in Benedict Canyon, was the Manson Family back in the sixties. But Manson told his followers he was Jesus Christ, not Satan."

"And on that cheery note . . . ," said Gordon.

Eager to be rid of the cop, Gordon headed to the front door in a not-so-subtle hint for Gaetz to leave.

"You can use the Satan reference in your article, Mrs. Carney," said Gaetz, angling after Gordon.

The floor shuddered.

"Whoa," said Gaetz, halting in his tracks. "Did you feel that?"

"Must be a quake," said Gordon, uncertain.

"I hope it wasn't too near. We'll be swamped with calls all day at the station if it was in the immediate area."

The floor stopped shaking.

"Looks like it's done," said Gordon.

Gaetz resumed striding to the door. "Make sure you take Brady to the hospital and get him a tetanus shot. You can't take chances with rat bites. I've been bitten by dogs, and I know the drill. Animals have bacteria on their teeth." He paused. "So do humans, actually."

Gordon exchanged looks with Karen, wondering if Gaetz had somehow figured out Brady had accused Karen of biting him.

"Will do," said Gordon.

"If I have time, I may drop in on you again later today," said Gaetz.

The last thing Gordon wanted, to be sure. He grimaced out of sight of Gaetz.

"Fine," Gordon muttered.

Relieved the cop was leaving, he watched Gaetz's black-and-white back out of the driveway.

"Thanks for not telling him Brady accused me of biting him last night," said Karen from behind.

Gordon turned around to face her. "Frankly, I wanted him to leave ASAP. Cops," he said, shaking his head. "Why does he keep sticking his nose in our business?"

"He *did* help me find out about the identity of the previous owner of our house. I owe him for that."

"He said he would drop by later," said Gordon, pulling a face.

"I don't want him to become a member of our family. I just wanted to find out what he knew about Deirdre Turner. Anyway, he didn't come here because of me. He came here because of that call Brady made to the station for help."

"Which was a report about your threatening him. He's terrified of you."

"I'm terrified of the demon in this house," she said, clutching Gordon's arm and pressing her body against him.

"It'll be all right."

"I feel like I'm being watched all the time," she said, taking in the living room walls as if they had peepholes drilled in them.

"Just don't go around tearing down the walls in the living room like you did in the bedroom. We'll never be able to sell this thing if you rip apart all of the walls."

"You don't feel eyes watching you?"

"I feel like we should move."

"I love this house. I'm not gonna let anyone force us out of it."

"You're terrified of it, but you love it? I don't get it."

"I'm terrified of the demon dwelling here. The unearthly presence. The millions of eyes looking at me."

Gordon was in the act of closing the door when he picked up on Armitage's Mercedes pulling into the driveway.

"Here comes Dr. Quack," he said.

"Stop calling him that."

"That business with the burning sage didn't do any good."

"He's just starting. Give him a chance."

Gordon grimaced.

Chapter 47

Armitage climbed awkwardly out of his car and made his way up the driveway, treading carefully because he couldn't see where his feet were stepping thanks to the encumbrance of his neck brace.

"Good morning, Doctor," said Karen.

"Good morning," said Armitage. "I have come to the conclusion we need to perform a séance before your family starts killing each other."

Karen widened her eyes at Armitage's unnerving revelation.

"Is it *that* bad here?" she said.

"I'm afraid so," said Armitage. "Smudging with sage usually exorcises a house except in extreme cases of demonic possession in which a violent and bloodthirsty entity is involved. I'm convinced this demon won't leave you alone till you're all dead."

"Why does it hate us so much?"

"That's what we need to find out. A séance should help us. I need to get in touch with the demon's motivation, its raison d'être, if you will."

"Is a séance dangerous?"

"No, no. I wouldn't do anything to knowingly expose your family to harm."

"'Knowingly,'" said Gordon. "You said *knowingly*."

"In the realm of parapsychology we can never be certain of anything. However, I can assure you I'm not gonna do anything to deliberately antagonize the demon. In any case, the demon itself cannot harm you. It can, however, possess your bodily vessels to cause harm to others and to yourselves."

"I'm not sure I want to go through with this," said Karen, fretting.

"I must warn you the alternative is your family murdering each other."

"It's not right for you to come here and threaten us," said Gordon, advancing on Armitage.

"I'm not the one threatening you, Mr. Carney. It's the demon. I'm merely warning you of the danger confronting your family."

"I don't believe in ghosts and demons."

"That's what my last client said," said Armitage ominously.

"Is that some kind of roundabout threat?" said Gordon, trying to put a lid on his resentment.

"I'm stating a fact, is all."

"All right. I'll take your bait. What happened to your last client?"

"Do you really want to know?"

"Yeah."

"He jumped out his mansion's third-story bedroom window."

"He fell to his death?"

"He hanged by the neck outside his bedroom window, Mr. Carney. The other end of the noose tied around his neck was tied to one of the legs of his bed."

"Do we have to talk about this?" said Karen, looking ill.

"Did he sit through one of your séances?" said Gordon.

"He refused," said Armitage. "He told me ghosts and demons were all a bunch of bunk."

"Are you telling me a demon forced the guy to commit suicide?"

"I'm telling you what happened at his house, which I determined to be possessed by a demon. He refused to take part in a séance to let me contact the demon and find out what it wanted."

"Why didn't you hold the séance without him?"

"He was the owner of the possessed house. A séance held without his presence would have been useless. Your entire family needs to take part in our séance for it to be successful."

"Brady too?" said Karen.

"Yes."

"I don't think we should expose the kid to danger," said Gordon.

"There is more danger to your family in *not* taking part in a séance. Everyone in your family must take part, or it won't work."

"If any harm comes to my kid, I'll hold you personally responsible, Doctor. If you really are a doctor—"

Armitage stiffened at the insult.

"Honey," said Karen. "I've checked his credentials. We went through this before."

"Whatever," said Gordon with a loud expulsion of breath, venting his frustration.

Chapter 48

Karen went to the foot of the stairs and looked up at the second floor landing.

"Brady, come downstairs," she called out.

"I was just down there," said Brady, sidling toward the newel, looking sheepish.

"Dr. Armitage is here. He wants to see you."

"Why?"

"We need you for a séance. It'll be fun. He wants to communicate with a ghost."

Brady descended the steps, not sure what he was getting into.

When Brady entered the living room, Armitage noticed the bandage swathing Brady's upper arm.

"What happened to your arm, son?" said Armitage.

"Something bit him last night while he was sleeping," said Karen.

"Mind if I look at it?"

"Why?"

"It might not be a bite."

"I looked at it," said Gordon. "There were teeth marks in his arm. See for yourself. What's the harm?"

Armitage unwrapped the gauze bandage and inspected the wound.

"Rather a large bite for a rat to make," he said.

"I woke up because of the pain and saw that woman walking down the hall outside my room in the middle of the night," said Brady.

"That woman is your mother," said Gordon, annoyed.

"Why were you walking around at that time, Mrs. Carney?" asked Armitage.

"I wasn't aware that I was," answered Karen, caught off guard by Brady's confiding in Armitage.

"She was sleepwalking last night," explained Gordon. "It's not the first time. She's been taking sleeping pills."

"I see," said Armitage.

He returned to inspecting Brady's wound then rewrapped it with the gauze.

"There could be another explanation," he said.

"I believe he bit himself," said Karen. "I don't go around biting people, that's for sure. You make me sound like a vampire or a zombie."

"Yes, it's possible he did. The demon could have possessed him and forced him to bite himself." Armitage paused a beat. "Or there could be another explanation."

"Let's drop the subject," said Karen, irritated that Brady had accused her of biting him. "Brady has an overactive imagination. He likes to tell stories. That's all."

"Is your son autistic?"

"Not that I know of. Why?"

"Autistic children sometimes bite themselves."

"Is there a test for autism?"

"I'm not a professional on the subject. I would ask your doctor."

"Brady seems normal to me," said Gordon.

"Autism is not debilitating. Some autistic people do quite well in life. But again, I'm not a professional on the subject."

"If he's biting himself, we need to fix that," said Karen. "He could seriously hurt himself."

"There could be another explanation for the wound."

"For somebody who's not an expert, you sure have a ton of explanations," said Gordon.

"Don't pay any attention to him, Doctor. He thinks he knows everything," said Karen, trying to silence Gordon with a scolding glance. "What is the other explanation for Brady's wound?"

"Stigmata," said Armitage.

"Stigmata?" said Gordon, not familiar with the term.

"Some sensitive people can cause scars and bites to appear on their own flesh by autosuggestion. Many of these people suffer from anorexia nervosa. Some cause self-inflicted harm."

"Like biting themselves," said Karen, sneaking a gander at Brady. "You see, I was right about him. He *did* bite himself."

"No, I didn't," said Brady.

Karen frowned. "When I want you to speak, I'll ask you a question, young man."

Brady sulked.

"People with stigmata don't bite themselves," said Armitage. "They make their wounds appear on their body through autosuggestion."

"See, I didn't bite myself," said Brady.

"But you made the wounds appear on your own body," said Karen. "That means you're responsible."

Armitage made a show of clearing his throat.

Chapter 49

"The Catholic Church believes stigmata appear on blessed people," declared Armitage. "The wounds usually occur in the same places where Jesus was crucified, namely in the wrists or hands. Or the wounds could appear in the forehead to represent the crown of thorns Christ wore when the Romans crucified him. Some people show stigmata by bleeding from their eyes, or their flesh bleeds for no reason. Which sometimes happens under the rib cage in the same area where the Roman soldier Longinus impaled Christ with a spear while Christ was nailed to the cross."

"We're not religious in this family, so why would Brady exhibit signs of stigmata?" said Gordon.

"I would say autosuggestion in his case," said Armitage, stroking his chin in thought. "He seems to be sensitive to suggestion. He could be vulnerable to the demon's demands. The demon could want Brady to bleed in order to terrify him."

"The demon's controlling him?"

"Yes, to a certain extent. That doesn't mean the demon has complete control of your son. If Brady caused the wounds to appear on his body, it was because the demon put the idea in Brady's head."

"Maybe that's why he thinks I'm not his mother," said Karen. "Because the demon is messing with his mind."

Armitage nodded. "Demons are experts at practicing deception. He could be pretending to be Christ and convincing Brady of it. But the demon's designs are evil. We must exorcise the demon from your house before a horrible catastrophe occurs."

"Is Brady in danger if he takes part in the séance?"

"I will protect him. As long as he doesn't break the ring of hands as we touch each other, he should be fine. Our power is multiplied as we hold hands."

"I'm confused," said Gordon. "Are you saying Brady bit himself without even knowing he was doing it?"

"It's entirely possible when dealing with a possessed house like this one," said Armitage. "Or Brady could have manifested the wound using the power of his mind, which is sometimes controlled by the demon."

"Brady can cause wounds to appear on people?"

"Not on other people. Only on himself. At times, the demon *is* possessing Brady and controlling him."

"Making him see things like hair coming out of a shower head?" said Gordon.

"Correct."

Brady shook his head in disagreement but was afraid to say anything on account of Karen's reprimand.

"You think Brady's the demon's target?" said Karen.

"I believe your entire family is at risk," said Armitage. "We must exorcise the demon without delay."

"Isn't a séance done at night?"

"It should be done in the dark," said Armitage, nodding. "You are correct. But we can't wait for the dark. You are in too much peril. We'll draw the drapes shut and get it as dark as possible before we proceed."

"Do you charge more for a daytime séance?" said Gordon, his face smug.

"We don't need your wisecracks now, honey," said Karen. "This is serious."

"What exactly is your profession?" Gordon asked Armitage.

"He's a medium," said Karen. "He gets in touch with spirits."

"I like to call myself an occultist," said Armitage. "I study parapsychology and the supernatural. Now let's shut the curtains and get down to business. The demon's hold over your family is getting stronger the longer you live here."

"I believe you're right about the presence of evil here. I found out Deirdre, the former owner of this house, belonged to a satanic cult."

"What?" said Armitage, taken aback. "In that case, you are in more danger than I thought. She must have conjured the evil entity herself with the use of the black arts, thus making the demon more powerful, since he was deliberately summoned. A demon's power is always enhanced when he is invited into a house."

"Why would she do such a thing?"

"We can only guess. Perhaps Deirdre was seeking immortality through Satan. Black magic is never to be dabbled with. The consequences are grave. Not only your lives, but your very souls are at stake."

"All right," said Gordon, tired of Armitage's self-importance. "Let's get on with it and get it over with."

"I concur. Speed is essential. Delay could be fatal for your family."

"Does it matter in the séance if I'm not religious?"

"It would help if you were, but keep your mind open. That way I should be able to contact the unsettled spirit. Any kind of negative energy resulting from doubt in anyone here will impede my efforts at communication with the demon."

"We need to find out what it wants," said Karen. "Then maybe it'll leave us alone."

"I fear not, Mrs. Carney. The demon already tried to kill you with the attack of the flies. He also tried to kill me, nearly breaking my neck in a car accident."

"Are you sure you're up to this séance, Doctor, with your injured neck? Don't séances exhaust mediums?"

Armitage smiled. "I'll be fine. My concern is for you and your family if we don't go ahead as planned."

"Don't you have a sidekick to help you?" said Gordon. "Somebody to pull the levers behind the curtains?"

Armitage glared at him. "There are no levers, Mr. Carney, unless you put them there. This is *your* house. You're talking about bunco artists pretending to be psychics. I'm not gonna stand for any more of your insults. It's *your* lives that are at stake, not mine. If you don't want my help, so be it."

Steamed, Armitage slewed around and headed for the front door.

"He didn't mean it," said Karen, upbraiding Gordon with a scowl.

She scrambled after Armitage to intercept him. "Come back, Doctor."

"Do you want to save your lives or not?" said Armitage, his visage grave. "Your immortal souls are at stake as well."

"I'm just having a little fun," said Gordon. "Don't mind me." Under his breath he added, "I still think you're a fraud."

"Draw the drapes shut and let's begin," said Armitage.

Chapter 50

"Help me close all the drapes in the house, Brady," said Karen as she drew the drapes over the picture window in the living room.

Brady scooted around the house, closing curtains.

"What about upstairs?" he said.

"Yes," said Armitage. "That will block any sunlight from shining on the stairwell and lighting the living room."

Brady ran up the stairs and closed all the curtains in the bedrooms. He hurried back down the steps.

"Someone needs to kill the lights after we sit down at the table," said Armitage.

"I'll do it," said Gordon.

He turned off all the lights except the one in the dining room and stood near the light switch while everybody else sat around the table.

"Put your hands flat on the tabletop so they're touching the person's sitting beside you," said Armitage. "All right, Mr. Carney, kill the lights and join us."

Gordon followed Armitage's instructions, found his way to his chair, sat down, and touched Brady's and Armitage's hands. Gordon wanted to sit next to Armitage to make sure the guy didn't pull a fast one to fake a demon's appearance.

The four of them sat in the dark.

"What are we supposed to do?" said Karen, sounding uncomfortable.

"Don't speak while I go into a trance," said Armitage. "I need absolute silence. Whatever you do, don't break the circle of hands."

Gordon glowered at Karen. He didn't know if she could see him. He was having trouble discerning her face. Just as well, he decided. She wouldn't be happy if she could see him. He couldn't believe she was falling for Armitage's con.

Armitage commenced humming.

"Spirit, I summon thee," he said. "What do you want here? What is your purpose?"

Silence.

"I'm freezing," said Brady, shivering.

"It *is* cold," said Karen. "I can see my own breath."

"Can I rub my hands together to get warm?" said Brady, grimacing.

"Do not break the circle," warned Armitage. "Be silent."

Gordon could feel his teeth chattering. He couldn't believe how cold it had become in a matter of minutes. He was going to end up with frost on his eyebrows if the temperature kept dropping. Even the tabletop was freezing. It was turning into a sheet of ice. The bone-chilling cold of its surface was turning his hands numb.

"The table is ice," said Gordon.

"Be quiet, I say," said Armitage. "Keep your hands on the table and do not under any circumstances break the ring."

"I couldn't move if I wanted to. I'm frozen stiff. I'm getting frostbite."

"Spirit, I summon thee," repeated Armitage. "Give us a sign to let us know you are present."

"Why's it so fucking cold?" said Gordon, his exhaled breath turning into grey mist in front of his face.

"Quiet," said Armitage. "Spirit?"

A chunk of plaster fell out of the ceiling and dropped onto the middle of the tabletop. Everybody sitting around the table started.

"Do not move your hands," intoned Armitage.

"I can't even feel mine, they're so cold," said Karen. "I don't know whether I'm touching anyone or not."

"State the nature of your business, spirit," said Armitage, recovering his composure. "Tell us your mission."

Armitage jerked his head back and gazed up at the ceiling, his eyes wide, his mouth agape.

"Death," he said in an eerie, androgynous voice.

Brady screamed in horror.

The table fell to rocking back and forth, making it difficult for everyone to keep holding hands.

"Death," came the eldritch voice again as Armitage continued to gawk at the ceiling.

Another chunk of plaster fell from the ceiling and struck the tabletop.

"Fuck this," said Gordon. "Somebody's gonna get hurt."

He broke the circle and bolted to his feet.

"No," cried Karen in protest.

"It's an earthquake," said Gordon. "Everyone, get under the table."

Brady scampered under the table.

Armitage fell backward as his chair toppled over. Impacting the floor with the back of his head he moaned.

"He told you not to break the circle," Karen berated Gordon.

"We're in the middle of an earthquake," retorted Gordon. "We could get killed if we don't seek cover."

"It's not an earthquake. It's the demon. It's contacting us."

"Demon shmemon," said Gordon, waving her off.

Karen ran to Armitage and hunkered down beside him.

"Doctor, are you all right?" she said.

Armitage moaned, his eyes shut.

Karen turned to Gordon. "Honey, help me get him up."

Gordon helped her lift Armitage and his fallen chair upright.

Chapter 51

"Somebody broke the circle," said Armitage, dazed.

"We had an earthquake," said Gordon. "The ceiling was falling on us."

"No earthquake. It was the demon. Its power is overwhelming. Like nothing I've ever encountered before," said Armitage, wincing and rubbing the back of his head.

"He can control earthquakes, huh?"

"Oh ye of little faith," said Armitage, exasperated. "It wasn't an earthquake. It was the demon."

"What does it want?" said Karen.

"It wants someone in your family dead."

"Which one of us?" said Karen, hanging on his every word.

"Somebody broke the ring before I could find out."

"Earthquakes don't have hidden meanings," said Gordon. "They have no significance. They're natural disasters. That's all. None of this jiggery-pokery."

Armitage kept rubbing the back of his head and wincing.

"Do you need to go to the hospital?" said Karen.

"Just a bump," said Armitage. "It's nothing."

"You might have a concussion."

"I'm fine."

"How come only you fell over?" said Gordon.

"The demon doesn't want my presence. It senses me as its antagonist."

"It was an earthquake," insisted Gordon.

"Didn't you see it?" said Karen.

"See what?"

"The demon's face. I saw it appear on the doctor's."

"Ectoplasm," said Armitage, nodding.

"I don't know what you're talking about," said Gordon.

"Tendrils like fog crept out of his open mouth and formed a cloud around his head in the shape of a woman's face," said Karen.

"You were hallucinating. I saw nothing."

"Didn't you hear her?"

"I heard Armitage speaking in a woman's voice, or an epicene voice, in any case."

"Didn't you see the fog around his face?"

"I saw vapor coming from his mouth as his hot breath met the frigid air. Just a cloud around his face."

"It was in the shape of a woman's face, sort of like Marilyn Monroe's."

"There you go with Marilyn Monroe again. You got that woman on your brain, always driving to her house in the middle of the night."

"She saw the ectoplasm emitted from my mouth," explained Armitage. "This is what happens during séances. It's how I communicate with the spirit world."

"I don't know how you got it so cold here, but I sure didn't see any spirits floating on your face."

"I'm not the one who made it cold. It was the demon. You heard it speaking through me."

"I heard your voice change into a falsetto. I couldn't really tell its sex."

"It was a creepy voice," said Brady, rubbing his shoulders, trying to keep warm as his teeth chattered. "It gave me goose bumps."

"Did you see a woman's face take the place of the doctor's?" said Gordon.

"I didn't see any faces. I was too scared. I had my eyes closed."

"How about the sixty-four-thousand-dollar question, Doctor? What does this demon want?"

"I don't know anything more than what it said. But I fear for your safety. What it wants is gonna cause suffering and death if you stay here."

"I thought you said you could get rid of it for us."

"It's hard to tell what it wants, because it practices deceit. Evil wraps itself in lies."

"I bet you know a lot about deceit, don't you?"

"I don't have to sit here and listen to your innuendoes," said Armitage, his feathers ruffled, rising unsteadily to his feet.

"Could somebody turn on the heat?" said Karen. "I'm gonna catch pneumonia."

"The demon has retreated. It will get warmer here in a matter of minutes."

Gordon stormed to the front door and flung it open to let in the warm air.

"Let's go outside and soak up some rays," he said.

Wearing a pained expression Armitage massaged his head.

"Are you all right, Doctor?" said Karen.

"Don't mind me. I'm exhausted, is all. Séances wear me out. They use up vast amounts of energy in mediums."

His mind muzzy, he staggered toward the door.

Karen hurried to his side to steady him.

"I'll be all right," he said, "once I get outside in the sun."

"We're lucky plaster from the ceiling didn't bonk us in the heads and crack our skulls," said Gordon.

"You must listen to me. The demon wants to cause you harm," said Armitage, approaching Gordon, who was standing at the open door.

"How can we get rid of it?" said Karen at Armitage's side.

"I'll have to try another séance. I don't have enough energy to do it now."

He meandered across the front lawn, looking shell-shocked, clutching his aching head.

"Make sure you go to a hospital to see if you have a concussion," said Karen, standing in the doorway, watching him.

He waved back at her, grimacing, but said nothing and climbed into his Mercedes SL roadster.

"Are you sure you don't want one of us to give you a lift?" said Karen, worried about him. To Gordon she said, "It's not safe for him to drive in his condition. He hit the back of his head hard on the floor."

"His wooziness may be part of his act," said Gordon under his breath.

"I'm fine," said Armitage, firing the Mercedes engine.

"Take care while you're driving," said Karen.

"You're the ones who need to take care. That demon wants to kill all of you. It wants blood, and it won't be satisfied until it gets blood."

Armitage backed his Mercedes out of the drive and drove away.

"And you want to bleed us white," muttered Gordon, watching him.

"He's trying to help us. Why do you keep dissing him?" said Karen, put out.

"So far he hasn't accomplished a thing."

"Nothing happens overnight. We need to be patient."

"Maybe we should just move. Let the demon have this house. It's turning into a decrepit piece of junk anyway. The walls are broken, the ceiling's falling down—"

"I love this house. I'm not gonna let anyone force me out."

"I can't figure you out," said Gordon, befuddled.

Excited, Brady pelted across the living room toward them.

Chapter 52

"I saw them in the bathroom," said Brady, his face working.

"Saw who?" said Karen.

"The two girls in that movie *The Shining*."

"What? What are you talking about? They don't exist."

"Come with me. I'll show you."

Karen exchanged looks with Gordon.

Brady cut across the living room and down the hall toward the bathroom, Gordon and Karen on his heels.

"Where are they?" said Karen, peering into the bathroom, unwilling to enter it, remembering her traumatic encounter with the nest of flies.

"They're gone," said Brady, mystified. "They were here again. I saw them."

"What do you mean 'again'?" said Gordon.

"I saw them that time the hair came out of the shower head and tried to strangle me."

Karen frowned at him. "You need to stop making up stories to get attention."

"Those two girls were actors in a movie," said Gordon. "They don't exist in the real world. Anyway, they'd be grown up by now. That movie was made over forty years ago."

"I saw them here," said Brady.

"I told you to stop making up stories, young man," said Karen. "Or I'll get mad."

Brady fled up the stairs to his bedroom.

"You don't have to scare the poor kid to death," said Gordon.

"He's got to learn that making up stories is wrong."

"Why? You make up stories and try to sell them to magazines."

"That's different. I admit they're fiction. Brady claims his stories are the truth."

"I don't know what's wrong with him. He sounds like he really believes what he's saying about those two girls," said Gordon, casting around the small, empty bathroom.

"He does it to get attention."

"Maybe we should take him to a shrink. He's been seeing some weird stuff, and he claims you're not really you."

"He doesn't believe what he's telling us. He knows he's lying."

"He never used to be like this till we moved here."

"Dad, look at me. I can fly," cried Brady.

"Where is he?" said Karen, unsure where his voice was coming from.

"It sounds like he's outside," said Gordon. "I don't like it."

Gordon tore out of the house and looked around for Brady, wondering how Brady could have gotten outside when Gordon had seen him run upstairs.

"Up here, Dad," cried Brady.

Gordon looked up and saw Brady standing near the eaves on the roof of the house. Gordon's heart froze. The blood drained from his face. One more step and the kid would fall to his death, Gordon knew.

"Don't stand so close to the edge," shouted Gordon, holding up his hands like a traffic cop, terrified Brady would lose his footing and fall off.

"They told me I could fly," said Brady, his face merry.

"There's nobody up there with you. Hold on. I'm coming up."

"Don't you want to see me fly?"

"No. Don't move."

Gordon bundled into the house and mounted the stairs two steps at a time.

"What's happening?" said Karen, watching him blow by her.

Gordon saw the ladder hanging down from the open trapdoor that led to the attic. He scrabbled up the ladder, crawled into the attic, and peered through the open dormer window at Brady.

Chapter 53

Brady had climbed out the window in the attic and was standing on the red pantiles near the edge of the roof, gazing down at the front lawn. It was twenty-odd feet from the window to the eaves, Gordon estimated. The roof shelved slightly downward.

Gordon shot to the window. He prayed Brady wouldn't fall on a loose pantile. Gordon didn't know what shape the roof was in. For all he knew, it might be as decrepit as the rest of the tumbledown house.

"Don't look down," he said, sticking his head out the window. "Turn around slowly and walk toward me."

"They said I could fly down into the front yard."

"No. Don't. Who told you? There's nobody up here but you."

"The two girls."

"Don't listen to them. Come back to the window."

"I want to fly."

"Don't move. Stay where you are. I'll come out and get you," said Gordon, fearing Brady might slip and fall if he moved.

"Can you fly too?" said Brady without turning his head to look at Gordon.

"Just stand there. I'm coming."

Gordon crawled out the attic window and stepped gingerly across the pantiles. He could feel one of them shifting under his foot. As he had thought, some of them were loose. He wasn't the right guy to do this. He had always had a fear of heights. Whenever he looked down from a skyscraper, he felt like the ground was pulling him down. He could feel gravity sucking him like water down a drain. The urge to jump was all but impossible to resist.

His heart jackhammering, he crept closer to Brady on the curved terra-cotta pantiles.

"Don't move, Brady," he said. "I'm coming."

"We can fly together," said Brady, smiling.

"Nobody's flying anywhere. I'm almost there," said Gordon, breaking into a sweat as he neared the roof's edge.

He didn't know if he could do this. He felt his legs locking up. He didn't think he could reach Brady if his legs continued to fight him. Every fiber of his being wanted to turn back and climb through the window into the safety of the attic.

Brady continued to stare happily down at the ground, preparing to fly down.

The kid was unaware of the extreme danger he was in, decided Gordon. One misstep . . . Gordon didn't want to think about it. He could see in his mind's eye Brady sprawled on the front lawn with a broken neck, his brains and blood leaking out his fractured skull. Gordon banished the spine-chilling image from his mind. He had to concentrate on reaching Brady.

Gordon inched toward the kid, feeling shortness of breath.

"Do you want to watch me fly now?" said Brady.

"*No.* Don't move," said Gordon, his face sweaty.

Gordon didn't think he could walk any closer to the edge. He was sure he would pass out if he got any closer. He was already feeling dizzy from looking down. He felt disoriented. Fear gripping him, he reached out toward Brady.

"Take my hand, Brady, and walk back with me to the window."

"I want to fly first. I've never done it before. Watch me."

"Stop."

"That woman's down on the lawn. She's motioning for me to jump."

What woman? Karen? There's no other woman around.

"Don't pay any attention to her," said Gordon frantically, continuing to reach toward Brady. "Turn around carefully and grab my hand."

"She wants to see me fly."

From his vantage point Gordon couldn't see past the eaves at who Brady was looking at. It had to be Karen. Why would Karen motion for Brady to jump?

"Don't pay attention to her," said Gordon.

"She's not my mom. I don't care what she says."

Karen. What the fuck are you doing? Are you trying to kill Brady?

"Listen to me," said Gordon, trying to reach farther toward Brady without losing his balance. His feet refusing to budge, Gordon still couldn't reach Brady from where he stood. "Concentrate on my voice. Turn around slowly and grab my hand."

Gordon felt sweat dripping off his face. One slip and the kid was done for, Gordon knew. A few more inches and he could grab Brady's shoulder if he could only reach farther without falling over. He screwed up his face with the effort it took to reach one more inch.

"What's taking you so long, Daddy? I don't want to wait any longer to fly."

Gordon heard Brady's feet shifting on the pantiles.

No. Clenching his teeth Gordon lunged toward Brady's shoulder, got a firm grip on it, and yanked Brady toward him, stumbling on the loose pantile beneath his left foot. Gordon slipped and fell to his knees, but he continued to hold fast to Brady, despite the pain in his knees as they struck the pantiles.

"What are you doing, Daddy? I want to fly down to the ground."

Brady tried to break free from Gordon's grasp.

Gordon yanked Brady's shoulder hard and pulled him down on his back on the pantiles.

"Ow," said Brady, wincing. "You're hurting me."

"Listen," said Gordon, shifting his grasp downward and getting a firm grip on Brady's wrist. "We're going to the window. It's not safe out here."

"You're hurting my arm."

Gordon struggled to stand up without losing his grip on Brady and hauled Brady to the window with him.

"I want to fly off the roof," whined Brady.

"Birds can fly. People can't. Climb through the window."

"The girls said I could fly."

"There aren't any girls out here. Just you and me. Now go through the window."

Gordon thrust Brady toward the window.

Shaking his head Brady climbed through the window into the attic, followed by Gordon.

Once inside, Gordon heaved a huge sigh of relief.

"You nearly gave me a heart attack," he said, brushing sweat from his brow.

"The girls wanted to see me fly."

"What girls?"

"They were in the hall below the attic trapdoor."

"I saw no one in the hall."

"They told me to go onto the roof and jump, so they could see me fly."

"Let's get out of the attic. It's hot in here. Don't ever try a stunt like this again."

"The girls—"

"If you see those girls again, don't pay any attention to them. They're not there. You're imagining them. Now climb down the ladder into the hall."

Chapter 54

When Gordon and Brady went downstairs to the living room, Gordon confronted Karen, who was standing near the open front door looking outside.

"Did you tell Brady he could fly?" said Gordon, fuming.

"What?" said Karen, appalled. "Why would I do such a stupid thing?"

"You were standing on the front lawn motioning for me to jump and fly when I was on the roof," said Brady.

"That's enough of that," said Karen, fit to be tied. "No more of your horrible stories. Why do you hate me so much?"

"I saw you. The girls said you wanted to see me fly."

"What girls?"

"He's seeing things," said Gordon. "There aren't any girls upstairs."

"He's making things up, is what he's doing. And it's got to stop," said Karen, stamping the floor with her foot.

"He never used to do this till we moved here," said Gordon, mulling it over. He turned to Brady. "Apologize to your mother for saying bad things about her."

"She's not my mother," said Brady.

"There you go again," said Gordon angrily. "Tell her you're sorry or you'll be confined to your room for the rest of the day."

"I'm—sorry," Brady managed to say before he cut and ran.

"How do we train him not to make up stories about people?" said Karen. "It's a terrible habit he's picked up."

"I don't know where he got it from," said Gordon. "He seems normal in other respects. I don't get it."

Karen surveyed the house. "This house. We have to exorcise it. Armitage said it has it in for us."

"So it's making us go crazy? Is that what you're saying?"

"You heard him. He said the demon wants to kill us."

"How? How can some ghost or whatever it is kill us?"

"It sent the flies to smother me."

"Ghosts can't control flies," scoffed Gordon.

"What makes you an expert on ghosts? You don't know what they can do."

"They can't do anything, because there aren't any."

Karen eyed him with disdain. "You're just ignorant."

"You're the one who's ignorant. Ignorant and superstitious."

"Brady is becoming a disruptive force here because of his constant need for attention."

"Would it hurt you to pay a little more attention to him? After all, he's your son."

"I have to concentrate on my writing. I'm not gonna let my career go to waste because of a spoiled son."

"Maybe that's why he thinks you're someone else—because you spend so little time with him."

"I'm not gonna let my writing talent go to waste. The only way to make it grow is to nurture it by continuing to write and to perfect my craft."

"If you're such a great writer, how come none of the magazines will buy any of your stories?"

"It takes time to get noticed in this business."

"By the time you get noticed you'll be dead and buried."

"You're a big help."

Gordon threw up his hands. "What's happening to us? We never used to be at each other's throats day and night."

"Now do you believe there's a demon here, trying to destroy us? Maybe it was the demon that caused Deirdre to drown her babies."

"She was emotionally disturbed. Don't blame it on a demon."

"Why not? Why couldn't it have been the demon that was driving her insane?"

"The cop said she was involved with a satanic cult. They might have brainwashed her to kill her kids. I'll accept that possibility, but there was no demon involved."

"I'm telling you there's something wrong with this house."

"Yeah, it's falling apart."

"That's not what I mean. And you know it. There's an evil entity present. We need the medium to come back and exorcise it."

"He's in no condition to do anything. He could barely walk out of here after his séance."

"He was tired. He'll get back his energy and help us."

Gordon cocked his head. "What's that sound?"

He approached the foot of the stairs and looked up at the landing. He could see Brady holding up the wooden pole with a hook on it that he used to pull open the trapdoor in order to lower the ladder to the attic.

"No," cried Gordon.

He stormed up the stairs and snatched the pole from Brady's hands. "You're not going up there again."

"The girls—"

"There aren't any girls. Now go back to your room."

"But . . ."

Gordon flung the pole through the trapdoor opening and heard it clatter above him on the attic floor.

"You're not going in the attic again without my permission," he said.

He telescoped the ladder back up into the attic, shutting and locking the trapdoor. Now he and Karen were the only ones who could open the trapdoor with the help of a chair to reach it and lower the ladder.

Disheartened, Brady retreated to his bedroom.

Chapter 55

That night Gordon had trouble sleeping. It was windy out, and the house creaked every time a strong gust swept over it.

His eyes snapped open as he heard Brady's voice borne on the wind, sounding far away.

It was coming from the roof, he realized with horror. He couldn't make out what Brady was saying.

Gordon bolted out of bed. The kid somehow must have opened the attic trapdoor and climbed onto the roof. But it was impossible. There was no way Brady could have gotten the pole to open the trapdoor, because the pole was in the attic. Then how?

Gordon glanced at Karen to see if she had heard Brady's cry. She was out cold, knocked out by her triazolam.

"I'm gonna fly tonight," said Brady's faint voice as the house creaked in the Santa Ana winds.

That was what it sounded like he was saying anyway.

Gordon bounded into the hall and eyeballed the trapdoor. It was shut. Then how could Brady have gotten into the attic?

"The wind will help me fly farther," said Brady's disembodied voice.

Gordon got a chair from his bedroom, placed it under the trapdoor, climbed onto the chair, and yanked open the trapdoor, which lowered the ladder. Terrified Brady would jump off the roof before Gordon had a chance to save him, Gordon scrambled up the ladder. He raced to the open window and craned outside in search of Brady.

Gordon didn't see anyone.

He heard weeping.

Where was Brady?

There was only one way to find out.

Gordon climbed out the window onto the pantile roof. He stepped across the pantiles in his bare feet, hearing the tiles clatter as they shifted beneath his steps. The wind buffeted him as he made his way to the edge of the roof. The leaves of the eucalyptus trees soughed in the wind, helping drown out Brady's weeping. Gordon could still hear his son's sobs, though. They sounded like they were coming from below.

His heart pounding out of control, Gordon edged closer to the eaves in order to look down at the front yard, where Brady's wails seemed to be emanating from. Gordon was too far away from the eaves to be able to peer over them and down into the front yard.

He hated heights in the first place, and now he was contending with the howling wind as well. He wasn't even sure if he was totally awake. The whole thing seemed surreal. A weeping, disembodied voice riding the bursts of wind. Brady's voice.

One of the pantiles shifted under Gordon's foot. In a cold sweat, Gordon thought he was going to lose his balance and get blown off the roof. His body tense with adrenaline, he managed to steady himself. He craned his neck. He still couldn't see the front lawn from his coign of vantage thanks to the eaves blocking his view.

Had Brady jumped off the roof, thinking he could fly, and crashed on the lawn? Was Brady sobbing because he had injured himself in his fall? How could he even be alive after such a long fall?

Gordon needed to move closer to the eaves in order to see Brady on the lawn. Gritting his teeth, Gordon struggled to slide his foot forward. His fear of heights was paralyzing him.

What if the pantiles near the eaves were loose and slid off the roof when he stepped on them? He would break his neck when he hit the ground. That's what. He didn't want to look down at the lawn, but he forced himself in order to see Brady. The edge of the roof continued to obstruct his view of the better part of the lawn. He felt gravity pulling him toward the lawn, urging him to jump. No. He had to fight it. He told himself to think of something else.

"Dad," said Brady, startling Gordon.

It sounded like Brady was behind him. How could Brady be behind him?

"What are you doing out there?" said Brady.

Stiffly Gordon craned his neck around.

Brady was standing in the attic, peering through the window at him with fear-wide eyes.

What the hell? wondered Gordon. He had to return to the window. He didn't hear the sobbing anymore. Whoever had been sobbing on the front lawn wasn't Brady. Was he half asleep? Had he dreamt the sobbing? Maybe he was sleepwalking like Karen.

The wind continued to batter him, threatening his balance. He needed to get off the roof before he fell.

He circumspectly edged toward the open window, testing each tile with his feet to make sure none of them would slide or break when he stepped on them. He didn't know how much weight these tiles could support. Probably not a lot. A sudden gust of wind could rip one of the tiles loose as well. The wind obliged him by gusting harder, making his skin crawl, the hairs on his arms standing on end. He stood motionless, waiting for the wind to die down, concerned its potent force might cause him to slip on a tile and fall head over heels off the roof.

The wind slackened.

At a snail's pace Gordon made it back to the window. He took a deep breath and crawled through the window into the attic.

"I thought I heard you on the roof," he said.

"I couldn't sleep because of the noise the wind is making," said Brady. "I went to get a drink of water and I saw the trapdoor open. I climbed up the ladder to see what was happening."

"I'm lucky you did."

"I know you told me not to come up here—"

"Forget it. I'm glad you did. I thought I heard your voice calling me on the roof. Let's get out of here."

"Where's Mom?"

"She's sleeping."

"I mean, my real mom."

The house groaned in the churning wind.

Gordon heard pounding beneath the attic floor.

He and Brady tensed.

"Is somebody trying to break in?" said Brady, frightened, grabbing Gordon's hand.

"I'll go down first and check it out," said Gordon, his pulse ramping up.

Chapter 56

Gordon peered through the trapdoor opening, saw nothing untoward, and clambered down the ladder.

The pounding was coming from his bedroom, he realized.

He cast around the hallway for a weapon. He didn't see anything. Fine, he knew how to kill with his bare hands if he had to.

He darted inside his bedroom, prepared to confront an intruder. He wished he had brought his SIG with him when he had left the bedroom. Instead it was stashed in his closet.

In the darkness he saw the silhouette of someone hammering the wall, pounding holes in it and crumbling the plaster.

He lunged toward the person, intending to disarm them, and realized it was Karen.

"What are you doing?" he said, confounded.

Hammer in hand, Karen turned to look at him with unseeing eyes. She said nothing. She returned to hammering the wall, bashing the Sheetrock into fragments and dust.

"What are you doing?" he demanded.

"FBI. CIA," she muttered in a monotonic voice, continuing to wield the hammer. "Bugs."

"Stop it. You can't see anything in the dark. What's the point?"

"FBI. CIA," she said in a daze.

"Are you sleepwalking again?"

"FBI—"

"I know, CIA. Put the hammer away and go back to bed."

She paid no attention to him. With her eyes blank she looked and acted like a zombie.

He latched onto the hammer handle and jerked it out of her hand to prevent her from destroying the rest of the wall.

"They're bugging us," she said. "They can hear everything we say."

"You're not awake. You don't know what you're doing. Go back to bed."

He snatched her wrist and ushered her back to their queen-size bed.

Remaining in a trance she didn't resist him.

He figured it was pointless to try to rouse her from her drug-induced sleep. Anyway, he didn't want to wake her. He wanted her to sleep. Then he could sleep, he decided, yawning. He felt exhausted. His adventure on the roof had enervated him.

He saw Brady peeking into the bedroom with saucer eyes.

"You can go back to bed now, Brady. Everything's fine."

If only that was true.

The house had other ideas.

Gordon heard a loud slam downstairs. Adrenaline coursing through him, he sprang into his closet, snagged his SIG P224, and bounded down the steps to the living room, gun in hand, expecting to confront a burglar.

He saw the broken front door blowing back and forth on its hinges, slamming again and again into the wall.

The damn wind had dislodged the door from its broken latch. He needed to get a repairman to repair the latch.

In the meantime he retrieved a leather recliner and carried it to the wind-buffeted door. He closed the door and braced the recliner against it to keep it from opening.

It would have to do until tomorrow. He wasn't going to call a repairman at this time of night.

He searched the living room to make sure no one had entered it.

Seeing no one he trudged wearily up the stairs to his bedroom, fighting to keep his eyes open.

Chapter 57

Gordon woke up late the next morning.

When he went downstairs to breakfast, he saw Karen sitting in the living room watching TV.

"I thought you had to do your writing," he said. "Why are you screwing around watching TV?"

"I can't write when the well is dry."

"Sounds like an excuse not to work."

"You don't know anything about writing."

"You keep blaming Brady for getting in the way of your writing. He's not the one monopolizing your time now. It's the TV."

"A lot you know. This happens to be research for my next story, which is a horror story."

"So what are you watching?" said Gordon, checking out the TV screen. "How to Write a Horror Story?"

"You're not funny."

"Isn't that Marilyn Monroe in that movie?"

"Right. It's one of her first movies, and I believe one of her best roles. It's called *Don't Bother to Knock*. She plays an emotionally ill babysitter who tries to kill a girl."

"I didn't know she made horror movies."

"It's not really a horror movie. It's a psychological thriller— like *Niagara*. That's another one of her movies. She didn't do just musicals and comedies."

"You're an expert cineaste now?"

Karen ignored his sarcasm.

"In many ways *Don't Bother to Knock* mirrored Marilyn's life," she said. "She was a deeply disturbed woman who grew up without a father. As the child Norma Jeane Mortenson, she felt lonely and abandoned by her paranoid schizophrenic single mother. When she grew older, Norma Jeane transformed herself into Marilyn Monroe, the movie star everyone loved and adored, especially men. But deep inside she was still the lonely and insecure Norma Jeane Mortenson. She had a dissociative identity disorder between two diametrically opposed personalities that waged war with each other—the shy introverted girl and the extroverted self-confident movie star."

"That's a mouthful."

Karen gave him a look, annoyed at his interruption. "In the end she couldn't take it anymore. She couldn't resolve the unending conflict between her two polar opposite personalities, and it killed her."

"Now you're a psychiatrist."

"It's not easy being a writer. I have to psychoanalyze characters."

"Yeah, I guess it's hard work watching movies all day," said Gordon, looking at the TV.

"You should talk. All you do is sleep all day."

"I had a rough night," said Gordon, becoming irritable. "I almost fell off the roof, and I caught you tearing down another wall in our bedroom."

"I don't know what you're talking about."

"You were sleepwalking again. Instead of going for a drive you hammered holes in the wall while you were asleep."

"Well, there *are* bugs in the wall. If you refuse to hire someone to remove them, then I'm elected."

"Have you found a single bug in the wall?"

"Not yet. They're well hidden. The FBI and the CIA know what they're doing. They're good at their job of eavesdropping on people. They were monitoring Marilyn Monroe for years without her knowledge. Every time she went to Mexico they knew about it."

"Maybe they had good reason to monitor her. I heard she was a communist and smuggled illegal drugs out of Mexico."

"Maybe the feds think the same thing about us."

Or maybe they suspected he was a hit man, decided Gordon, becoming apprehensive. Had the government somehow caught onto him? Could Karen be right that the feds were monitoring him? This was foolish. He was becoming as paranoid as Karen.

"You haven't found any bugs, because there aren't any," he said.

"How can you be so naïve?"

"You need to get off this Marilyn Monroe kick you're on. You're gonna end up as nutty as her. She was mentally unbalanced."

"She knew the truth. She had dirt on the Kennedy brothers, and she was gonna spill the beans to the media. The Kennedys couldn't let that happen, so they ordered her murder."

"They're all dead. It happened many years ago. It doesn't concern us. We need to get on with our lives."

"How can we? This house won't let us. We can't escape its history."

"A house can't make us do anything."

"A house like this can. It has a demon," said Karen, scoping out the living room as if it was alive and would attack her any moment.

Gordon didn't want to argue about demons again.

"I'm gonna grab some breakfast," he said, ducking into the kitchen.

"Fine. I can't do my job if you keep interrupting the movie. We only get one life to live. If we don't live it the way we want, we're not gonna get a second chance. Are you listening to me?"

Gordon ignored her. He had to take out Childress. He had to do it today. The Zetas weren't going to wait any longer. It wasn't going to be easy. Childress had cops protecting him because of Gordon's failed assassination attempt in the *Los Angeles Times* parking lot. Gordon figured the judge didn't feel safe without protection nowadays.

Gordon had never missed a kill shot on a target till Childress. Gordon couldn't understand it. If he could get settled in at this new house, maybe things would work out better for him. Why was so much crap happening here? It was a beautiful house in a beautiful location. Yet nothing but crap happened here.

From the kitchen he glanced into the living room at the broken ceiling where chunks of plaster had dislodged during the séance and nearly beaned him and his family.

The exterior of the house was beautiful. The same could not be said of the interior, which was disintegrating. In a way it was like Marilyn Monroe. Beautiful on the outside but messed up inside.

And what was going on with Karen? She seemed like a different person here. What was with her obsession with the former tenant Deirdre Turner and with Marilyn Monroe?

He thought he heard water running.

He looked at the kitchen sink. The faucet wasn't running.

He frowned.

Chapter 58

He left the kitchen, following the sound. He traced it to the bathroom. Entering it he saw the faucet in the bathtub running.

"You left the water running in the bathtub," he called out to Karen.

He crossed the floor to the tub and turned off the hot and cold water handles. The water stopped running. The tub was half filled with water.

"I was getting Brady's bath ready," said Karen from behind him, startling him.

"Jesus, you don't have to sneak up on me," he said, wheeling around to see her.

"Why did you turn it off? The tub isn't full yet. Brady likes a full tub of water."

"I thought he just had a bath. Why does he need another one?"

"He says he won't take another shower in this bathroom because of the hair he saw coming out of the shower head and strangling him."

"I thought we decided he made that up."

"He didn't make up the part about not wanting to take a shower here again. He didn't say he wouldn't take a bath, though. I'm not gonna have a smelly son running around our house. He needs his bath."

She passed Gordon and turned on the hot and cold water handles in order to fill up the tub.

She had a weird look on her face, decided Gordon. She was smiling, but she looked out of it. Maybe she was still feeling the effects of the sleeping pills she had taken last night.

"How many pills did you take last night?" he said.

"Uh—I don't remember. What difference does it make?"

"It's gonna make a difference if you take too many. You could end up like your new hero Marilyn Monroe, dead from an overdose."

"I feel fine."

"If you're so fine, why do you keep sleepwalking? It must mean you have problems bothering you."

"Come downstairs for your bath, Brady," she cried out the bathroom door.

"Why can't he take a bath by himself? He can take a shower by himself. Why do you have to be here with him?"

"He wants me to."

"I don't need a bath," cried Brady from upstairs.

"It doesn't sound like it," Gordon told Karen.

"Do as I say, Brady," yelled Karen, contorting her face with anger. "Come downstairs and get clean."

"No wonder he thinks you're someone else when you yell at him like that."

"He shouldn't disobey me. It's a bad habit to get into."

"I don't think you should wash him in the mood you're in."

"Don't you think I have better things to do? I have to work on my writing. I'm sacrificing my valuable time to help him."

"He almost fell off the roof yesterday. Can't you treat him decently instead of trying to intimidate and belittle him?"

"I'm not letting him take over my life at the expense of my career."

"Don't you understand? He's telling people you're trying to *kill* him. That's not right."

"That's him making up stories."

"But why would he want to make up such an awful story about you?"

"Ask him." Karen brushed past him out the door. "*You* give him a bath. I need to get back to writing. I can't deal with everybody sabotaging my career."

"And don't forget to watch the rest of your movie."

Without looking back she gave him the finger.

He reached over the rim of the bathtub and turned off the hot and cold water handles.

He tensed when he felt someone grabbing his head and shoving it underwater, forcing him to his knees. He had no idea who was attacking him. He hadn't seen or heard anyone enter the bathroom. Whoever it was was strong. Gordon couldn't break away from the attacker's grip around his neck.

Gordon couldn't breathe. He didn't know how much longer he could hold his breath. He stuck his hands into the water till they touched the bathtub rubber mat. He pressed upward to push his head out of the water. Nothing doing. The attacker was too strong.

Gordon flung his hands out of the water and thrashed them behind him, trying to poke the attacker in the eye to blind and disable him. To his surprise he couldn't locate the attacker's head. He kept reaching backward with his hands but felt nothing but air. And yet he could feel someone thrusting his head underwater.

He couldn't hold his breath any longer. He began inhaling water. It flooded into his lungs, burning them.

He reached underwater and groped along the bottom of the tub until he located the stopper with his fingers. Grabbing the stopper he yanked it out, draining the water. He kept gripping the stopper in his hand to prevent the attacker from snatching it and replacing it in the tub's drain.

As the water level lowered, he coughed water out of his lungs. Feeling the pressure on the back of his neck ease up, he jerked his head out of the remaining water and took deep breaths, coughing out bathwater fitfully.

He wheeled around to confront his attacker. Astonished, he saw no one behind him.

Could it have been Karen? He had no idea she was so strong. And yet who else could it be? Karen was the only adult in the house other than him. Brady didn't have the strength to hold Gordon's head underwater.

Blowing water out of his mouth, Gordon shook his head. He snagged a towel on the rack and wiped his head dry.

Wiping water off his hands with the towel, he entered the living room and saw Karen lying on her back on the sofa watching the movie on TV.

How could she have got back here so fast and look so relaxed? She should look flustered from all the energy she had expended to subdue him in the bathroom. Engrossed in the movie, she wasn't aware of his presence—or pretended she wasn't.

He finished drying his hands on the towel and flicked it onto her face.

"Hey," she said, bolting upright on the sofa, ripping the towel off her face. "What's the big idea?"

"Were you just in the bathroom?"

"No. I'm watching the movie. Can't you see?"

"Somebody tried to drown me in the bathtub."

Karen looked around the house frantically. "Is there an intruder in the house?"

"I didn't see anyone in the bathroom with me."

"Wait a minute. Are you saying I'm the one who did it?"

"I don't see anyone else in the house big enough to hold my head underwater."

Karen bridled. "It wasn't me. I can't believe you would even think I would do such a thing."

If it wasn't her, who could it have been? wondered Gordon. Flummoxed, he pulled a face.

"I'm telling you, I didn't imagine it," he said.

Karen thought about it.

"Maybe it was the demon," she said in a foreboding tone.

"You blame everything on the demon. You don't take responsibility for anything."

"I'm not taking responsibility for something I didn't do."

Gordon heard knocking on the front door.

Chapter 59

Gordon watched Karen answer the door.

"Why is this recliner blocking the door?" she said.

"The wind kept blowing the door open last night," said Gordon, following her. "I put it there."

"Can you move it so I can open the door?"

Gordon leaned over and pulled the recliner out of the way.

"Who is it?" said Karen, looking at the door.

"Lieutenant Gaetz."

Not that nosy cop again, decided Gordon. Had someone ID'd him as the shooter who had waylaid Childress?

Gordon's palms commenced sweating.

Karen let Gaetz in.

"Good morning," said Gaetz, wearing a brown blazer, a button-down white shirt, and black slacks.

"Good morning," said Karen.

Gaetz inspected the door. "I see you still haven't fixed your door. Has there been any trouble here?"

"No trouble," said Gordon.

He wasn't about to tell Gaetz Karen had tried to drown him. The last thing Gordon wanted was Gaetz poking around in his life. Gaetz might uncover information linking Gordon to contract killings in his past.

"Is Brady OK?" said Gaetz.

"He's fine."

Gordon remembered Brady had said Karen had tried to drown him in the bathtub. Maybe Brady wasn't making it up. After all, someone had tried to drown him too. If it wasn't Karen, who the hell could it have been?

"That's good to hear," said Gaetz. "Do you mind if I ask him?"

"Sure," said Karen. "Go ahead."

Gaetz searched her face.

She called Brady's name.

"I'm here," said Brady at the head of the stairs.

"Could you come down and say hello to the lieutenant?"

Brady tentatively descended the steps, his expression uncertain. He reached the floor.

Gaetz approached him. "Is everything OK with you, young man?"

"Fine."

"No more rat bites at night?" said Gaetz, eyeballing the bandage that swathed Brady's arm.

"Uh—no. She didn't . . . ," Brady trailed off.

"She?" said Gaetz, puzzled.

Brady sneaked a glance at Karen.

"We decided it was a female rat that bit him," said Karen.

"Oh," said Gaetz, not convinced. He leaned down toward Brady. "Is that what you meant?"

Gordon caught Karen glowering at Brady out of Gaetz's sight.

Brady gulped. "Uh—yeah."

"Your parents are treating you nice?" said Gaetz. "No more death threats?"

"That's right," said Brady, shifting nervously.

"You see, Lieutenant," said Karen. "No problems. Are you satisfied?"

"It wasn't my main reason for coming here," said Gaetz, turning toward Karen. "I've been digging into Deirdre Turner's files and uncovered interesting material. I had forgotten all about her case, but your questions about her revived my interest."

"Is that so? What did you find?"

Chapter 60

"Deirdre wanted to be part of the in-crowd in Hollywood," said Gaetz. "She wanted desperately to belong to the film community. She thought it would further her career to be seen with A-list celebs."

"Could I offer you a cup of coffee?" said Karen.

"I stopped at Starbuck's before I drove here," said Gaetz, waving her off.

"At least have a seat while we talk."

"Don't mind if I do."

Gaetz sat on the sofa.

Discomfited, Gordon wanted Gaetz to leave. It annoyed Gordon that Karen was making the guy feel at home, encouraging him to stay. He would keep coming back if she was too pleasant to him. Of course, Karen didn't know she was married to a hit man.

"As I was saying, Deirdre found out that a lot of members of the film community had joined a satanic cult," said Gaetz. "It prompted her to join the cult to advance her career."

"It sounds like she was going off the deep end," said Gordon. "I doubt I'd join a satanic cult to advance my career."

Though he had to admit his career was hitting the skids, Gordon didn't see how a satanic cult could help.

"There's no question she was having psychological problems," said Gaetz. "A well-adjusted mother wouldn't kill her babies."

"Who else is in this cult?" said Karen.

"It's a secretive society," said Gaetz. "I don't know any names. I don't know if even the members know each other's names. They wear robes and masks. That type of club."

"I don't understand," said Karen, rucking her brow. "How could it advance her career if nobody knew she was a member?"

"As I understand it, the other members have to approve a new member. They have to know the person's name before they can make a decision on their induction into the cult."

"Once they are admitted, they hide their faces?"

"Right."

"Why do they hide their faces?" said Gordon.

Gaetz looked blank. "I don't know what goes on at their meetings."

"Did they get mad at her for some reason?" said Karen.

"Why do you say that?"

"Maybe the cult put a curse on this house."

"If she was a member, why would they?"

"Who knows? Maybe she violated one of their rules."

"I couldn't say."

"The problem is there's a demon present in this house, her house. We haven't been able to get rid of it."

"Demon?" said Gaetz. "How can you tell?"

"An occultist told us."

"What do you know about this cult, Lieutenant?" said Gordon.

"Not much. They keep to themselves. But I did learn that their leader claims to be the son of Charles Manson."

"A good reason not to join," said Karen, shivering. "Cults give me the creeps." She paused. "Do you know if the FBI was investigating her or the cult?"

"Not to my knowledge, even though she was convinced the feds were monitoring her," said Gaetz. "Her conviction was part of her paranoid schizophrenia, according to her shrink."

"Did you consult with the FBI, regarding Deirdre's murder-suicide?"

"There was no reason to. Everything was clear-cut. Deirdre drowned her girls and killed herself. There was never any question of it. This wasn't a case that would interest the FBI. It didn't have national security implications, and it didn't involve more than one state. It was a local issue."

He rose to his feet. "Well, I'll be on my way. I thought this info might help you with the article you're writing about Deirdre."

"Yes," said Karen. "Thanks for telling me. Her desperation to be accepted as part of the in-crowd is interesting, and it explains her motivation to join a satanic cult. Why do these movie people want to join such dreadful cults?"

"I guess it's a fad. A lot of movie actors joined that sick self-improvement cult NXIVM. They thought it empowered them, when in reality it debased them and cost them a fortune."

"Isn't that the cult where they branded members?" said Karen with disgust.

Gaetz nodded yes, his face glum. "It was a racket. Their boss will rot in jail for the rest of his misbegotten life. They sentenced him to 120 years. Makes me proud to be a cop."

Gaetz inflated his chest.

"Why did Deirdre kill herself after joining this satanic cult you're talking about?" asked Karen.

Gaetz shrugged. "Who knows? It obviously didn't work out for her."

The house fell to shaking.

Everybody stood still.

"Another quake," said Gordon, concerned. "We just had one yesterday. Is this house on a fault line?"

"Not that I know of," said Gaetz. "But I'm no seismologist. You'd have to ask an expert."

The house settled.

"I guess that's my cue to leave," said Gaetz,

He made a beeline for the front door.

Chapter 61

Karen watched Gaetz get into his cruiser and pull out of the driveway.

"Why does anyone join these crazy cults?" said Gordon, approaching her from behind.

"I guess they have low self-esteem," said Karen. "Like people who get rejected a lot. Actors get rejected a lot. They must think the cult can improve their sense of self-worth."

"I wouldn't be caught dead in one of those places. No telling what goes on in them."

Brady ran past them and started playing catch with his baseball and outfield glove on the front lawn.

A few minutes after Gaetz drove away, Karen was surprised to see another car pull into the driveway. A white Tesla.

"Who's that?" said Gordon.

"Not a friend of yours?"

"Nope."

A middle-aged woman with a pixielike face and flaming red hair, her lips smeared with bright scarlet lipstick, climbed out of the Tesla and approached them. She wore jeans and a Kelly green blouse. She eyed Brady and smiled.

She swung her gaze toward Karen.

"Hello," she said, a twinkle in her blue eyes. "Is Deirdre home?"

"Deirdre?" said Karen.

"Deirdre Turner," said the woman, looking a tad embarrassed.

"She doesn't live here anymore," said Gordon.

"Oh, I'm so sorry. I had no idea. I'm Sophie Lemon. I'm a friend of Deirdre's."

Not a very good one, decided Karen. Sophie didn't even know Deirdre was dead. They couldn't have been very close.

"We're the new owners," said Karen.

"I'm so sorry to bother you. I haven't seen Deirdre in ages. I wanted so much to talk to her. Do you know her new address?"

"Forest Lawn," said Gordon.

"Huh?"

"He means, she's dead," said Karen, shooting a reproachful glance at Gordon for his crass black humor.

"Dead? Deirdre?" said Sophie, flustered. "Goodness. She was so young. What in the world did she die of?"

"An acute lack of oxygen," said Gordon.

Sophie looked bewildered.

"She died of an overdose of sleeping pills," said Karen.

"How awful," said Sophie. "She was one of the community. We'll miss her."

"Community?" said Karen, pricking up her ears.

"The Hollywood film community. She was an actor. Like me. I'm also a producer. Are you in the Biz?"

"I'm a writer," Karen found herself saying without thinking.

She was the only one who knew she was a writer. Nobody else knew but her, for the time being anyway—until she sold one of her works. It was up to her to enlighten others about it. It was a punishing business with all the rejection she had suffered pursuing her career.

But in the end she would succeed. It was a matter of conviction and convincing others she was who she believed she was. You couldn't convince anyone of anything unless you yourself believed it.

"That's wonderful," said Sophie. "What do you write?"

"Crime thrillers. Mysteries."

"Sounds terrific. You'll fit right in. What is your name? Maybe I've heard of you. I do a lot of reading. I'm always searching for possible scripts."

"I doubt it. My name's Karen Carney."

"Ah. I see," said Sophie, looking blank. "We all loved Deirdre."

"If you loved her so much, how come you didn't even know she was dead?" said Gordon.

Karen elbowed Gordon in his ribs for his rudeness.

"I've been incommunicado, you see," said Sophie. "I was out of the country for the past year, filming a movie in Croatia."

"How exciting," said Karen.

"For a moment I thought you were gonna say Transylvania," said Gordon, grinning.

"It's cheaper to film in Croatia than here," said Sophie, ignoring him.

"It must be exciting shooting a movie," said Karen, agog.

"I have to admit I'm glad to be back. I don't speak Croatian. It wasn't easy making myself understood."

"But creating a work of art is so stimulating."

Sophie glanced at Brady. "And this is your son?"

"Yes," said Karen. "Brady, say hello to Sophie."

"Hello," said Brady.

"Hi, Brady," said Sophie. "Nice to meet you."

He resumed throwing his ball up in the air and catching it in his glove.

Chapter 62

"What is the name of the movie you made?" asked Karen.

"What? Oh, they haven't decided on a title yet," answered Sophie.

"Isn't that strange?" said Gordon, squinting his right eye in an expression of disbelief.

"Not at all. I'm not even supposed to be talking about it. The producers don't want me to give away any of the story. They don't know the release date yet."

"Oh well, the producers," said Karen. "You can't disobey them."

"Not if I want to work on another picture."

"Is this your first movie?" asked Gordon.

"As a matter of fact, it is," answered Sophie. "I got the part soon after I joined the club."

"You had some good luck," said Karen.

"What club?" said Gordon.

Sophie searched Karen's face. "Maybe you would like to join our club, since you're in the Biz."

"Thanks," said Karen, smiling, pleasantly surprised by Sophie's invitation.

"Joining could boost your career. You could make a lot of contacts at our club. Most of our members are movers and shakers in the Biz."

Gordon pooh-pooed the idea of joining. "We're not very clubby."

"It's all about making connections in the Biz."

"What is the name of your club?" said Karen, maintaining her interest in Sophie's offer.

"The Styx Club," said Sophie.

"The sex club?" said Gordon, fascinated.

"The *Styx* Club."

"Oh," said Gordon, bored.

Without looking at him Karen slapped Gordon's wrist.

"And you say Deirdre belonged to it?" asked Karen.

"Most definitely she did," answered Sophie. "It's always sad to lose a member, now that I know she isn't with us anymore," went on Sophie, her voice becoming somber.

"How much are the dues?" said Gordon.

"Well, nothing's free in this world."

"Ain't it the truth."

"We're not talking about money, though."

"No?"

"We're talking about tradeoffs."

"I don't understand," said Karen.

"For instance, if you have created something we like, we will let you join our club on the condition that we get your creation."

"Oh, I get it. Like a screenplay or something?"

"Sort of. Have you written a screenplay?" said Sophie with bright eyes.

"Yep."

Gordon gave Karen a look.

She was aware that he knew she had never written a screenplay, but she wanted to find out about this Styx Club. And she knew she could write a screenplay. She could easily adapt one of her short stories into a screenplay. She had taken a screenplay-writing course at the USC School of Cinema. She thought it would be an interesting career. Her professor had disabused her of the viability of a career in screenwriting, a high-risk business at best, though he had liked one of the brief scripts she had written for the class.

"If we like your creation, we will not only let you join our club, we'll also move heaven and earth to market it for you," said Sophie.

"Wow," said Karen. "It sounds incredible."

"It sounds too good to be true," said Gordon.

"The sky's the limit in Hollywood," said Sophie. "Screenplays rake in good money."

"How much could mine make?" asked Karen.

"A good screenplay can sell for millions. *Basic Instinct* sold for three million bucks."

Karen gasped.

"Pie in the sky," said Gordon, trying to bring Karen back down to earth.

Deep down Karen knew Gordon was right. The chances of her making three million bucks on her first screenplay were slim and none. But other people did it. Why not her?

"I guess he's not the creator in the family," said Sophie.

"No. He's the one with the money," said Karen.

"To be honest, there's always the strong chance we won't like your script. In which case we won't be offering you membership in our club."

"I see," said Karen, her enthusiasm deflated.

"Don't sell yourself short. It's always worth a chance. The worst that can happen is they reject your membership."

"It sounds hinky to me," said Gordon, crossing his arms on his chest. "I never heard of such a club."

"Membership is by invitation only," said Sophie. "We don't advertise. We don't accept applications from just anybody."

"I can see why," said Karen. "You would be swamped with people wanting in."

"So sad about Deirdre," said Sophie, disconsolate. "She was a valuable member of our club."

"It's a shame."

"Well, whip your screenplay into shape. We'd love to read it. The sooner the better."

"I will."

"Would tonight be all right?"

"Tonight?" said Karen, doing her best to imitate a deer caught in headlights.

"How about tomorrow, then?"

"Uh, why yes," said Karen, gulping. "No problem."

She would have to write the entire script in one day, she realized, overwhelmed at the prospect.

"Nice meeting you, Brady," said Sophie, waving good-bye to him as she returned to her Tesla.

"Screenwriter, my ass," said Gordon under his breath.

"I'll adapt one of my short stories," said Karen, waving and smiling at Sophie, who drove out of the driveway onto the road.

"You'll have it by tomorrow?" said Gordon, incredulous.

"I'll work day and night on it."

"Look, this woman comes out of nowhere and says she can help you become a famous screenwriter. Does that sound believable in any sense of the word?"

"It's not just a screenwriter career I'm interested in. This club Sophie's talking about could be that satanic cult Deirdre belonged to."

"All the more reason to avoid it."

"I want to know what would drive her to kill her own children. Maybe this cult had something to do with it."

Gordon stared at her. "If that's true, they're dangerous. You don't know what you're getting yourself into. These cults can fuck up your head. I bet that's what they did to Deirdre. What if they want to brand you like that NXIVM cult?"

"Gathering as much information as I can about Deirdre will help me write a good article," said Karen, obsessed with the idea. "The more facts I can cram into it, the better my chances of selling it."

"You're not even writing an article. You said it was a cover story to get Gaetz to open up to you about Deirdre's murder-suicide. You write fiction, not nonfiction."

"I can try my hand at nonfiction. I might have better luck at it than I've had at fiction. Why not?"

"I'm telling you you need to step back and think about this with a clear head."

She turned on him. "There you go again, trying to get me to stop writing. Always interfering with my career. You and Brady," she snapped, glancing at Brady, who was still playing catch in the front yard.

She heard the baseball smack Brady's leather glove as he caught it.

"I want you to be realistic, is all," said Gordon. "Screenwriting is a long-shot business, especially for someone like you who's never written a script. You'd be better off playing the lottery."

"Screenwriting isn't just dumb luck. You have to know what you're doing."

"How would you know?"

"I'll show both you and Sophie. I'll have the script finished by *tonight*," said Karen, empowered by her burgeoning self-assurance.

Chapter 63

Brady walked down the hall, carrying his baseball glove and ball. He heard a voice in the bathroom, whose door was ajar.

"You two get good and clean," said the woman.

It sounded like Karen, Brady decided, but he couldn't see her yet, because the door was blocking his vision. Who was she talking to?

He crept toward the bathroom. He didn't want her to see him.

Through the crack between the hinge side of the door and the jamb, he could discern her sitting on the toilet.

"Hurry up," she said. "We don't have all day."

He didn't know who she was talking to. She wasn't talking to him. She didn't even know he was there. He had made sure she couldn't hear him sneaking up on her.

Past the ajar door he could make out the bathtub, which was filled to the brim with water. He couldn't believe what he saw in the water.

"You two, don't have too much fun in there," said Karen.

Brady saw two bodies floating upside down in the water. The bodies of two girls. Their blonde hair splayed out and drifted in the bathwater like jellyfish tentacles while their yellow dresses billowed out.

His heart in his mouth, he froze, fearing Karen might hear him. Of course, he knew she wasn't Karen. That woman claiming to be Karen wasn't his mother. And there she was sitting in the bathroom talking to two dead bodies floating in the tub.

"Are you two almost finished?" said Karen.

Why was she talking to them? wondered Brady. They couldn't talk back. She acted so calm and matter of fact while two corpses floated in the tub. What was wrong with her?

"Don't splash water on the floor and make a mess," said Karen.

Who were those two girls? Couldn't the woman pretending to be his mother see they were dead.

"Calm down, Theresa," said Karen. "Stop bothering Frieda."

Brady didn't know what to do. Should he call the cops? Two dead girls were floating in the bathtub. They must have been dead. They were floating face down. How could they breathe if they were face down in the water? They weren't moving either. They had to be dead.

Then why was Karen talking to them?

Goose bumps sprouted on his flesh.

What should he do? The girls had to be dead. He couldn't save them. There was no point in running into the bathroom and pulling them out of the water.

"Frieda, stop retaliating against your sister," said Karen. "Be a good girl and behave yourself."

Was his mother going crazy? What would she do if he entered the bathroom? Was she the one who had drowned the girls? She had tried to drown *him* before. She would probably try again if she saw him now.

Brady skulked away from the bathroom. He didn't want Karen to find him.

He dashed through the house, frantic in his haste to find Dad. Dad would know what to do.

Brady couldn't find him in the house. He scrambled outdoors and looked around for him. He spotted Gordon, who was sitting in the driver's seat of his rental, preparing to leave.

Brady pelted to the driver's-side door.

"Dad, there are two dead girls in the bathtub," said Brady, his face flushed.

"What? Take a deep breath and calm down."

Brady followed his father's advice, except he didn't feel calm. He kept seeing those two drowned girls.

"Now tell me what happened," said Gordon.

"There are two dead girls floating in the bathtub."

Gordon clambered out of his rental.

"This better not be one of your stories," he said.

They rushed into the house to the bathroom.

Karen was standing in front of the sink, gazing at the mirror on the medicine cabinet door and brushing her hair.

"What's wrong?" she said when she saw Gordon and Brady charging toward her.

Gordon peered past her at the bathtub. It was empty.

He frowned at Brady. "The tub's empty."

"Of course, it's empty," said Karen.

"There were two dead girls floating in it," blurted Brady.

He darted past Karen to the bathtub. He saw it was empty. How could that be? How could Karen have had enough time to take the bodies out and hide them? He scoped out the bathroom. No sign of dead bodies. He didn't understand. He knew he had seen the two dead girls.

"He told me he saw two dead girls floating in the tub," said Gordon.

"Are you making up stories again, Brady?" said Karen. "I told you to stop doing that. This has got to stop."

"You were talking to them," said Brady.

"I was the only one in the bathroom till you two showed up."

"You called them Theresa and Frieda."

"Weren't those the names of Deirdre's kids?" Gordon asked Karen.

"Yes. He's a very impressionable boy. He's seeing things."

Brady pointed at the tub. "They were floating dead in the—"

"Stop it," said Karen. "Apologize to your father for lying to him then go to your room."

"I didn't lie."

"Go to your room now and don't come down till you're ready to apologize to your father."

"But—"

"You don't want to be next, do you?" she hissed.

Gordon stared at Karen. "What's that supposed to mean?"

"It means, be a good kid and do as you're told. We can't have him telling lies about us. He called the cops on me last time for threatening to kill him. Another lie. I'm his mother for Chrissake. That's unacceptable behavior."

Gordon didn't look satisfied with her answer but said nothing.

Brady hung his head and retreated up the stairs to his bedroom. He had no idea what was going on. He was certain he had seen those two girls floating on their stomachs in the bathtub. And now the woman who said she was his mother was threatening to drown him. In his mind's eye he saw his own body floating dead in the full tub.

Nobody believed him when he said she wasn't his mother. How could he convince anyone? She had everyone else fooled, because she was the spitting image of his mother. But it wasn't her. This woman was a monster. And he believed with all his being that she would kill him. The two floating dead girls in the bathtub were a foreshadowing of his own impending death. It reminded him of that movie *Invasion of the Body Snatchers*, and he was little Jimmy Grimaldi who didn't believe his mother was his mother. Jimmy Grimaldi was right. Jimmy Grimaldi knew the truth.

What happened to Jimmy Grimaldi in that movie? Grimaldi became one of the pod people.

The thought depressed him.

Was he going to become one of the pod people? Or was his fake mother going to kill him like she had threatened?

An ice-cold shiver of fear shot down his spine.

Chapter 64

Karen sat in front of her laptop propped on the desk in the study, writing her screenplay for her crime short story "Killers and Corpses," which *Ellery Queen Magazine* and *Alfred Hitchcock Magazine* had both rejected. No matter. She liked the story. She thought it was one of her best, brimming with irony and white-knuckle suspense. *EQ* and *AH* be damned.

It was just a matter of adapting the story for the screen. She had learned how to format a script at her college class at USC Cinema. She had also bought a book about dramatic writing by Lajos Egri for the class.

The problem was since it was a short story, there wasn't going to be enough material to fill a feature film. She would need to add a couple of characters and maybe a subplot or two. Not a problem. Time was the problem. She feared she didn't have enough of it.

A fly flew around her face. She batted it away with her hand, missing it of course. She was never any good at hitting flies with her hand. They always seemed to dodge the blow. In any case, the fly flew to another part of the room.

It sat on the windowsill and stared at her with its bulbous metallic blue and green eyes.

She had work to do. She returned to her script.

She had to produce the script at lightning speed if she was going to have it ready by tonight. She wasn't sure she could meet such a tight deadline. The finished script might have to wait till tomorrow. Sophie had said tomorrow would be OK, but from the sound of her voice Karen thought Sophie didn't really mean it. It was clear Sophie wanted the finished script by tonight. Any later might doom Karen's chances of acquiring representation from the movers and shakers at the Styx Club.

Karen had never sold a script, but she knew from reading newspaper articles about it that you had to have powerful people flogging your script for it to have half a chance of selling or being optioned. Even if someone bought the script, there was no guarantee a movie would be made of it. Just the optioning of it would be a major accomplishment. Not just anyone could get a script optioned in Hollywood. Show business was an even tougher business to crack than publishing, and she had yet to sell one of her short stories.

She would be a fool to pass up this golden opportunity to sell a script to the movies. Sophie was giving her a chance to get her foot inside the door, a chance most people never got, a chance most people would kill for. Karen had to put her nose to the grindstone, crank out the screenplay, and have it completed by tonight.

The fly buzzed around her head again. She blew it away from her face, trying to concentrate on typing her script on her laptop. To no avail. The fly kept buzzing around her head. In fact, another fly joined it.

She swiped at the flies, annoyed at them for disrupting her concentration. She happened to glance at the window ledge where the first fly had alighted. She was surprised to see that a dozen more flies had joined their comrade perched on the ledge.

Where were all the damn flies coming from? The window was open, but the screen was closed and should be keeping them out of the study. What were they doing in here? She didn't have any food on her desk. What had lured them into the room?

She sensed with creeping dread that the flies on the ledge were staring at her. Which was silly, she knew. Flies had such weird-shaped eyes you couldn't tell where they were looking. And yet she could have sworn all of them were staring at her.

Why would they be staring at her? It made no sense. Flies didn't stare at people. They could care less about people. All they cared about was stuffing their stomachs. A pile of dog shit was more worthy of staring at than a human.

There were now at least a hundred of them standing on the window ledge staring at her, rubbing their legs the way flies do in anticipation of a meal.

She had to ignore them and get back to work.

But she couldn't get it out of her mind that the flies were staring at her. Not only that, the number of flies standing on the window ledge was increasing, despite the screen in the window being closed.

The study was beginning to fill with the sound of buzzing flies.

Stricken with anxiety, she flashed back to the day the flies had attacked her in the bathroom and all but smothered her. Were they getting ready to launch another assault on her?

Hundreds of flies were now flying around her head, gorging her mind with their incessant, nerve-racking buzzing. Several flies landed on her face. She brushed the creatures off with her hand and spat out another fly that landed on her lips.

She couldn't write under these conditions. Agitated, she stood up, swatting at the flies circling her.

How could she write her script with these stinking flies pestering her?

A nimbus of flies surrounded her head. It was becoming difficult for her to see through them as their numbers increased. Were they going to try to smother her again? She needed to get the insecticide from the bathroom and fumigate the study—if she could see her way to the bathroom through the mask of flies becoming glued to her face.

The flies smelled fetid.

She needed to get them off her.

Chapter 65

Struggling to breathe she stumbled in the direction of the doorway, holding her hands outstretched in front of her, trying to feel her way like a blind person.

What good would the Raid serve against the flies swarming around her face? She couldn't spray insecticide on her face without getting the toxic poison in her eyes and blinding her.

Where was Gordon?

"Gordon," she tried to scream through the flies blanketing her face.

Flies flew into her open mouth and crawled across her tongue with their skinny legs and down her throat, choking back her scream. She pounded on the corridor walls to get Gordon's attention. Where was he? She kept shambling forward. She had to find the bathroom. If she moved too quickly, she would trip and fall. Unable to see, she had to inch forward. She felt like she was going in the right direction. She should eventually reach the bathroom.

She continued groping in front of her.

She blew out air to clear the flies from her face so she could breathe. On the nail, flies flew into her mouth. She coughed vehemently, choking on the onrush of flies cramming themselves down her throat. With disgust she felt their tiny legs crawling along her throat, tickling her.

She wanted to puke.

Where was the bathroom? She must be getting closer to it. She had to keep walking. It was becoming more difficult to breathe. If she passed out, the flies would smother her.

She felt a doorjamb. It must be the bathroom.

She sidled through the doorway, feeling for the medicine cabinet above the sink. Woozy, she struggled to breathe, her heartbeat racing.

She found the medicine cabinet. She crab-walked past the sink until her foot thumped against the porcelain side of the bathtub.

Lifting her left foot she stepped into the tub. She followed suit with her right foot.

She would pass out any second from lack of air. Coughing a cluster of flies out of her mouth, she turned on the hot and cold water handles full blast. Water gushed out of the showerhead. She eagerly faced it, flooding her face with water and washing off the mask of flies.

She continued hacking as she began breathing normally again. The shower washed the last flies from her face.

She had never heard of flies that were attracted to human faces. Human feces, yes. But not human faces. She noticed the flies were dispersing, repelled by the water.

She stepped out of the tub, coughed another fly from her throat, and spat it into the toilet. Feeling ill she knelt in front of the toilet and vomited a slumgullion of flies and undigested food, bursting to eject every last fly out of her stomach and throat.

"Brady, come here," she yelled through her gastric acid–coated mouth out the bathroom doorway.

"Coming," he said.

He descended the stairs and froze midway when he saw her standing drenched in the bathroom, holding a can of Raid toward him.

"Take this and spray the study to kill the flies there," she said. "And bring my laptop to me."

He continued staring at her in befuddlement.

"What's wrong?" she said.

"Your clothes are wet."

"I had to get the flies off. Where's your father?"

"I dunno."

"Come here and get the Raid," she said, continuing to hold out the Raid can.

He descended to the ground floor and approached her like she might try to bite him any second.

"There's nothing to be afraid of," she said.

He snatched the Raid from her hand and scampered to the study.

From where she stood it looked like most of the flies had left the study.

She watched him spray the study, close her laptop, retrieve it, and return it to her.

She accepted the laptop from him and told him to spray the bathroom with the Raid. She knew she couldn't get any more work done in the study thanks to the sickening stench of insecticide that was permeating the place.

Laptop in hand, she left the house, crossed the lawn to the carport, flung open her Beetle door, and scooched onto the driver's seat. She would work inside her car, where she wouldn't have to breathe the toxic fumes of insecticide.

She slid her seat backwards, placed her laptop on her lap, and fell to typing the scene she had been working on when the flies had attacked her. She wasn't going to let a bunch of pesky flies prevent her from finishing her script. She could write just fine in her Beetle.

```
INT. SUBURBAN HOME - BATHROOM - NIGHT
   Three cops find two girls' corpses
swarming with flies and floating face down
in a bathtub full of water. Two of the cops
hold their noses because of the stench. The
third cop grimaces.
```

Chapter 66

Karen saw Marilyn Monroe's naked white body nailed to a cross. Marilyn's head was canted to the side, her mouth with full red lips hanging agape. Her platinum blonde hairdo dug like a crown of thorns into her forehead. Bright carmine blood from the pricks trickled down the creamy flesh of her cheeks. More blood was dripping from Marilyn's wrists where the rusty tenpenny nails had impaled them and was pattering on the ground.

But Karen didn't hear the pattering. She heard another noise. It was coming from the driveway.

Karen woke up when she heard the noise. She was so exhausted from writing that she must have dozed off and begun dreaming about Marilyn Monroe. Karen realized she was sitting in her Bug, her laptop open on her lap.

In the VW rearview mirror Karen could see Armitage's Mercedes pull into her driveway and park.

Armitage clambered out of his car and stumbled onto the front lawn, looking like a drunkard heading for a fall.

She wondered how many drinks he had had. He was going to get into another accident if he kept driving after drinking.

Armitage made for the front door of the house.

"I'm over here, Doctor," said Karen, powering down the driver's-side window of the Bug.

Armitage wheeled around at the sound of her voice and located her. He lurched across the lawn toward her.

"Are you OK?" she said.

"As a matter of fact, I'm having trouble seeing," he said.

With all your drinking I'm not surprised.

"I seem to have gone blind in one eye," he said.

Karen gasped. "Oh no. How awful."

"I had a killer headache after I left your house yesterday. I went to sleep. And when I woke up, I realized my left eye couldn't see."

"Do you think it had something to do with this house?"

"Yeah, I do," he said, turning around to scope out the front of the house. "The demon haunting this house is extremely powerful. I wouldn't be surprised if he has the power to blind me."

"Maybe you shouldn't come back here, then," said Karen, concerned for Armitage's health.

"I'm not done with this demon yet."

"Flies attacked me in my study. They tried to suffocate me again."

He turned to look at her. "I was afraid the demon would strike again."

"We have to stop it before it hurts someone."

"I agree. But stopping it is gonna be difficult. A demon with this much power needs an equally powerful adversary to vanquish it. It has successfully overpowered my attempts to exorcise it so far. Its power is increasing, I fear."

"Where does that leave us?"

Armitage fetched a long sigh. "Your husband says you're a somnambulist."

"What's that?"

"You walk in your sleep."

"He told me I've been walking in my sleep. I'm not aware of it."

Armitage nodded. "Where do you go when you sleepwalk?"

"I'm not aware I'm going anywhere. Gordon says I drove to Marilyn Monroe's house in Brentwood while I was asleep."

Armitage pricked up his ears. "Why would you go there of all places?"

"I'm not sure. However, I've been researching Deirdre Turner and I found out she was obsessed with Marilyn Monroe. Deirdre wanted to be successful like Marilyn, but she wasn't having any luck. She also thought Marilyn didn't commit suicide. Marilyn had everything to live for. She was basking in success. Why would she kill herself?"

"I thought it had something to do with Bobby Kennedy jilting her."\

"Which is why Deirdre thought the CIA and/or the FBI assassinated her."

"I don't understand."

"After Bobby jilted her, Marilyn threatened to dish the dirt on the Kennedy brothers. She had tapes of her conversations with Bobby and the president. She threatened to go public with the tapes. The Kennedy brothers feared their careers would be tarnished and ordered her assassinated."

"I thought she overdosed on sleeping pills."

"Ah, that's what you were supposed to think. In reality, the assassin gave her an enema of chloral hydrate and Nembutal, which killed her."

Armitage mulled it over. "It is as I feared. When you somnambulate, the demon is possessing you. You're not yourself when you're sleepwalking. The demon is controlling you. Are you taking medication in order to fall asleep?"

"A little."

"I suggest you stop taking it. It's enabling the demon to possess you. If you keep letting it possess you, you won't be able to cast it out any longer."

Karen pursed her lips. "I won't be able to sleep without my Halcion."

"Aren't you supposed to take it for only a couple of nights at the most? Isn't it addictive if you take it too often?"

"My doctor said I could take it for six months without becoming addicted. He said another one of his patients had taken it for that long without any problems."

"What kind of a doctor is this?"

"Internal medicine."

"OK. But the bottom line is the other patient wasn't being possessed by a demon. You are."

"How can I drive while I'm asleep? Why don't I have an accident? I don't understand."

"You're not the one doing the driving. You're a shell occupied by the demon. The demon is doing the driving."

"Jesus. You're scaring me."

In fact, he was scaring the hell out of her. How was she supposed to work on her script if she was scared to death?

"Why does the demon want me to drive to Marilyn Monroe's house?" she said.

"Deirdre's obsession with Marilyn must have something to do with it."

"Can you help me fight the demon off?"

"The thing is, the demon wants me dead," said Armitage. "If it succeeds in killing me, you'll be on your own against it."

"I hired you to exorcise it. You said you could do it."

"I haven't given up, but this is the worst case of a possessed house I've ever encountered. Your family's lives are in grave danger."

Armitage withdrew a handkerchief from his back trouser pocket and wiped sweat off his face with it.

"I don't have time to fret over it," said Karen. "I have to get this script done." She stared at her laptop keyboard. "This is a once-in-a-lifetime opportunity given me by a friend of Deirdre's. I'm not gonna pass on it."

Armitage eyeballed the house. "There must be a way to exorcise this house." He turned to Karen. "Your best defense is for you and your family to continue to resist the demon. Stay awake and stay vigilant."

Karen looked up from her laptop at him. "Are you telling me we can't go to sleep?"

"Staying awake would be the best defense. I realize everybody needs sleep, but when you're asleep, the demon can possess you."

"Well, I'm staying awake tonight, because I'm gonna finish this script tonight come hell or high water and hand it in to the club."

Armitage cocked up his head with interest. "Club?"

"It's a club that advances the careers of people in the Biz. It's called the Styx Club."

"Never heard of it."

"It's a top secret club. One of Deirdre's friends told me about it."

"Keeping occupied is the best defense against the demon. By keeping occupied with your work, you are preventing the demon from finding an opening and possessing you." Armitage paused. "I better go. I need to have an ophthalmologist look at my eye. Maybe he can explain why I suddenly went blind in it."

"Good luck."

Chapter 67

Armitage floundered across the lawn to his Mercedes, stumbling several times on the grass and regaining his balance.

Karen felt sorry for him. He looked like he was having a lot of difficulty functioning with only one good eye. She had to admit she was losing hope in believing he would be able to exorcise the house. The house was getting the better of him, destroying him a little bit at a time. It was horrible to watch. Was it doing the same thing to her? she wondered with a shiver slinking down her spine. Maybe it was, and she wasn't conscious of it.

In the rearview mirror she watched the half-blind Armitage reverse out of the driveway. A passing car honked at him in warning. Armitage braked his Mercedes. He pulled out of the driveway after the car left.

Karen returned to typing her screenplay with a vengeance. She needed a cup of coffee to keep her going. She had read that Balzac used to drink coffee all night long to keep himself awake in order to keep writing. She would be exhausted in no time at this rate of speed. Her body would collapse from fatigue without a hit of caffeine from time to time.

A shot rang out.

Her side-view mirror exploded.

Terrified, her eyes starting from their sockets, she ducked as glass from the mirror burst through the driver's-side open window and showered her.

Gordon came storming out of the house, spotted the broken mirror, and, whipping out his piece, scoped out the surroundings, his eyes alert, casting around for the shooter.

Not seeing the assailant, Gordon bucketed over to Karen.

"Are you all right?" he said.

"Yeah," she said, raising her head, willing her rapid heartbeat to slow down. "I think so. The bullet didn't hit me."

She climbed out of the Bug and flipped over her laptop to dump the mirror fragments off the keyboard onto the ground.

"That was close," said Gordon, wedging his SIG in his waistband.

"Do you always go around armed with a gun?"

"I thought you were in danger," said Gordon, dodging the question.

"Why would someone try to shoot me?"

Karen couldn't get her head wrapped around it. First, a demon was trying to possess her, and now someone tried to blow her head off.

Gordon received a text on his cell phone and checked it out.

"Do you know who tried to kill me?" said Karen.

"An unhappy client," said Gordon, reading the text. "Diego."

"Can you take care of it, or do I have to buy a gun?"

"I'll take care of it. I know what he wants."

"What type of clients are you dealing with?"

"Uh—*determined* is one way to describe them."

"*Bloodthirsty* is another."

"I don't see the shooter anywhere," said Gordon, scanning the neighborhood. "I think it was just a wakeup call."

"With a bullet? Couldn't he have used a phone instead?"

"Why are you typing in your car?" said Gordon, wishing to drop the subject.

"Didn't you hear me screaming before? Flies attacked me again when I was in the study."

"I was out in the backyard for a while. Out of earshot, I guess. What happened?"

"I got them off me before they could smother me."

"We need to have the entire house fumigated. We should move, is what we should do. This has got to be the straw that broke the camel's back."

"I love this house. I'm not running away in fear."

"It's turning into a deathtrap. We might not be able to survive another night in it."

Karen brushed the mirror shards off the driver's seat with the side of her laptop, climbed back into her Bug, and resumed typing.

"I'm behind schedule," she said. "I have to finish my script."

"Will you listen to reason? What good is selling a script if we all die in this house of horrors?"

"The doctor is helping us."

"Helping us to the poorhouse."

"You're exaggerating. We're not that bad off."

"The house is falling apart."

"It's a beautiful house. Now let me do my work." She looked up at him, anger smoldering in her eyes. "Or are you trying to sabotage my career like Brady?"

Gordon threw up his hands. "Not this again."

He stalked away in exasperation.

Karen hit the ground running. Her fingers fairly flew across the keyboard. She would not be denied. No more interruptions. She would finish this screenplay or die trying.

She was not going to miss out on the biggest break fate would ever deal her in her writing career. What were the chances that she would move into a house owned by an actor who had top-of-the-line connections with Hollywood pooh-bahs and that one of the actor's friends would invite her—*her* of all people—to meet these pooh-bahs in person?

No way was she going to pass up this opportunity.

Chapter 68

Gordon stood in the backyard and used his cell phone to call Diego.

"What's the big idea?" said Gordon in a lather. "Why'd you try to blow away my wife?"

"It wasn't me."

"Bullshit. Right after someone tried to kill my wife I got a text from you that told me to do the job or else."

"I wasn't the one who shot at her. A sicario did."

"Hired by you."

"He's gonna wipe out your entire family one by one if you don't take out Childress. I'm through playing patty-cake with you. You're taking too long on this job."

"I'm dealing with a personal matter."

"Well, drop it and do your job," said Diego, livid. "I'm paying you good money to do a job."

"That doesn't give you the right to shoot my family," said Gordon, his blood boiling.

"Reneging on your contract gives me every right to take out whoever I want. Nobody double-crosses me and gets away with it."

"I'm not double-crossing you. I just need a little time."

"Don't you want to get paid? You're not getting a nickel from me unless you do the job."

"You made your point. Now leave my family out of this."

"I'm more important than your family. I'm the most important person in your life at this moment. Understand? Do the job, and we have no problem. I'll even let your family live."

Gordon could barely rein in his fury. He couldn't believe Diego had sent a sicario to whack out Karen. Hopefully, it was nothing more than a warning shot. But what if the sicario had actually tried to whack her and had missed? The thought burned in Gordon's craw.

He debated whether he should take out Diego after he did Childress. But then Diego would never hire him to do another hit. Diego was a good client even if he was a cold-blooded asshole. He always ponied up after a hit, not like some of Gordon's former clients.

"You're not funny," said Gordon, seething.

"I wasn't joking. I'm beginning to think you're losing your nerve, Carney. Is that what this is about? Have you lost your talent for killing?"

Maybe he had, decided Gordon. He didn't know what was happening to him. He had never missed a target before. And it was playing on his nerves, leading him to overthink everything and filling him with self-doubt about his profession. Ever since he had moved into this house he had started screwing up. *This house. This house. Always this house.*

Diego cackled like a hen. "Is that it, Carney? Are you turning into a pussy? Grow a pair of cojones."

Laughing, Diego terminated the call.

Palms sweaty, Gordon eyed his cell phone in his hand. Was Diego right about him? Was he losing his nerve? He was about to pocket his cell when it vibrated.

He answered without looking at the caller ID.

"I've had it with you harassing me," he barked before Diego could speak.

Only it wasn't Diego.

"What are you talking about?" said Karen at the other end of the line.

Gordon quashed his temper.

"I thought you were someone else," he said, sounding apologetic.

"I forgot to tell you that Armitage went blind in one eye. He came over to tell me our lives are in grave danger."

"I'm beginning to think he's a psycho. These quack mediums all have mental issues. I'd bet dollars to donuts his blindness is psychosomatic. Mediums are borderline lunatics. A lot of them are candidates for straitjackets in bughouses."

"He's on the right track if you ask me. He told me the demon was possessing me every time I sleepwalked. It was the demon that was telling me where to drive. I was a shell doing the demon's bidding. That's why I have no memory of sleepwalking."

"I can't bring myself to believe in demons and possession."

"Then why's Armitage going blind?"

"It's psychosomatic. He's psyching himself out with his parapsychology routine. Mediums are mentally disturbed. They can't handle reality. They think demons are plotting against them, because their lives are so messed up. Armitage is one step away from being institutionalized for the hopelessly insane."

"No. That's wrong. He's on the right track. There *is* a demon in our house."

"I grant you that our house is a mess. It's dilapidated. It's not fit for living in."

"*And*, don't forget, it's possessed by a demon."

Gordon made a sound of dismissal. "If it's possessed by anything, it's possessed by flies. It's infested with insects. It needs to be torn down thanks to structural damage. It might have termites too, for all we know."

"You need to open your eyes and see what's going on."

"My eyes are as clear as the sky. I can see exactly what's going on. Armitage is scamming us out of our money, using fear tactics to make us think our house is haunted by some hideous demon that nobody can see. It's a con game. A protection racket. He's scaring us into paying him to protect us with his exorcism."

"I'm convinced he believes what he's telling us. He contacted the demon in the séance."

"He's a borderline psycho. He has multiple personalities, and he's talking to his other personality in his so-called séances. Some of these psychos are super clever. They even have themselves conned."

"Why are you so mean?"

"I hate to break this to you, but Hollywood is full of scammers. It's the world capital of scams."

"I have to go back to work," she said in a huff.

"You're the one that called me. I didn't call you."

She hung up.

Chapter 69

Where did the time go? wondered Karen. It was getting dark. She couldn't type in the dark in her car—unless she turned on the dome light, which didn't provide enough light to see to type. She was already suffering from eyestrain. She would have to go inside to continue typing.

An empty cup of coffee stood on the center console. She needed a refill. Her stomach rumbled. She hadn't eaten all day. She had been living on coffee.

She yawned.

She was nearing completion of her screenplay. She was exhausted from typing so many pages, but she knew she could complete the script tonight and deliver it to the Styx Club. They would be impressed by her speed at finishing the script and meeting her deadline.

She had no idea she could type so fast.

Incentive. It was all about incentive. Selling a screenplay was a major incentive. Even if they offered her just an option, she *would* get paid. *Paid for her writing.* A dream come true. The thought exhilarated her.

Her cell phone chimed in her purse.

She took the call.

"Hi, Karen," said Sophie. "Have you finished your screenplay?"

"It'll be done in an hour," said Karen, wiped out.

"Excellent. I knew you could do it. I bet it's awesome."

"I believe it is," said Karen, and meant it.

"I'm glad to hear it. Our club is gonna have a meeting in the Santa Monica Mountains tonight. I want you to join us. Bring along your script, of course, so we can have a look at it. We want to be the first to see it."

"The mountains?" said Karen, baffled.

"We're having a campfire in the woods. We'd like you to join us."

"How can you read my script at a campfire?"

"Don't worry about it. We'll have scores of bamboo tiki torches at the campsite, enough to provide plenty of light for reading."

The idea of reading by torchlight didn't appeal to Karen. She would get a headache if she had to read under light provided by flickering flames. Oh well, she wasn't the one who would be doing the reading. If the club members wanted to strain their eyesight, so be it.

"You're outdoorsy types, I guess," she said.

Sophie laughed. "You could say that. It won't be all business. It will be fun too. We like to mix business with pleasure."

"Sounds exciting."

"Oh, it will be. And if we offer you representation for your script, it will be even more so."

Karen couldn't wait to meet the high-powered, elite Hollywood club members.

"I'm looking forward to it," she said.

"Excellent. I'll pick you up in an hour."

Sophie hung up.

Karen took her laptop into the house in order to finish her script with adequate lighting. She met Gordon in the living room. She set her laptop down on the sideboard.

"Surprise, surprise," he said. "I thought you were gonna stay in your car all night."

"There's not enough light for me to type in the Bug. My eyes are getting bloodshot."

"I can imagine."

She beamed. "Sophie's picking me up tonight and taking me to meet the Styx Club members in the mountains."

"In the mountains?" said Gordon, frowning.

"They're having a campfire jamboree or something. They like to mix business with pleasure at the club. They're gonna offer to buy my script there."

"Sounds hinky to me."

"It's the Biz. You know how they are. They're movie types. They like to make things exciting."

"I better go with you. I don't like the idea of your going alone to meet strangers at a remote mountain camp. You might be in danger."

"That's ridiculous. I'll be fine. These are movers and shakers in the Business. It's all on the up and up."

"How can you be sure?"

"Sophie will be with me."

"You just met her today."

"What's wrong with that? You're a worrywart."

"How am I gonna know where you are if you get into trouble? Some place in the mountains. I'll never be able to find you."

"Nothing's gonna happen to me."

Was he trying to sabotage her career again by preventing her from going to the jamboree? She felt a surge of resentment.

"At least keep your cell phone on, so I can track you in case you run into trouble," he said. "I have an app that can track your phone."

Karen shrugged, wondering why he was so stressed about her. "I guess I could do that, but how are you gonna know if I'm in trouble?"

"Call me if you need help."

"No problem."

"I'm serious. I never heard of this club and to me that's reason to be suspicious."

Chapter 70

"You should be happy for me," said Karen. "A lot of money could be coming our way if they offer me representation. They're not gonna take on a script unless they have a strong belief they can sell it to the movies. These people are connected. They ought to know what they're doing."

"According to Sophie—who you just met," said Gordon, unconvinced. "Hollywood hucksters are a dime a dozen in these parts."

Why did he always have to fight her when it came to her writing career? she wondered.

"There you go being suspicious of everyone again," she said.

"I still think I should go with you."

"I need another cup of coffee, so I can finish before Sophie gets here. She's picking me up in an hour."

"This is happening way too fast. I don't like it."

"You're too suspicious of people."

"You're a total unknown. You can't just write one screenplay and sell it right off the bat. It doesn't happen like that."

"Why not? This is the movie business. Anything can happen."

"They haven't read anything you've written. How can they possibly say they're gonna like it sight unseen?"

"They're gonna read it tonight. Then they'll make their decision about representation."

"My mind's made up. I'm going with you."

Karen bridled. "Sophie didn't invite you. You're welcome to ask her if you can go. But you have to accept her decision if she says no."

A dark cloud hanging over his head, Gordon paced around the room. "Fine."

Brady trotted down the stairs. "When are we gonna eat dinner?"

"I have to finish my screenplay," said Karen. "I'm getting another cup of coffee."

She retreated to the kitchen.

"I'll fix something for us, Brady," said Gordon. "Your mother's busy."

Brady followed her with a wary eye.

"This is gonna work out for us big time," said Karen. "You'll see."

Gordon met her in the kitchen.

"How do you know this Styx Club isn't the satanic cult Deirdre belonged to?" he said.

"Actually, I think it is. This is why I need to find out what's going on there as part of my research of Deirdre. I need to find out as much as possible about her to determine why she committed the heinous crime she did."

"Aren't you worried this is a satanic cult you're attending?"

She rounded on him. "I don't believe in Satan. Do you?"

"No. But these cults can be rough. The Manson Family was a cult. They murdered innocent people in horrible fashion, breaking into Roman Polanski's house, stabbing the occupants hundreds of times, and smearing their blood all over the walls. They carved up the actress Sharon Tate and her unborn baby for Chrissake."

"That was back in the sick sixties. Everybody was tripping on acid. They don't do that kind of thing anymore. Anyway, this might not be the satanic cult that Deirdre joined. It could be a polar opposite club exclusively for Hollywood hotshots."

She poured herself a cup of coffee and drank it, trying to keep herself from collapsing from exhaustion. She glanced at her wristwatch.

"Oh no," she said. "I didn't know how late it is. I need to finish my script before Sophie gets here. She'll never forgive me if it's not done. Don't bother me while I work on my script."

Clutching her cup of coffee, she retrieved her laptop from the sideboard in the living room and strode into the study.

She sniffed the air. She could smell the residual stench of the insecticide Brady had sprayed earlier. She made sure the windows were open for adequate ventilation and returned to work, feeling safe from any more flies attacking her. She didn't think inhaling the insecticide would make her sick as long as the windows were open. The noxious stink had subsided since Brady had sprayed many hours ago. She figured she could stand it for less than an hour.

Then she would be off on an exhilarating trip with Sophie to the mountains for the welcome opportunity to breathe crisp, clean fresh air.

Chapter 71

Sophie arrived one hour later on the dot after she had called Karen.

Karen was in the process of finishing her screenplay when she heard knocking on the front door. She ran out of the study to answer it, apprehensive that Sophie might write her off as a prospective member and leave if she didn't open the door right away.

Karen flung open the door.

"You're right on time," she said breathlessly. "Come in."

"Do you have your screenplay ready?" said Sophie, entering the living room.

"All I have to do is print it and bind it."

"Wonderful. We don't want to be late for the jamboree. The other members wouldn't like it."

"Of course not. I'll be ready in a minute."

Karen dashed back to the study to print out her screenplay.

"I thought I heard someone at the door," said Gordon, entering the living room.

"Yes, I'm here to pick up Karen," said Sophie.

"This jamboree sounds like it's gonna be a blast. I can't wait. I love hiking in the mountains and eating toasted marshmallows."

"Uh," said Sophie, flustered. "I'm afraid there's a misunderstanding."

"What do you mean?"

"The invitation is for your wife because she has completed a screenplay that we would like to read."

"Well, I'm her husband, and I'd like to tag along if you don't mind."

"Uh, that's the thing. We do mind. Unless you also have a script for us to read."

"Of course, I don't. She's the writer in the family, not me. But I'd like to go along. How come I have to miss out on the fun?"

"I hate to disabuse you, but this isn't a vacation. It's a business trip."

"I thought you were having a campfire, barbecuing, and partying."

"If we agree to represent your wife's script, we will have a short celebration, but I can't guarantee the members will like her script."

"I don't mind if there's no party. I'll stay out of your hair if that's what's bothering you."

"Did somebody say a campfire?" said Brady, descending the stairs.

"Hello, Brady," said Sophie, approaching the staircase. "Would you like to come with your mother?"

"I like campfires."

"I bet you do."

"I want to go."

"Wonderful."

Karen hustled into the living room, gripping a hundred-odd sheets of typing paper in her hand.

"I need to puncture three holes in the papers so I can insert brass studs into them to bind the script," she said.

"No problem," said Sophie. "We're not gonna deduct points because the script is improperly bound. Do you have a big paper clip? That'll do for the time being. If we like the script, we'll have a professional bind it for you before we submit it to the studios."

Despite her exhaustion, Karen beamed. She couldn't believe this was happening. With these Hollywood powerbrokers backing her she had an excellent chance of selling her script. She was not so naïve that she didn't know it was all about connections when it came to the Biz.

"You're welcome to bring Brady with us," said Sophie, smiling at Brady. "He says he'd love to come along."

"I'm looking forward to sharing your moment in the spotlight," said Gordon.

"We seem to have a misunderstanding," said Sophie, looking pained. "Our invitation is for you, Karen, not your husband. But we understand you have a child that needs looking after, and you are welcome to bring him."

"I know," said Karen. "It's not a problem." She turned to stare at Gordon. "I told you you weren't invited."

"I'm sure Sophie can make an exception for your husband," said Gordon.

"I'm afraid it's not up to me," said Sophie. "Our club is private. We have strict rules. Membership is by invitation only."

"But I'm her husband," protested Gordon.

"There are no exceptions. You were not invited."

"Wait a minute. Let me get this straight. Brady is invited, and I'm not. What's that all about?"

"We don't want Karen to have to hire a babysitter because of our invitation to join our club," said Sophie.

Karen was in a quandary. She had no intention of taking Brady with her. She didn't understand why Sophie had invited him. If she took him with her, they wouldn't get back till long past his bedtime. Brady had nothing to do with the writing of her script. Why was he being invited to share the limelight with her?

"I don't think Brady should go with us," she said.

Disappointment registered on Brady's face.

"Will you be able to find a babysitter at such short notice?" said Sophie.

"Gordon will stay home with him," said Karen.

"I have a better idea," said Gordon. "Why don't we all go to the jamboree? We can make it a family affair."

"This isn't a proper outing for Brady," insisted Karen. "He can't stay up past his bedtime."

"It's up to you, of course," said Sophie. "He's your son."

"I won't be staying up past *my* bedtime if I go," said Gordon. "Why can't I go?"

"We already discussed this, Gordon," said Karen. "Why are you making a scene?"

"It makes no sense," said Gordon. "We're married. What's the problem?"

Sophie glanced at her wristwatch and gasped. "Oh dear. We're gonna be late. We have to leave this minute to get there on time. If we're just one minute late, they'll revoke your invitation for membership."

"What kind of nutbag club is this? One minute late and you're fired? They act like they're your boss. Give me a break."

"Stop making a scene, dear," said Karen, tapping her foot in pent-up aggravation.

"Rules are rules," said Sophie. "As I said before, our rules are very strict."

"You sound like a bunch of screws running a joint," said Gordon.

Can you stop sabotaging my writing career for once in your life? thought Karen, struggling to restrain a spiteful outburst at Gordon's expense.

"Grab a paper clip for your script and let's be off," said Sophie, hustling toward the front door, ignoring Gordon.

Karen bolted into the study, managed to find a large triangular paper clip in the desk drawer, clipped the script's pages together, and skedaddled after Sophie, not without glaring at Gordon for making waves.

As she flashed by him, he snagged her elbow, bringing her up short.

"What are you doing?" she flared.

He lowered his voice. "Ask yourself, what kind of club allows your son to attend but not your husband? Does that make any kind of sense?"

"Let me go," said Karen, struggling to free her elbow. "You heard her. They have strict rules."

"They make no sense."

"If you make me late, I'll kill you. And tell Brady I'll kill him."

Gordon gaped in awe. "What's got into you?"

"This is my career. It's important to me. Now let me go."

"At least remember to take your cell phone," he whispered, releasing her.

It was in her purse, which she grabbed on her way out the front door. She dashed outside, worried Sophie would pull out of the driveway without her.

Sophie's Tesla engine was already idling as Karen threw herself against the passenger's-side door, latched onto the handle, and yanked the door open.

"Fasten your seat belt," said Sophie as Karen slid into the shotgun seat.

Karen did so.

"Are you sure you don't want to bring Brady?" said Sophie. "He's a cute kid. I'm sure he'd enhance your chances of being approved by the club."

"It's past his bedtime," said Karen, puzzled.

She didn't understand how her son could improve her chances of being accepted by the club. She saw no connection between the two. Writing a screenplay had nothing to do with her son.

Sophie shrugged. "It's your decision. I'm only trying to help you succeed. I want you to put your best foot forward. But I want to be absolutely sure you understand that this club is almost impossible to join. You need everything going for you to be invited as a member."

"I understand," said Karen.

But she didn't understand—at all. Oh well, it was Hollywood. Not much made sense in the wild and crazy world of the Biz.

Sophie backed her Tesla out of the driveway at speed and peeled out down the street, oblivious to traffic around her.

At this rate they might not arrive at the mountain campsite in one piece, decided Karen, grinding her teeth and latching onto her armrest with a viselike grip.

Chapter 72

Gordon was more worried than ever after he watched Sophie rocket down the street out of sight.

It made no sense to him that Sophie would invite Brady but not him to the club meeting. He hoped Karen knew what she was doing. She had become so obsessed with becoming a famous screenwriter that she had developed tunnel vision, not caring about her family anymore.

He couldn't believe his ears when she had threatened to kill him and Brady. She was acting out of character, and it was unnerving him. Whether she liked it or not he was going to follow her to this so-called power tryst of Hollywood fat cats. It could very well be the satanic cult Deirdre Turner had joined. Why didn't Karen see the connection? He knew what her answer would be. She was doing research on Deirdre. He found Karen's behavior reckless. Maybe it was the triazolam she was taking. It could be affecting her psychologically. His shrink had told him triazolam could alter a pill popper's personality. The move to the new house was stressing Karen too. It was stressing the whole family.

What if her research jeopardized her life? Didn't it concern her? If so, she wasn't showing it. She must have believed Sophie and her club were on the level when they requested a look at her screenplay in order to represent it.

But why would they request to see a script written by an unknown who had never written a screenplay before? And at such short notice? They sounded like they could be scammers. But what was the scam? Maybe it would come later. Maybe they would ask her for money in order to represent her.

He had made up his mind he was going to follow her even though she had refused to let him accompany her.

He produced his cell phone and checked his tracking app to make sure it was showing her whereabouts on the screen. The app seemed to be working.

He looked at Brady.

"I have to go out," Gordon said, approaching him.

Gordon didn't like the idea of leaving Brady at home alone, but he liked the idea of taking him to a for-all-intents-and-purposes dangerous rendezvous even less. He didn't want to expose the kid to danger. Gordon figured Brady would be safer at home. The problem was the front door still had a busted lock on it.

"OK, Dad," said Brady.

"After I leave, slide the recliner against the front door and don't let anybody in."

"OK."

Gordon knew a determined intruder could break through the front door with ease. A recliner propped against the door wasn't going to keep them out.

How much danger was Brady in if left alone at home? Was this a dangerous neighborhood? The lieutenant had said something to that effect when he had noticed the broken lock on the door.

"Are you gonna be OK if I leave you alone for a little while?" said Gordon.

"Yeah, sure."

"Is everything OK?" said Gordon, noticing Brady looked nervous.

"I'll be all right if those two girls don't come here again."

"What two girls?"

"Theresa and Frieda." Brady shrugged. "I saw their dead bodies floating in the bathtub, so maybe they're gone now."

"I didn't see any dead bodies in the tub."

"They were there, and Mom was with them."

Brady had an overactive imagination, decided Gordon. That was all. It was normal in a child.

"I doubt you'll have to worry about them," said Gordon.

"Yeah, they're dead. Somebody took their bodies away, I guess."

Gordon put his hands on Brady's shoulders and gazed into his eyes. "You don't have to sweat about your mother killing you. She didn't mean it. She isn't gonna kill you."

"She's not my mother."

"Why do you keep saying that?"

"Because she isn't. She looks like her, but she's not her."

"This must be a product of your overactive imagination. You'll get over it. But rest assured, she won't kill you. I'm gonna have to talk to her about her threatening us, because it's out of line."

"She can't do anything to me if she's not here."

"Right." Gordon glanced at the front door. "I don't like leaving you alone here with that door broken, but Karen might be in danger. I have to make sure she's OK."

"I understand."

It was time for Brady to grow up tonight, decided Gordon.

"Come with me," he said, ascending the staircase.

Brady followed him.

Chapter 73

Gordon entered his bedroom, opened his louvered closet, took down a metal box from the top shelf, and showed it to Brady.

"This is a gun safe," said Gordon.

Brady watched with interest.

"If a stranger breaks into the house, you're gonna have to defend yourself," went on Gordon. "There are bad people in this world and they want to harm you."

He hoped he wasn't scaring the kid, but Brady had to find out sooner or later. Gordon hoped for Brady's sake that he never met any of these bad people in his life, but Gordon also knew it was a pipe dream to think the world was full of loving people who wished to help you.

Gordon punched in the combination to the safe, opened the lid, and laid the safe on the counterpane on the bed. He removed the SIG P365 stored in the safe.

"If a stranger breaks into the house, use this gun on him," said Gordon, showing the SIG to Brady. "You have the right to protect yourself."

Brady stared with fascination at the piece.

Gordon removed a fresh magazine from the safe and inserted it into the SIG magazine well.

"Before you fire this gun, you need to disengage the safety," he said, demonstrating the procedure. "Understand?"

Brady nodded, watching.

"I hope you don't need to use this, but you need to be able to defend yourself," said Gordon. "After the safety is disengaged, you aim the gun and squeeze the trigger. Do you understand?"

"Yeah," said Brady, widening his eyes as he observed the SIG. "This is like *The Rifleman* on TV."

"Are they still rerunning that old Chuck Connors western?"

Brady nodded yes. "It's in black and white."

"OK, watch me. Fire it like this," said Gordon, demonstrating the two-handed Weaver stance.

Gordon engaged the safety and handed the SIG to Brady. "Feel it in your hand."

Brady accepted the gun and gripped the stock.

"Don't aim it at anyone unless you plan on shooting them," said Gordon, brushing the gun barrel away from himself with his hand, "even if the safety is on."

"Got it."

"Try aiming it like I did. Aim at the closet over there."

Brady followed Gordon's example, aiming the pistol at the closet with one hand bracing the other.

"Good," said Gordon.

Gordon took the gun from Brady and replaced it in the gun safe.

Brady noticed the shattered walls that Karen had hammered in the bedroom.

"What happened to your walls?" he said with alarm.

"Never mind. I'm gonna leave the gun safe open on the bed, so you can grab the gun quickly if you need it. The safety is engaged. You'll have to disengage it to fire the gun. Do you understand?"

"Yeah."

"The magazine holds ten 9mm Luger rounds. As you can see, there's another full magazine in the safe."

"OK."

"The gun is loaded and ready to shoot."

Gordon racked the slide and jacked a round up the spout, preparing the gun for firing.

Brady nodded yes.

"I doubt you'll have cause to use this," said Gordon. "I'm not sure what time I'll be back with your mother. I suggest you stay awake until we're back. I hope it's not late."

Gordon had a loaded SIG P224 holstered on his ankle. Since he had no idea what he was going to encounter at the jamboree, he had stuffed several spare magazines into his cargo pockets.

Needless to say, he had plenty of misgivings about the club jamboree or whatever it really was. He could be driving headlong into a satanic ritual, for all he knew. This Styx Club was hinky to the nines, as far as he was concerned.

"If you see anything suspicious outside, call me on your cell phone," said Gordon.

"Like what?"

"Like strangers walking in front of the house."

"OK," said Brady with a worried expression.

Gordon patted him on the shoulder. "I doubt you'll see anyone. I just want you to be on your guard tonight."

"Why can't I go with you? I like campfires."

"It's too dangerous. I'll be back with your mother later tonight. Everything will be fine."

Gordon didn't really believe the last part. He expected to run into a shit show at the campsite.

He waved good-bye and took leave of Brady.

When he slid into his rental driver's seat, he inserted his cell phone into the plastic cup holder so he could see the tracking app while he was driving. He didn't want Sophie to get too big a lead. He wanted to make sure he could find her when she arrived at her destination. On the other hand, he couldn't get too close to her, because he didn't want her to spot him tailing her. The darkness was his ally, preventing Sophie from seeing his rental behind her.

He fired the ignition, reversed out of the driveway, and drove in the direction of the signal on the tracking app, which showed a map of the immediate area with a blinking dot that signified the location of Karen's cell phone.

He couldn't see if Brady was looking out the window at him, but he waved good-bye at the living room window in case Brady was standing there watching him in the darkness.

Chapter 74

Brady didn't relish the idea of being left home alone in the middle of the night at a house he wasn't familiar with. Every time the house creaked he jumped.

He told himself there was nothing to be afraid of. At least Karen wasn't here. She scared him more than anything else the way she kept threatening to kill him and kept wanting to give him a bath. He feared he'd end up like those two girls Frieda and Theresa who had drowned in the bathtub. He didn't want to see them again.

He turned on a horror movie on TV to take his mind off everything else that was going on in his life. He watched *Alien*. Probably not a good movie to watch when you were home alone, but he felt like watching a horror movie. He recalled an ad for the movie: In outer space nobody can hear you scream. Could anybody hear him scream in this house?

He settled back on the sofa in the family room and watched Sigourney Weaver on TV. Trapped in her spaceship, she had to battle the slavering monster to survive.

He thought he heard a car pull into the pebble driveway.

Maybe Dad had come back, he decided, eager to greet him at the front door when Dad entered the house.

On the other hand, Dad shouldn't be back so soon. He had just left.

Brady needed to find out who it was before he slid the recliner away from the front door to allow the person inside.

Adrenaline surging through his body, he sprang off the sofa to the picture window in the living room, and, hiding behind the curtain, peeked outside at the front lawn.

A man clambered out of the driver's seat of the car parked in the driveway. It was hard for Brady to see the guy's face in the night. He could see the guy's neck brace, though. It had to be Dr. Armitage.

What was Armitage doing here at this time of night?

Armitage stumbled across the front lawn, lurching back and forth like a wino. He stood staring at the house for several minutes. Then he brandished his fist at the house and yelled at it, cursing it.

Brady didn't like it. He didn't understand what was wrong with Armitage, who looked consumed with anger.

Should he get the gun? Was Armitage dangerous in his agitated state? Would he try to break into the house with murder on his mind?

Brady heard his heartbeat thundering in his ears. He didn't know what to do. Armitage didn't have a gun, but he could easily overpower Brady with his adult strength.

Brady decided to call Dad.

Fishing out his cell phone from his trouser pocket, Brady speed-dialed Dad's number.

Brady breathed raggedly as he watched Armitage berating the house.

What the hell was wrong with the guy? He was acting like a maniac.

Chapter 75

"Hello," said Gordon, driving his rental and answering his phone.

"Dad, there's somebody here in the front yard," said Brady, his voice urgent.

"Who?" said Gordon, breaking into a sweat, wondering who would be at the house at this time of night.

"It looks like the doctor. He's wearing a neck brace."

"Armitage?"

"Yeah."

"What's he want?" said Gordon, puzzled.

"He's standing in the front yard and yelling at the house."

"What?" said Gordon, frowning, trying to get his head around it. "Is he trying to get inside?"

"No. He's just standing outside screaming at the house and shaking his fist."

Something was wrong, decided Gordon. He didn't know whether to turn back or not. Was Brady in danger? Gordon couldn't turn back. He had to reach Karen when she arrived at the campsite. He would never be able to reach her in time if he had to turn back and return to the house to help Brady.

"Does he look dangerous?" said Gordon, trying to understand the nature of the threat if indeed there was a threat to Brady.

Maybe Armitage was plastered, decided Gordon.

"He's angry," said Brady.

"Does he have a weapon?"

"I don't see one, but it's dark. It's hard to see outside."

"Does he know you're in the house?"

"I dunno. I don't think he saw me. I'm hiding behind the curtain and looking out the window at him."

"OK. Has he tried to get inside the house?"

"No. He's still standing on the lawn yelling at the house."

"What is he yelling?"

"He's cursing the house. He says it's the house from hell. He says he's cursing it before God."

Gordon couldn't decide if Armitage was dangerous to Brady. For sure Armitage wasn't acting normal. Maybe he had had one too many.

"Does he look like he's drunk?" said Gordon.

"He's having trouble walking. He could be drunk."

Gordon couldn't figure out if he should tell Brady to get the gun. Brady might overreact and shoot Armitage for no reason. Maybe the guy was simply venting, because the house was frustrating his professional efforts to exorcise it.

Gordon kept his eyes on the road as he negotiated the upcoming turn on Sunset, sodium vapor streetlights arching in front of him lighting the way.

"Oh no," cried Brady.

Setting his teeth, Gordon said into his cell phone, "What is it? What happened?"

Gordon heard choking on the other end of the line.

"What happened, Brady? Talk to me," said Gordon, his eyes frantic as he tried to hear what was going on with Brady.

"I—I—threw up," said Brady. "I couldn't help it. It's terrible."

"What's terrible? What happened? Tell me for Chrissake."

Was Armitage strangling Brady? It was the only explanation he could come up with.

Gordon heard more choking on the phone.

He pulled over to the shoulder of the road, trying to think what to do. Should he turn back to the house? Thoughts were whirling through his head. He couldn't concentrate. What was happening to Brady? If Armitage was strangling Brady, Gordon would never get back to the house in time to save the kid.

"Brady, what's happening?"

"I threw up again," said Brady, struggling to talk. "It was awful."

"What?" cried Gordon, frustrated at his inability to help Brady from such a distance.

"I saw him. Holy shit. He . . ."

"He what?" said Gordon, hanging on Brady's every word.

"I saw him. He said, 'If thine right eye offends thee, pluck it out.' I heard him. He screamed it really loud. Then he"—Brady gulped—"uh, he gouged out his right eye with his fingers and flung it at the house."

Brady broke into tears.

Appalled, Gordon could see Armitage in his mind's eye stumbling around the front yard, blind, wailing, his mind gone.

Overcoming his revulsion at the idea of Armitage gouging out his eyeball, Gordon felt a measure of relief. A blind Armitage couldn't do Brady any harm. Gordon wouldn't have to return to the house to protect Brady.

"All right, calm down," said Gordon. "What's he doing now?"

"He stumbled around and tripped. Now he's sitting on the lawn, moaning, his face in his hands."

"Does he look dangerous?"

"Ugh. Blood's pouring out of his empty eye socket—"

"Did you hear if he was cursing you?"

"He was screaming at the house, not at me. I can't stand looking at him. It's awful. I'm gonna be sick again."

"Don't look at him anymore. You're gonna be OK. Karen told me he was already blind in his left eye. Without his right eye, he can't see a thing. He can't harm you. If you think he's gonna harm you, find a good place to hide and keep quiet. He'll never be able to find you without being able to see."

"OK," said Brady, gasping for breath.

"So calm down. Forget about him."

"Just leave him on the front lawn all night?"

"I'll take care of him when I get back. Get some popcorn or pretzels and a Coke and watch TV and relax. Forget about him."

"OK."

Easier said than done, figured Gordon, but a blind man couldn't be a threat to Brady, no matter how ghastly he looked sitting on the front lawn.

Gordon said good-bye, hit the rental turn signal, and pulled into traffic.

Sophic had put additional miles between him and her, but his app was continuing to track her. He wondered what the range on the app was. If she drove out of range, he would never be able to find her. He picked up speed in an effort to close the gap between them.

He wasn't surprised Armitage had lost his marbles. Any guy who was seeing ghosts must be halfway to the bughouse in the first place. Just another psycho medium who went around the bend.

No, Gordon wasn't surprised at all. All that parapsychology mumbo jumbo. Nobody but a cuckoo bird could believe in it.

He had more important things to think about—like how to save Karen's bacon from the scammers in Sophie's club. He was becoming more and more certain there was no way they could be legit.

One hand on the wheel, he felt with the other for his SIG in his ankle holster to reassure himself he was prepared to do battle.

Chapter 76

Karen watched Sophie hang a right into a lighted, half-filled parking lot in a woodsy section of the Santa Monica Mountains. Sophie parked her Tesla beside a Bentley. Everywhere Karen looked she saw Ferraris, Porsches, Mercedes G-Wagens, and other high-end vehicles.

The club members weren't hurting in the financial department.

"Why are we stopping?" said Karen, clutching her script in one hand. "I don't see a campsite here."

All she could see were oak trees and sycamores surrounding the parking lot.

"We have to walk the rest of the way," said Sophie. "This is where all the club members park. From here we follow a hiking trail to the campsite."

They clambered out of the Tesla, cut across the parking lot, and climbed onto a tortuous hiking trail that snaked up the mountainside through oaks, sycamores, and underbrush. Sophie used a flashlight from her purse to help them see the dirt path in the dark.

"Where is everyone?" said Karen, taking in the deserted forest that surrounded them.

"They're already at the campsite waiting for us."

After they reached a ridge in the mountain, they could see a small ravine below them. A ring of Tiki torches lit a flat area in the ravine.

Karen saw people in black satin robes with cowls pulled over their heads milling about. Beneath their cowls the members were wearing filigreed masks encrusted with gold leaf and studded with diamonds like the one Tom Cruise wore in *Eyes Wide Shut*.

Masks never failed to creep her out.

Karen and Sophie descended the trail to the ravine.

"Watch your step,"

"Why are they wearing robes and masks?" said Karen.

"To protect their identities. Like I told you, this is an ultrasecret club where members don't want their identities divulged."

"Then how do you know they are who they claim to be?"

"They can't get into our club unless their identities are verified before they receive an invitation from us to join."

"Why don't I have a robe?"

"You haven't been accepted as a member yet, because we haven't read your script."

"I see," said Karen, and shook her screenplay in front of her. "Here it is."

"And we will be happy to read it," said Sophie as they made their way to the campsite.

Karen could smell the lemon odor of citronella burning in the Tiki torches.

She felt anxious circulating with people wearing robes and masks. She had no idea who they were. They could be anybody. She didn't understand why they didn't want to be seen. This could very well be the satanic cult Deirdre had joined, even though they claimed to be a club of Hollywood hotshots.

She was getting cold feet. Maybe she shouldn't have come here.

Sophie escorted her to a group of members sitting on benches at a redwood table with the light from Tiki torches flickering above, casting shifting shadows over them. A campfire was burning near one of the tables.

"Give them your script," said Sophie.

Karen approached the table, her palms sweaty, and placed the script on the tabletop.

"Where is the rest of your offer?" said a baritone-voiced member sitting at the redwood table.

"What do you mean?" said Karen, baffled. "My script is my offer to join your club."

Baritone looked at Sophie, expecting an explanation.

"She refused to bring her son with her," said Sophie.

Now Karen was really confused. What the hell were they talking about? What did Brady have to do with joining this club?

Baritone turned to Karen. "You need to make an offer for us to consider you as a member."

"My offer is my screenplay. The way I understand it is if you like it, you agree to represent me as a screenwriter and allow me to join your club."

"You misunderstood."

Karen glanced at Sophie. "That's what Sophie told me."

"Perhaps *offer* isn't the right word," said Sophie. "You need to make a *sacrifice.*"

"I don't understand," said Karen, more perplexed than ever.

"I asked you politely to bring Brady with you, but you refused," said Sophie.

"I didn't want to keep him up past his bedtime."

"Then you must not want to join our club," piped up a falsetto voice from a shorter member sitting beside Baritone.

"Of course, I do. I wouldn't have come all this way if I didn't. Aren't you gonna read my script? I brought it here especially for your members to read," said Karen, becoming annoyed at their brusque treatment of her.

"You should have brought your son," said Falsetto.

"Why? He has nothing to do with my screenplay."

"Are you being deliberately obtuse?" said Baritone.

"I resent your insults. I'm gonna leave if you keep treating me like this."

"Let me remind you, you came here of your own free will," said Sophie. "Nobody forced you to come."

"I accepted your invitation to join your club."

"Then you need to give us something important to you," said Baritone.

"I did. I gave you my screenplay to see if you would represent it."

"It's not important enough."

"Not important?" said Karen, indignant. "I worked my fingers to the bone to get that script written on time. How dare you say it's not important?"

"I'll say it again. It's not important enough. We're talking about blood."

"I sweated blood to complete that script for you."

"We're not speaking figuratively."

Karen felt herself sweating. What the hell was this guy talking about? This so-called club was making her skin crawl. By no means was this the reception she had expected. Why would they offer her an invitation if they didn't want her to join their club?

Despite her qualms, she chose to plow ahead with her other reason for coming here—to find out more about Deirdre.

"Was Deirdre Turner a member of your group?" she said.

"Why is that your business? We don't divulge other members' names."

"Why not? What difference does it make now that she's dead?"

"She has a point," said Sophie.

"Deirdre wanted desperately to join us, but she was unwilling to make the sacrifice to join," said Falsetto.

"I'm tired of beating around the bush," said Baritone. "If you want to join our club, you must give us your son."

"What?" said Karen, dumbfounded.

She felt her knees turn to jelly. She felt she might collapse any second. What in the world was he talking about?

"You must sacrifice your son to Satan," said Baritone.

Karen didn't know what was keeping her standing. His words made her blood run cold. She felt like she was standing outside herself watching herself in disbelief. This couldn't be happening in this day and age. Sacrifices to Satan? It was insane. It was something out of the Middle Ages. Did these people really believe in Satan?

One thing was certain. This was indeed the satanic cult the lieutenant had told her Deirdre had joined. But they said they had refused to allow Deirdre to join. Then why had she killed her two girls? To protect them from being taken and sacrificed by the satanists?

"I'm not sacrificing my son to anyone," said Karen, stiffening her spine. "I want my script back. I'm leaving."

Falsetto snagged the script from the tabletop and tossed it into the campfire.

"This is what I think of your script," she said.

"What are you doing?" cried Karen, aghast. "I practically killed myself to finish that script."

She rushed to the fire to snatch her script from the flames, but one of the hoods seized her and hauled her away from it.

"Bastards," hissed Karen, struggling to no avail to break free.

"We want your son," said Baritone. "We will do nothing to help your career if you don't sacrifice your son. If you give Satan your son, doors will open for you in Hollywood. How do you think we became so rich and successful in Hollywood? Do you think it was just hard work that brought us success?" He laughed. "You fool. We all made sacrifices to our great leader after he allowed us to pleasure ourselves with all sacrifices beforehand."

My God, decided Karen. Who were these sick bastards? Pedophiles?

She wanted to puke at the thought of giving them Brady to sodomize. These people were aberrant in every sense of the word. No wonder Deirdre had murdered her own children. Anything to protect them from these sick freaks. Poor Deirdre. How did she get hooked up with these deviates?

Karen should never have trusted Sophie.

Gordon had been right. This was a club born in hell.

"You have a handsome boy," said Sophie. "The great one will lavish you with fame and wealth for your sacrifice. You will become the most famous and sought-after screenwriter in Hollywood."

"You're insane," said Karen.

"If we're insane, why do we have so much fame and money?" said Baritone. "We are idolized by society."

"Because they don't know how depraved you are."

"Your outdated and narrowminded morality is preventing you from fulfilling yourself and achieving success beyond your wildest dreams. Free yourself from the lies of the religious morality inculcated on you since you were a child and join us."

"I demand to be let go," said Karen, setting her jaw with determination, even though she was on the verge of passing out with nerve-shredding fear.

"Not before we bring your son here for you to watch while we pass him around and then plunge the sacred knife into his heart and sacrifice him to the all-powerful one," said Baritone, stretching his arm upward and brandishing the dagger he had drawn from his robe.

The full impact of his words hit her like a screaming Lamborghini.

She fainted.

Chapter 77

When Karen came to, she smelled a campfire burning.

She found herself bound to a chair and facing a bonfire that hadn't been lit yet. Underbrush gathered and used to fuel the bonfire was piled in a ring around a wooden crucifix with a naked brunette with striking looks hanging from it, her face a mask of agony as blood trickled from her wrists and from her feet that were nailed to the cross.

Sophie, Baritone, and Falsetto approached Karen. Baritone and Falsetto remained robed, hooded, and masked. Sophie remained dressed as she was when she had picked up Karen at home.

"This is Anne," said Baritone, indicating the brunette. "She's an aspiring actress. We invited her to join our club. She refused to give us her little girl. Now she must pay the price. Doors would have opened wide for her if she had accepted our invitation. Instead she refused."

"I don't blame her," said Karen, quivering with terror.

"This is your fate—unless you sacrifice your son Brady to us."

"You are the most horrible people I've ever met."

"Don't look a gift horse in the mouth," said Sophie. "This is a once-in-a-lifetime opportunity for you. For good things to happen in life, sacrifices must be made. Haven't you learned that by now?"

"I promise you doors will open for you," said Baritone. "You will get offers of vast sums of money for your script if we agree to shop it for you. You will meet wealthy and famous celebrities in show business. However, we can't agree to help you unless you give us your son."

"It's detestable for you to even ask me such a question."

"How do you think *we* became successful? We all had to make sacrifices to make it in Hollywood. Everyone dreams of making it in Hollywood, but few are willing to make the sacrifices necessary to achieve their dreams. You have that chance. Don't pass it up. You will never get a chance like this again."

"I don't believe everyone in show business had to sacrifice their children to make it big in Hollywood."

"You're naïve. You think hard work and talent are all you need to become successful in the movies? It's not that easy. You need doors to open for you. We're the ones who can open those doors for you. Otherwise, those doors will be slammed in your face and you will be a pariah, no matter how hard you toil on your project."

Anne whimpered in pain on her cross.

"Help me," she said in a pitiful voice. "Please."

"She could have been a brilliant success in Hollywood as a movie star if she had given us her child," said Baritone, dismayed. "What a waste for such a beautiful woman. This is what happens when you're too full of yourself and refuse to make sacrifices in order to succeed in your chosen career."

"You are dreadful to even ask such a godawful thing of me," said Karen, appalled. "All you want is my child. *That's all?* My only child. He's all I have in the world. How dare you?"

"Making it in Hollywood isn't easy," said Baritone evenly. "Only a very select few make it. You can become one of that chosen elite if you make a sacrifice. All you need to do is make one sacrifice. Only one."

"For all I know, you could be crooks running a pedo ring. You walk around in hoods with your faces covered. You want me to take your word that you're famous Hollywood movers and shakers."

"Some things you have to accept on faith. You have to believe if you want to succeed in the cutthroat film business. Other people would give their eyeteeth to get an offer from us to join our club. But you're so high and mighty you turn it down."

"I'm not giving my only child to a cabal of sadistic perverts wearing robes and masks."

Baritone fetched a loud sigh. "That is unfortunate indeed. Do you understand what the alternative is?"

"The alternative is a clear conscience."

Baritone shook his head no. "The alternative is your turn on the cross. You will end up sacrificing yourself, but instead of getting a fantastic job in showbiz, you'll get to die by fire. The most horrible way to die. You will burn as a witch like Anne, I'm afraid. But it is your choice, and you make it freely. Nobody is forcing you to do anything. You have chosen the cross for yourself."

"If we were really monsters like you say," said Falsetto, "we wouldn't be giving you choices. We would simply take your child without asking you."

"Maybe you can't do it that way," said Karen. "Maybe your ritual is not acceptable to Satan unless a mother voluntarily sacrifices her child."

"How clever of you, but not so clever that you will survive this night without giving us what we want from you. If the mother is dead, we don't need anyone's permission to sacrifice her child on the great one's altar."

"You will never have my permission," said Karen, gripped with fear, her face stippled with beads of sweat that glistened under the wash of light from the Tiki torches.

"It's your choice," said Baritone. "Being burned alive at the stake or becoming an awe-inspiring success in the movies with everybody in the media hanging on your ever word. You'll be as famous as Taylor Swift if you join us."

"And all I have to do is give you my child to rape and kill. Fuck you."

Baritone raised his hand.

Now what? wondered Karen, her heartbeat accelerating. Was he going to slap her? She didn't care. She wasn't going to change her mind. She couldn't imagine Brady being assaulted by this coven of sodomites. She would never let them have him. Never.

Chapter 78

At Baritone's hand signal, Karen could see robed members gathering around Anne, who writhed on the cross, trying to free herself. They fell to chanting. Karen couldn't make out their words. It sounded like a dirge. It could have been Latin like one of those dirges on *The Omen* soundtrack. She couldn't be sure, because she didn't speak Latin.

They were preparing to set Anne on fire. Karen wanted to look away, but, bound in her chair, she was forced to watch the obscene ceremony that was about to take place before her. She rocked in her chair, trying to turn it around. No soap. She couldn't turn away.

Sickened at the prospect of watching Anne burned alive, Karen upchucked on her chest.

"Now see what you've done," said Falsetto, chiding her. "We're not gonna clean you up. This is all on you. You could be rich and successful like us. Instead you want to be a poor loser who will die in poverty and oblivion."

"You're stinking pervs. I don't care how much money and power you have."

"You have no ambition," said Baritone. "You lack the burning desire to succeed that all successful people in their craft have in this business. Without it you'll never achieve your goals."

"You are a scammer. The law will catch up with you and throw the lot of you murderers in jail."

Baritone guffawed. "The law is on our side. Lieutenant?"

One of the robed, masked figures in the semicircle stepped toward Karen and removed their mask.

Karen started when she saw Lieutenant Gaetz.

She thought she was going to have a heart attack.

"The choice is yours, Karen," said Gaetz.

"Judge?" said Baritone, chuckling.

Another robed figure stepped forward and revealed himself.

It was Judge Childress.

She recognized him from a news report she had seen on TV about an assassin who had tried to kill him.

She felt like she was suffocating. They were all part of this sick cult. It wasn't just Hollywood movers and shakers. It was powerful people in government as well. She had become enmeshed in a conspiracy of pooh-bah perverts.

"Believe me, Karen," said Baritone. "It's worth the sacrifice. Everyone in our club would agree. We're giving you the chance of a lifetime. Don't pass it up. Nobody here regrets what they did to become a member of this exclusive fraternity."

"We want you to succeed, Karen," said Falsetto. "We want you to become the best paid and most famous screenwriter in Hollywood. *And we can make it happen.* All you have to do is make one sacrifice. Your writing career will take off like you wouldn't believe. It will shoot into orbit like one of Elon Musk's missiles." She snapped her fingers.

"This is a nightmare," said Karen. "Can't you see how depraved you are?"

"All I can see is how stupid you are for refusing to join our club."

"Let's show her what's in store for her if she continues her stubborn ways," said Baritone. "Light the bonfire."

"No," cried Anne, fear contorting her face. "No. For the love of Christ, no."

"You're beseeching the wrong lord," said Baritone, chuckling. "Christ rules in heaven. Satan rules on earth."

"Liar," cried Anne. "Christ rules all."

"The world is Satan's kingdom," said Baritone, spreading out his arms. "All that you see before you is his. He is the supreme ruler here. Christ has no say on earth. You can meet Christ in heaven after you're dead, for all the good it'll do you. Money and power, not Christ, rule this world. Sacrifice your child to us, and you will receive tons of money—more money than you could ever imagine. It will all be yours."

"Never," gasped Anne, and fell to weeping. "Never."

"Satan rewards his followers with wealth and fame. Christ rewards his followers with nothing. Evil reigns on earth. Good reigns in heaven, where everyone is dead. Only a fool would say no to our offer to join our cult."

"Never. *Yea, though I walk through the valley of the shadow of death, I will fear no evil—*"

"Spare me, you halfwit," cried Baritone in an access of rage. "Burn, baby, burn."

Baritone motioned to one of the robed figures who was standing near the combustible brush heaped around Anne's cross.

The figure leaned forward and lit the bonfire with a lighter.

Anne's deafening shrieks sliced the night air, echoing across the mountain like the squalls of a terrified gull trying to escape, drowning out the cackling of the blazes leaping at her feet.

Karen couldn't stomach it. She could feel Anne's fear like it was her own. She wanted to plug her ears to blot out the nerve-racking sounds, but her hands were tied. There was nothing she could do, she decided, slumping her shoulders in despair in her first-row seat at a carnival of bloodcurdling horrors.

"Is this how you really want it to end, Karen?" said Baritone, shadows of bonfire flames flickering across his hooded face, the gold filigree in his mask glittering. "There's still time for you to change your mind. Anne's fate is yours if you don't."

"You're barbarians," muttered Karen, crestfallen.

"Satan rules on earth. What more proof do you need?"

"He rules you, you bastards."

"Only toward our enemies. If you're not with us, you're against us. In that case, we cannot permit you to go on living and spill to the world the secrets we have revealed to you."

Anne's shrieks knifed through Karen's brain, causing her physical as well as emotional distress. Karen gritted her teeth.

"You must stop this," she cried, unable to endure Anne's suffering.

"It's too late for Anne to save herself. Once on the cross, you can never get off it. Ask Christ," said Baritone, chortling. "Give us Barrabas. Ha-ha. Anne should have changed her mind before her crucifixion."

"You people are insane."

"You're the one who's insane for passing up such an unbelievable deal," piped up Falsetto.

"We're trying to help you, Karen," said Baritone. "Can't you see that? We'll get Brady whether you give him to us or not. No matter what you do, you lose him. Our power is stronger than yours."

"Then why bother to ask me for him?"

"Because Satan wants willing followers. A willing follower means more to him than a vanquished foe like Anne." Baritone glanced in disgust at Anne as she burned on the cross in agony. "Say hello to Jesus for me, Anne."

He turned back to Karen. "This is why he rewards his followers with wealth and power."

Were they going to raid her house and kidnap Brady, regardless of her decision? wondered Karen, thinking the unthinkable. That was what it sounded like, according to Baritone. She thought of Brady home alone. If she wasn't scared to death before, she was now. He was a defenseless kid. What they were going to do to him defied belief. It was unconscionable. There had to be a special place in hell for the torturers of children.

Would the doors in Tinsel Town really open for her if she joined the cult? Somehow she doubted it. It was all probably a big scam run by pedos seeking new members and, more importantly, new sacrifices. Now she was sounding like Gordon, thinking everything was a scam. In any case, she realized she didn't care about the damn Tinsel Town doors. What she cared about was her son Brady.

"Why not make the best of it and give him to us of your own accord?" went on Baritone. "Then success will be yours in your chosen field of screenwriting, and everyone will be happy. Why do you want to get closed doors and cold shoulders for the rest of your life?"

Karen shut her eyes and screamed at the top of her lungs. Maybe someone would hear her, like a camper on the mountain who had nothing to do with this evil cult spawned in the bowels of hell.

Chapter 79

Gordon was driving through the parking lot in the Santa Monica Mountains where Sophie had parked her Tesla. He was inspecting the cars when he recognized Sophie's Tesla. At the same instant, he started at the sound of a scream.

He parked his rental, clambered out, and gazed in the direction of the scream, all of his senses alert. It sounded like the scream had emanated on the other side of the mountain ridge. Since her voice had echoed around the mountain, he couldn't be sure where it had originated.

He checked the location app on his cell phone. The app indicated Karen's cell phone was on the other side of the ridge. He picked up on a mountain trail that snaked up the ridge. He whipped out his SIG from its holster. He sprinted to the trail and tore up it, using the flashlight on his cell phone to light his way, his heartbeat thumping against his ribs like a frantic bird trying to break free from its calcium cage.

He couldn't be sure, but it might have been Karen's scream.

He heard another scream knife through the mountain air. It sounded like a different woman's voice. Maybe this voice was Karen's.

How was he supposed to know? He rarely heard Karen scream, though she had screamed when the flies had tried to suffocate her in the bathroom. The second scream sounded more like Karen's.

Hopefully, neither voice was hers.

He knew this Styx Club was up to no good. Karen should have taken his advice and stayed away from it. Too late now.

Gun in hand, he belted up the dirt trail. He had to get to the crest of the ridge to be able to see what was happening on the other side. He hoped he wasn't too late.

Breathing hard he reached the crest, hid behind an oak tree, doused his flashlight, and surveyed the ravine below, where Tiki torches arranged in a circle lit a glade.

Taken aback, he spotted a naked woman nailed to a cross with a bonfire burning at her feet. The flames were lunging toward her, turning the flesh on her legs red and black. The bastards were burning her alive. Was it Karen? He couldn't make out her face from this distance. The woman on the cross had brunette hair, but maybe it had been blonde before it had caught fire and become charred. In which case, it could be Karen being burned alive.

The woman shrieked. The agony in her yell made his skin crawl.

He couldn't tell if it was Karen's scream.

A ring of onlookers looking like giant crows in their black robes and hoods were chanting as they watched the woman burn.

The satanic cult.

He had to save Karen.

He backed and filled down the mountainside, periodically hiding behind oaks as he descended to the ravine. He couldn't use his cell phone flashlight lest it give away his presence to the cultists. He proceeded slowly on the dark trail to avoid tripping on exposed roots.

The woman on the cross unleashed a particularly nerve-shattering scream and passed out, tilting her head onto her shoulder. As she hung immobile, the flames consumed her flesh. She had passed out from agony and sheer horror, he decided. Beyond saving, she would die soon.

It couldn't be Karen, he decided for no reason. Maybe because he was blinded by hope. Nevertheless, the closer he got, the surer he became that it wasn't Karen. It didn't look like her body. On the other hand, maybe the searing heat of the flames had altered the shape of her body and scorched her flesh, making her figure impossible to identify.

Sweat streaming down his face, he neared the basin of the ravine. There were no trees in the glade. If he attempted to cross it to reach the campsite, the cultists would see him. For the first time as the cultists broke their circle around the bonfire, he noticed another woman sitting bound in a chair facing the burning woman. He hadn't been able to see her before because the robed cultists surrounding the burning woman had obscured his vision.

Even though her face was twisted with agony as she watched the other woman burn, Gordon recognized Karen. He breathed easier. She was still alive. What was the cabal's plan for her? Were they going to nail her to a cross and burn her alive too?

Standing behind an oak trunk, he tried to signal her, but he had to be careful not to be seen by the robed cultists. Fortunately, they were preoccupied with watching the brunette burn at the stake, her flesh boiling, crackling, and turning to soot. None of them had spotted him yet.

He needed to make his move while they were enthralled with watching their sacrifice. The burning woman would serve as his diversion.

He took deep breaths to calm himself. He would need to remove Karen's ropes before he could save her.

He reached down his leg, lifted his trouser cuff, and withdrew a knife from a leather sheath fastened to his ankle. He couldn't waste any time once he reached her. He had to cut her free and take a powder with her before the cabalists knew what had happened.

He gagged on the odor of the burning woman's flesh that wafted toward him on a breeze.

He signaled again to Karen, who was twisting her head, trying to look away from the fire-engulfed brunette. He didn't want her to scream, which would attract the attention of the cabalists. He wanted them to concentrate on the burning woman before he would approach Karen to free her. Waving to Karen he ducked behind the oak he was using as cover.

It looked like she might have seen him. He peeked around the oak and held his forefinger in front of his lips, motioning her to be quiet. Even though she was visibly shaken by her ordeal, she seemed to acknowledge him. On the other hand, he doubted she could see him in the dark. Neither the wash of the light thrown by the bonfire nor by the tiki torches reached him.

He couldn't wait much longer for his suicide mission—if that was what it was. As the bonfire flames finished devouring and charring the sacrifice's flesh, the cabalists would become bored and turn their attention to their next victim, which Gordon figured was Karen.

Gun in one hand, knife in the other, Gordon decided it was now or never. He broke into a sprint from the stand of oak trees and made a beeline for Karen. If those bastards wanted a fight, they were going to get one they would never forget.

Chapter 80

Now that *Alien* had ended, Brady was watching *The Thing* on TV when he heard the sound of running water coming from the bathroom.

He was the only one at home. He didn't remember leaving the water running. He better check it out, even though he didn't want to miss the movie with its gripping paranoia. Whose body was the Thing assuming? Kurt Russell couldn't trust anyone in his crew. Thing-inhabited crew members were as bad as pod people, decided Brady, because they weren't human anymore. The Thing took over human bodies and replaced them with itself.

When you got right down to it, the pods and the Thing wanted to do the same thing. They wanted to replace humans. The pods wanted to replace people with their exact doubles, who lacked emotions, and the Thing wanted to replace humans by inhabiting their bodies.

It was creeping out Brady just thinking about it.

He tore himself away from the movie and made for the bathroom to check out the leak or whatever it was.

Standing in the bathroom doorway, Brady could see water gushing out of the bathtub faucet into the tub, which was already full. The dead bodies of Theresa and Frieda were floating naked on their stomachs in the water. The sight of the two girls filled him with fear.

Why did they keep coming back to the bathtub? And how could they? They were dead. They drowned over a year ago.

Having trouble breathing he edged toward the bathtub on rubber legs to turn off the water as it was starting to flow over the tub's rim, even though he couldn't stand the idea of getting too near the floating corpses.

Maybe he was dreaming the two girls.

As he neared the faucet, Theresa startled him when she flipped over onto her back, blew water out of her mouth, and scrabbled out of the tub. Dripping wet she stared at him with black sightless eyes.

Brady stopped dead in his tracks, the ice-cold hand of fear squeezing his heart.

How could she not be dead after all these years? This was impossible, and yet there she was standing not more than two feet in front of him.

At that moment, Frieda righted herself in the tub, blew out water from her mouth, and stood in the tub, facing Brady.

Paralyzed with fear, Brady stared at the two drowned girls that weren't drowned.

He told himself to run like hell out of the bathroom, but it did no good. He couldn't move. What did they want? What were they going to do to him?

He wished Mom and Dad were here. But they weren't. He would have to take care of this by himself. He couldn't depend on anyone to come to his rescue.

The two girls didn't attack him. They just stood and stared at him with their dead doll's eyes, water dripping down their naked bodies, whose flesh was shriveled like prunes because the cadavers had been floating in the water for such a long time.

Continuing to face them he started inching backward toward the door.

They kept watching him with their big, black, dead eyes.

Go away, he thought. *Go away and die somewhere else.*

Water was flooding onto the linoleum. There was nothing he could do about it. The two girls weren't going to let him shut off the water. They showed no interest in turning it off themselves.

They continued staring at him without following him.

"Mom will get mad if you flood the bathroom," he found himself saying.

Why was he talking to corpses? They can't be there. He was imagining them.

He closed his eyes for a minute then opened them.

The two girls were still there, standing dripping wet, staring at him with no expressions on their dead faces.

"No," he said, shaking his head.

They weren't really there. They couldn't be. He was seeing things.

He dashed back to the living room to watch the movie. Maybe if he stayed away from the two girls, they would leave him alone, or they would vanish. Yes, they would vanish, because they weren't there in the first place. Something that wasn't there couldn't hurt you.

He saw headlight beams sweep across the closed curtains in the living room.

Maybe Mom and Dad were back.

Just in time.

Jacked up, he ran to the window to peek out the curtain.

He saw Dr. Armitage kneeling motionless on the lawn in the powdered moonlight, seemingly looking at the house, his face blood-streaked, one of his eye sockets empty. But he couldn't be looking at the house, because he was blind.

A car was pulling into the driveway, frosting the lawn with headlight beams.

It must be Dad, decided Brady, feeling like leaping for joy. He got set to run out and meet him, but now that he could see it better he realized it wasn't Dad's car.

The driver climbed out of the front seat.

A frisson ran down Brady's spine. His mouth felt dry. He couldn't swallow.

The driver had the head of a hog and wore a black silk robe that rippled in the moonlight.

He stalked across the lawn, whipped a long carving knife out of his robe, gripped Armitage's head by the hair, yanked Armitage's head back, tore off the neck brace, and slit the doctor's throat from ear to ear.

Brady covered his eyes and tried to blot out the shocking image of blood erupting from Armitage's carotid artery. But the image wouldn't go away. He kept seeing the brutal scene repeat itself in his mind.

Even worse, Hog Head was cutting across the lawn toward the front door, the carving knife in his hand dripping fresh blood from its blade. Hog Head paused to wipe the blood-smeared blade on the grass then kept making for the front door. In the next instant, Brady saw a robed guy wearing a wolf head climb out of the shotgun seat of Hog Head's car.

Brady knew he had to keep them out, no matter what. Once they got inside the house, he was dead meat. The problem was the broken lock on the front door. He thought fast.

Coming up with an idea, he bounded to the kitchen, flung open the bottom cupboard, retrieved a coil of nylon clothesline from it, and bounded back to the living room. He uncoiled the clothesline, wrapped it around the front doorknob, tied a knot in it, and flung the other end of it around a steel lamp fixture mounted to the wall next to the doorjamb. He wrapped the clothesline around the fixture several times then wrapped it around the doorknob again and knotted it.

Brady stepped back and viewed his handiwork. He doubted it would keep the strangers out, but it should slow them down.

He wasn't going to wait there to find out. He fled upstairs.

Chapter 81

Armed to the teeth, Gordon was charging down the incline toward Karen, who by now had seen him. The cult members were still enthralled with the immolation of the brunette on the cross, watching her sooty flesh smoke. Gordon hoped she wasn't still alive. Death by fire had to be agonizing because it took a while to die, and the pain . . . he didn't want to think about it. Could you feel your eyeballs boil out of their sockets when they caught fire?

He would reach Karen soon.

As long as the cultists didn't turn around and try to stop him, he would make it.

His eyes blazed as adrenaline shot through his system.

"It's Brady," cried Karen, undiluted horror engraving her face. "They're gonna torture and sacrifice him."

"What?" said Gordon, stunned.

"Brady's the one they want, not me."

And Brady was home alone, decided Gordon with alarm.

There was nothing he could do about it now. He had to get Karen out of here before the cultists nailed her to a cross and barbecued her. Like a man possessed, he sliced through the ropes binding Karen.

Out of the corner of his eye he noticed one of the cult members turning around. He wasn't wearing his hood over his face. It was Childress, Gordon realized in shock, and Childress was looking at him. Gordon couldn't believe his eyes. It defied belief that the judge would be a member of this bloodthirsty cult.

"Hurry," said Karen, pulling her arms free from the severed ropes.

Only her legs remained bound.

Overcoming his astonishment at seeing Childress, Gordon set to work with his knife on the ropes tying Karen's legs to the chair.

"Can't you help that poor woman?" said Karen, eying the flaming brunette on the cross.

"It's too late for her," said Gordon, finishing releasing Karen.

"At least put her out of her misery."

Gordon saw the anguished woman open her charred, weeping eyes on her sizzling face. He had thought she was already dead. It would have been better if she was. It would have put an end to her suffering.

At that moment Childress hollered to alert the others to Gordon's presence. The rest of the cultists wheeled around to see Gordon.

Gordon trained his SIG on the burning woman's head and shot her, knowing she was beyond salvation, the raging flames bent on consuming her flesh and bones.

The cultists charged Gordon and Karen.

Gordon opened fire, downing Childress with a shot to the chest.

Gordon and Karen broke into a run across the gorge to the tree-studded incline that led back to the parking lot.

Gordon shot two more cultists, who crumpled.

Realizing their danger, the rest of the cultists stopped pursuing him and fled for cover.

They must not have been armed, decided Gordon.

But then a shot rang out.

Gordon realized it was Lieutenant Gaetz who was shooting at him and Karen with his LAPD FN 509. Despite his surprise at seeing Gaetz in a cultist robe, Gordon returned fire while running, which threw off his aim. Who were the other cult members? What manner of nightmare was this? Was everybody he knew a member? Who *wasn't* involved in the conspiracy? The idea boggled his mind.

Gordon reached an oak, ducked behind it, and, taking steady aim, fired back at Gaetz.

Wincing, Gaetz dropped to his knees, firing two errant shots.

Gordon didn't see any of the other cultists pursuing him. They were in hiding—for the moment, anyway.

"Come on," he told Karen, producing his cell phone and flicking on its flashlight.

He lit the trail as they burst up the mountainside as best they could in the night.

"We have to save Brady," she said, at her wits' end.

Gordon glanced back over his shoulder. The cultists were slowly sneaking out from their hiding places and staring up at him and Karen. Gordon figured they were mustering their courage to give chase. He saw one of them pelt to Gaetz, who sprawled on the grass, thrashing in pain thanks to his bullet wound. The cultist scoffed up Gaetz's FN 509 and bopped after Gordon and Karen.

Gordon fired a shot at him but missed.

Emboldened by their possession of the FN 509, the other cultists raced after their armed member.

Gordon and Karen kept ascending the slope.

"They might have guns in their cars," said Gordon, pumping his legs up and down on the dirt mountain. "We have to get out of here."

"Brady," said Karen. "We have to get Brady. Sophie knows where we live."

"I can't believe she's a part of this."

"She's a full-fledged member."

Gordon felt his cell phone vibrate in his hand. He didn't have time to take a call. On the other hand, it might be urgent.

He saw that it was Brady calling.

"Hello, Brady," Gordon said breathlessly.

"Dad," cried Brady. "Hog Head's here. What am I supposed to do?"

"What?" said Gordon, baffled. "What's Hog Head?"

"What's happening?" said Karen in anguish.

"It's Brady. He sounds hysterical. He's not making sense."

Gordon put the call on speaker.

"Hog Head slit the doctor's throat," said Brady, and burst into tears.

"Oh my God," said Karen.

"Wolf Head's with him."

"Where are they now?" said Gordon.

"They're coming to the front door."

"Keep your voice down. Don't let them hear you. Understand?"

"Yeah," said Brady, lowering his voice but continuing to sound terrified.

"Where are you?"

"In the living room. I was watching *The Thing*—"

"Go upstairs to my bedroom," said Gordon, knowing there was no time. "You need to get my gun and use it like I told you."

"They must be cult members after him," said Karen, stricken. "They were ready to kidnap him in case I didn't sacrifice him voluntarily to the cult."

"Get my gun and find somewhere to hide," Gordon told Brady.

"Where?" asked Brady.

"You're good at finding places to hide. If they find you, shoot them with the gun. No matter what they tell you, they want to hurt you."

"Oh no."

Gordon hated to say this, but, "If there are too many of them, make sure you save one bullet for yourself."

"What?" gasped Karen, staring at Gordon in horror.

"We can't let him fall into those perverts' hands."

"I don't understand," said Brady.

"Don't let them take you alive," said Gordon. "The people coming for you are pure evil."

"OK," said Brady tentatively.

"The bullet for yourself is only a last resort. Shoot through your open mouth into your brain. Got it?"

"Yeah," said Brady, his voice faint.

"Go now. Don't be scared. We're coming to help you. Stay calm and hide. We'll be there soon. Bye."

"I can't believe you told him to kill himself," said Karen, aghast.

"Can you imagine what those freaks would do to him if they got him?"

The blood drained from Karen's face.

Chapter 82

Gordon and Karen climbed over the ridge crest and, despite their searing lungs and the darkness, ran down the dirt trail that wound to the parking lot. Karen tripped and fell, barking her knees. She rolled partway down the trail then brushed herself off and got up.

"I can't run much farther," she said, winded.

"We have to reach the car," said Gordon below her on the trail, looking up at her.

He also looked past her farther up the mountain to see if any of the cultists were catching up to them. So far he didn't see any. They hadn't reached the ridge crest yet. It wouldn't take much longer for them to mount it.

Hanging her mouth open, gasping, Karen resumed her journey down the trail.

"We gotta help Brady," said Gordon, watching her from the parking lot.

Karen doggedly kept trotting down the mountain trail, trying to avoid tripping on roots.

Gordon scoped out the cars in the parking lot. He tried to think of a way to block them from leaving, but he couldn't come up with an idea. If he couldn't block them, he needed to disable them.

Knife in hand, he set to work slashing one tire on each car. He knew he wouldn't have time to slash all the tires on each car. The cultists would be here soon. And for sure one of them had Gaetz's piece.

Gordon figured one flat on each car would disable the fleet, enough so the cultists wouldn't be able to keep up with Gordon's rental. It was the best he could come up with on such short notice. If he had had more time, he would have at least slashed two tires on each vehicle. He settled for one tire and went about his business as Karen continued hustling down the trail.

Karen emerged onto the asphalt parking lot.

She hunched forward, grabbing her knees and trying to catch her breath.

The crack of a gunshot broke the bosky silence of the mountain.

Gordon slewed toward the sound. Another gunshot ensued. Gordon saw the muzzle flash of the fired pistol and picked up on the silhouette of a cultist at the top of the ridge aiming Gaetz's FN 509 at Karen. Gordon returned fire at the cultist, who ducked behind an oak.

"Are you OK?" said Gordon, wondering if Karen had been shot.

"Yes," she said.

"Let's go," Gordon cried.

They dashed toward the rental.

He reached it before her and flung open its doors in preparation for her arrival.

Gordon and Karen piled into the rental. Karen claimed the shotgun seat.

Gordon heard two gunshots as the shooter barreled down the mountain trail toward the parking lot. One of the bullets sparked off the asphalt surface of the parking lot near Gordon's rental and ricocheted.

Gordon fired the rental's engine.

"Did you disable all of the cars?" said Karen, fastening her seat belt.

"Yeah. They can still run, but they won't handle very well. They're gonna be running on their rims. I hope it slows them down enough so they can't catch up to us before we reach home."

He backed out of his parking space, braked, sped to the exit, hung a right, and peeled away from the parking lot, burning rubber and fishtailing.

"We never should've left Brady alone," said Karen, her eyes bleak as she stared out the windshield.

"I know," said Gordon without being aware of what he was saying thanks to his concentration on the road in front of him.

He refused to think about what he should have done, knowing doing so would accomplish nothing and only slow him down. He had to reach Brady before the cultists kidnaped him.

"I had no idea people could be so depraved," said Karen, disconsolate. "You read about them in the papers, but I've never met anyone *that* evil until now."

"Who was that beautiful woman nailed to a cross?"

"An actress who wanted to make it big in Hollywood but decided it wasn't worth sacrificing her children for."

"I don't know how Deirdre got mixed up with these slimeballs."

Karen faced him. "She wanted fame and glory in the movies like Marilyn Monroe."

"How could a cult give her fame and glory?"

"They claim they can open doors in Hollywood if you sacrifice your children to them."

"And you believe that bullshit?"

"Unfortunately, yes. Remember *Rosemary's Baby*? Remember how Rosemary's actor husband got his break in that play he auditioned for but didn't get the role?"

"The coven of witches helped him with their black magic and caused the original actor chosen for the part to go blind. Rosemary's husband got the part. But that was a movie."

"There are rich pervs in Hollywood who'll do anything to get their dirty little hands on children. I'm sure they have enough power that they can open doors of showbiz movers and shakers to any actor they want, or to any screenwriter, for that matter."

"I don't see how that explains Deirdre drowning her own kids."

Staring out the windshield Karen mulled over the matter.

"I believe I understand now why she did it," she said. "At first I thought it was because she was so obsessed with Marilyn Monroe that she was trying to copy Marilyn by killing herself and she didn't want to leave her children motherless."

"Now what do you think?"

"The cultists demanded her girls as sacrifices or they wouldn't allow her to join their twisted satanic cult. In exchange they promised to open doors in Hollywood for her and make her a movie star. But Deirdre turned them down. Instead of offering her girls to the cult, she killed them herself to prevent the cult from getting them. She took her own life when she realized she loathed herself for what she had done and she felt too awful to go on living without them. She died with a tormented spirit."

"Jesus."

"I believe it's that spirit that's haunting our house. A spirit that's filled with guilt and grief for what she did to her own children. A spirit that's filled with rage at her unjust life. In short, a spirit that can never rest in peace."

"The demon that's possessing the house, according to Armitage?"

Karen nodded yes.

"I don't believe in demons," said Gordon, "but I *do* believe in perv cultists. I just saw them at work." His face bathed in sweat, he accelerated. "We need to get to Brady. Fuck me if they get him. I'm the one who left him alone."

Gnashing his teeth he slammed the headliner with the heel of his open hand.

"I got carried away with my writing and forgot about Brady," mumbled Karen as if to herself, her head bowed.

Chapter 83

Brady was upstairs retrieving Gordon's SIG P365 from the master bedroom when he heard a bang at the front door.

His heart thumping on steroids and all but deafening him, Brady figured the bang was Hog Head trying to enter through the front door. Thanks to the clamor of his heartbeat, Brady couldn't tell if Hog Head had broken into the house yet.

It was only a matter of time. Brady knew the broken door wouldn't last long under duress.

Brady had to act fast.

He grabbed the spare magazine in the gun safe and stashed it in his trouser pocket. He grabbed the pistol and snugged it inside his waistband. He didn't like the idea of shooting someone, but Dad had told him Hog Head was coming to harm him. And Brady had seen Hog Head slice the doctor's throat. Brady knew he had to shoot Hog Head when the guy came for him.

In the meantime he had to find a hiding place.

He thought about crawling under the bed, but he figured that would be the first place the intruders would look. He had played hide and seek many times. He had a good idea how seekers thought. He figured Hog Head would look under the beds and in the closets.

Thoughts raced through Brady's head.

Maybe he should confront the intruders on the staircase. He could shoot them as they ascended the steps. But what if they had guns and shot back? He had never shot a gun in his life. His aim would be lousy. On the other hand, the intruders could be professional gunslingers. Brady didn't like his chances.

Even if he shot Hog Head, how many more of the intruders were there? There was at least one more. He knew that much from having seen Wolf Head. There could have been even more of them in the car. They could have bundled out after Wolf Head when Brady wasn't looking.

He might be able to kill one of them with a lucky shot but not all of them.

He heard a lot of people talking on the front lawn but couldn't distinguish what they were saying. It sounded like more than two voices. Maybe they were going to surround the house and break into the front and the back at the same time.

The bottom line was he didn't know what they were going to do.

Confronting a gang of thugs by himself wasn't a good idea. It was best to hide.

But where?

He started when he heard furniture scuffing against the living room floor. The scuffing stopped. The clothesline was preventing them from opening the front door all the way, he decided.

He burst into the upstairs hall and scoped it out, seeking a hiding place. He noticed the trapdoor pole lying on the side of the hall. He glanced up at the trapdoor. *The attic.*

He snagged the pole, hooked it around the trapdoor handle, and pulled down the ladder to the attic. Carrying the pole in one hand, he climbed up the rungs. He placed the pole in the attic so the intruders wouldn't be able to open the trapdoor. He knelt down and peeked through the open trapdoor.

He heard a loud noise at the front door. Something crashed to the floor.

They must have kicked open the door, tearing the steel lamp fixture out of the wall in the process and slamming it to the floor. They would be inside the house in no time.

Riddled with fear, Brady pulled the ladder up into the attic, closing the trapdoor as quietly as he could. He knew he must not make any noise. When they came upstairs, he would have to remain stock-still or they would hear him in the attic. Once they found out he was hiding in the attic, he would be trapped.

He felt the gun in his hand. He would shoot them when they stuck their heads through the trapdoor. He would blow Hog Head's ugly face apart.

Brady wasn't going down without a fight.

He wondered if he should call Dad. Fishing his cell phone out of his trouser pocket, he debated the idea. What was the point? What could Dad do for him now? Brady was on his own.

Before he could place a call, he heard a voice down below.

"Come out, come out wherever you are," a man's voice crooned.

"We know you're here," said a female voice.

"Don't make this hard on us or you'll regret it."

Scared senseless, beads of sweat popping on his face, Brady heard the stair treads and risers creaking under feet climbing them. He held his breath. He must not move.

There was still a chance, no matter how small, that they might not find him, give up, and leave.

Who was he trying to kid? They knew he was here. Dad had said they wanted to harm him. They weren't going to leave without him.

He realized he felt faint from holding his breath.

He took a deep breath. He didn't care if they did hear him. He had to breathe.

He consoled himself with the thought that even if they suspected he was in the attic, they would not be able to lower the trapdoor without the pole which he had secreted in the attic with him.

"He's not under the beds," said the woman.

"Keep looking," said the man. "He's here somewhere."

"How can you be sure?"

"The TV's on in the living room. And I can smell his fear."

"He's not downstairs," said another man from the first floor.

There were at least three of them, figured Brady. The house was infested with them. He didn't like his chances.

Armies of goose bumps of fear pitched tents on his arms.

Where was Dad? What was taking him so long?

He realized his knuckles were turning white as he clenched the gun in his hand. He didn't want the gun to go off accidentally and alert the intruders to his presence. He relaxed his grip and withdrew his forefinger from the trigger.

A man's voice sounded like it was right below him and curdled his blood.

"He must be in the attic. Bring me a chair."

A chair, decided Brady, his face turning ashen. He hadn't thought they could reach . . .

Don't move a muscle, he told himself, eyeballing the trapdoor, training his gun on it with a shaky hand, and waiting with overwhelming dread for it to open.

Chapter 84

Gordon picked up speed in his rental.

"Are we gonna get there in time?" said Karen, staring out the windshield with popping eyes.

Gordon didn't know. It was windy. The Santa Anas were freshening, rocking the rental.

"We'll get there," he said, hoping he sounded convincing.

Had the intruders entered the house already? He figured they had, since Brady had reported that they had arrived at the house. There was nothing keeping them out. The front door was a joke. Brady's only hope at this point was to find a safe hiding place. But how long could he hide from a group of thugs who had access to the entire house?

Gordon figured the cultists would find Brady without question. It was just a matter of time. How much time? Gordon didn't want to think about it. Worrying was counterproductive.

He had to watch the speed limit on Sunset. Getting pulled over for speeding would mean a death sentence for Brady. Brady couldn't stay hidden forever. Time wasn't on his side.

"I can't believe this is happening," said Karen, continuing to stare out the windshield.

Gordon glanced at the rearview mirror, wondering if the cultists were chasing him. He didn't know how they could pick up his rental in the dark. He didn't think they could go as fast as him in their disabled cars with only three good tires. But the cultists drove expensive cars. Maybe some of those cars could drive fine on three wheels. Or maybe they had spares. Not all cars did these days. Or maybe they had tire repair aerosols in their trunks. But would that stuff work on a slashed tire?

Again, why worry? There were multiple scenarios that could be working against him. Why should he pepper his mind with all the forces arrayed against his success at saving Brady? He needed to focus his mind on the one thing—the need to reach Brady ASAP.

Despite himself he glanced in the rearview mirror again. He was looking for a luxury car hanging a tail on him. The good thing about luxury cars was they were easy to spot. Their fanciness made them stick out. And all the cultists had expensive tastes, he had noticed in the parking lot at their mountain retreat. Their cars' brighter xenon headlights should stand out from regular ones if they were behind him.

One pair of headlights stood out in the darkness on the black ribbon of road unwinding behind him. They could belong to someone else's luxury car though, not necessarily a cultist's.

"I can't believe how evil Sophie Lemon is," said Karen. "I had no idea people this rotten existed. I mean, I read about them in the papers and see them in the movies, but I've never actually encountered anyone so rotten they would recruit little children for a satanic pedo ring."

"Corruption is everywhere in this neck of the woods. Hollywood draws all types, including Manson types."

He had to admit he didn't expect to see Childress as a member of the cult. He knew the guy was corrupt from his taking graft from the Jalisco New Generation cartel but not so corrupt that he would join a satanic cult that molested and sacrificed children to Satan.

"I couldn't believe it when I saw the lieutenant there," said Karen, her face long with dismay.

"He must have been scouting out new victims when he saw Brady. It explains why Gaetz seemed so interested in Brady."

"I thought he was just being nice to our boy. Did you kill him?"

"I hit him. I don't know if it was a kill shot. I was shooting on the run."

She faced him. "Why do you always have a gun on you?"

There was a lot she didn't know about him, he decided, and it was best to keep it that way. She wouldn't be happy if she found out how he made his living.

"I believe in self-protection," was all he said.

"I'm glad you do. Otherwise, we'd both be burning at the stake," she said, shivering, thinking about it.

"We're out of there. Don't think about it."

"I can't imagine what they have in store for Brady," she said, her voice catching.

"They won't kill him at the house if what you say is true that they want to torture him during a satanic ceremony before they kill him as a sacrifice."

"Your pep talk leaves something to be desired." She paused a beat. "Maybe we should call Brady to see if he's OK."

"The chime of his cell phone might betray his hiding place if I rang his number."

"Wouldn't he have it on Mute?"

"Not necessarily. It's not worth the risk of calling him. He might have found a good hiding place. We don't want to give it away by ringing his phone."

He doubted Brady had a good hiding place, though. There were only so many places you could hide in a house, and there could be as many as a dozen cultists searching for him, which would cut down on the time it took to find him. Gordon didn't like Brady's chances.

Gordon strengthened his resolve and goosed the gas. He had to reach Brady.

"I'm gonna kill myself if we don't reach him in time," said Karen, woebegone. "It's my fault."

"It's *my* fault for leaving him alone."

Their rental Toyota followed the taillights that stretched before them, becoming another link in the mileslong bloodred chain that meandered to the Pacific Ocean.

Chapter 85

When Brady heard one of the intruders ask for a chair, he knew they would be able to reach the trapdoor and open it.

Sweat streaming out of his armpits and down his flanks, he frantically thought of a way to block the intruders. He cut his eyes around the attic, trying to find an answer.

He picked up on a steamer trunk some three feet from the trapdoor. Careful not to give away his presence, he stole across the attic to the trunk, hoping the floorboards wouldn't creak and give him away. He placed his gun on the floor and slid the trunk toward the trapdoor, not realizing how heavy the trunk was. It took all his strength to slide it over the trapdoor.

He hoped the thugs couldn't hear him sliding the trunk.

"What's that noise?" said a woman.

"What?" said a man.

"Someone's moving in the attic."

"The kid. He's up there."

Brady started when he heard the suppressed crack of a gunshot. Terrified, he backed away from the trapdoor and scoffed up his gun from the floor.

"You idiot," said one of the men.

"Why? He's up there."

"You might hit him. The boss doesn't want a dead kid for a sacrifice. He has to be alive and well."

The other man grumbled.

"How could the kid have gotten up there?" said the woman. "He can't reach the trapdoor."

"He must've used something."

"Open the trapdoor," said the woman.

"How do we know the kid doesn't have a weapon?" said Grumbler.

"He's just a kid," said the man who sounded like he was in charge, probably Hog Head. "You really think he's got a machine gun up there?"

"Ah, what do you know?"

"Shut up and open the trapdoor. We need to get moving. The boss wants the ceremony tonight. Something about the position of the full moon and the signs of the zodiac."

"I'm going."

"OK. Careful. The kid's up there with a machine gun and a bazooka ready to blow your head off."

"Very funny."

Grumbler mounted the chair, reached up to the trapdoor, unlocked it, and tugged it open. His eyes bugged out when he saw the steamer trunk slide through the opening, slam into his face, and knock him off the chair. The trunk slid down the ladder and crashed onto the floor beside Grumbler, who was sprawled on his back and flailing around.

"My leg," he cried. "I think it's broken."

"Shut up," said Hog Head. "The neighbors will hear you and call the cops."

"Jesus, it hurts."

"Keep it down or I'll whack you."

"Fucking kid. Let me at him."

"We know he's up there. Are you pussies afraid of a little kid? Come on, let's get him."

Gun in hand, Brady stole away from the open trapdoor to avoid being seen by the gang. They were armed, and he feared they might shoot him, no matter what they said about taking him alive. He had one advantage. They didn't know he had a gun.

"Leo, go up there, grab that kid, and bring him down," said the leader.

"No problem."

Brady gasped. He hadn't realized he had been holding his breath.

He trained his SIG on the trapdoor, waiting for the first guy to pop his head through the trapdoor opening, his entire body tense from the adrenaline pumping through it. He had to shoot the guy or Hog Head and his gang would kidnap and hurt him, according to Dad.

Brady didn't want to kill anybody, but he had no choice. Kill or be kidnaped and tortured.

Waiting for the guy to appear at the trapdoor, Brady felt his palm sweating on the pistol stock, making the stock slick to hold. He adjusted his grip on the stock. Where was the guy?

"What are you waiting for?" said Hog Head. "He's just a fucking kid."

"No problem."

Chapter 86

Brady watched the trapdoor aperture as Leo climbed the ladder and gingerly stuck his Fox Head above the attic floor and eyeballed the dim-lit room. Creepy Fox Head poked his silenced pistol in front of him.

"Give up and come here, kid, or I'll shoot you dead," he said, unable to see Brady, who was hiding behind a suitcase.

Brady squeezed the trigger, wincing in anticipation of the deafening report of the gunshot.

Leo's head dropped out of sight.

"Shit," he cried.

Brady couldn't tell if he had hit the guy. Somehow he doubted it. After all, he had never fired a gun before. You couldn't expect much from a rookie. His ears were still ringing from the crack of the gunshot.

"The little shit has a gun," said Leo.

"Did he hit you?" asked Hog Head.

"No."

"So what if he has a gun. His aim sucks. This is probably the first time he ever shot a gun at someone. He ain't Annie Oakley. Either go up there or get the fuck off the ladder."

"We don't have time to dick around," said the woman. "A neighbor might have heard the gunshot and called the cops."

"We're not leaving without the kid," said Hog Head. "The boss will skin us alive if we do."

"How do we get him?"

"Are you listening, kid?" said Hog Head. "I know you are, because your life depends on what I say. Do you want to go on living?"

Brady didn't answer.

"Answer me," said Hog Head, raising his voice. "Do you want to go on living or do you want us to kill you here and now?"

Brady said nothing. He was too scared to speak. His throat felt dry and tense with the fear that gripped him.

"Throw your gun through the trapdoor," said Hog Head.

No way, thought Brady, grasping his gun harder if that was possible. His grasp was so firm his hand felt stiff.

"If you don't throw that gun down here, we're gonna be mad when we get you," said Hog Head. "And *we will* get you. Then we're gonna whip your puny ass."

Brady thought about firing another shot to scare them away, but he didn't want to waste bullets. He didn't know how many members were in the gang.

He heard something behind him. Alarmed, he whipped his head around. Had the thugs somehow circled behind him onto the roof?

He scrambled to the window and peered outside.

Theresa and Frieda were standing on the roof in their yellow dresses, smiling at him.

"We want to see you fly," said Theresa.

Maybe they were right, decided Brady. This would be a good time to fly off the roof. The cult would never catch him if he did.

Brady scrabbled out the window onto the roof tiles and got to his feet under the night sky bathed in moonlight. A gust of wind brushed his face. The eucalyptuses swayed and soughed in the wind. From his perch he watched the treetops bend, paying obeisance to the moon.

The two wraithlike girls stood opposite him.

"We want to see you fly," said Frieda.

He knew he could fly. They had told him he could. All he had to do was walk to the edge of the roof and jump.

Inside the attic, the female cult member thrust her pig head through the trapdoor and cast around for Brady.

"I don't see him," she told the cultists below.

"He has to be there," said Hog Head. "He fired a gun. He's hiding. Crawl up there and bring him down."

Pig Head crawled into the attic and, crouching with her gun in her hand, checked out the attic for Brady. Not seeing him she approached the window, which she noticed was open. She saw Brady standing near the edge of the roof.

She turned around and yelled through her mask toward the trapdoor, "He's on the roof."

"What?" said Hog Head.

She repeated herself, louder this time.

"Well, get him," said Hog Head. "Make it snappy."

"Come over here," said Pig Head, motioning to Brady.

Brady drew a bead on her.

She disappeared behind the window jamb when she saw the piece in his hand.

"We want to take you to a barbecue in the woods," said Pig Head, pressing her spine against the wall inside the attic. "You'll have fun. Come inside, and we'll take a trip to the woods."

"I can fly," said Brady, looking at the two girls. "Theresa and Frieda want to see me fly."

Pig Head peeked around the jamb out the window.

"What two girls?" she said, confused. "You're standing out there by yourself."

"You're lying. They're here with me, and you can't touch us. I'm gonna fly for them."

"Kid, you can't fly."

"All I have to do is step off the edge of the roof and you'll never catch me."

"You step off the roof, you're gonna break your neck. If you know what's good for you, don't move." Pig Head turned around and hollered toward the trapdoor. "He's gonna jump off the roof."

"Fuck, no," bellowed Hog Head. "Grab him now and bring his punk ass down here. We blow this assignment, we're fucked."

A voice from the front lawn startled Brady. He all but lost his balance as he whirled around to see who it was.

It was Dad, standing below and looking up at him.

Chapter 87

"Don't move," Gordon called out, his SIG in his hand, his eyes bulging with apprehension as he stared at Brady.

Karen stood beside Gordon, her gaze locked on Brady standing precariously on the roof.

"I can fly down," said Brady.

"No," said Gordon, his heart skipping a beat.

For all the good it did, he motioned with his open hand for Brady to stop where he was on the roof, as though the gesture could somehow prevent Brady from moving.

"Hog Head and his pals are inside," said Brady.

Even as Brady spoke, Gordon picked up on a robed cult member in a vulture mask standing in the doorway of the house, training a piece on him and Karen.

Gordon double-tapped Vulture Head, felling the cultist.

Gordon's SIG locked back. Gordon ejected the spent magazine and replaced it with a fresh one from his cargo pocket. He racked the slide and chambered a round.

"You stay here and watch Brady," Gordon told Karen, and burst toward the front door, gun in hand, ready to fire at a moment's notice.

"Don't move, honey," Karen shouted up at Brady.

One of the tiles dislodged from the roof, plummeted to the ground, and shattered on the front lawn. Brady lost his footing for a second but regained it.

"Jesus," gasped Karen, flinging her hand to her mouth.

Gordon strode over Vulture Head's corpse and stormed into the living room, brandishing his SIG.

Spotting an armed cultist in a crow head at the foot of the stairs, Gordon blew the cultist's head apart with two bullets.

Determined to kill every last one of the bastards, Gordon stalked the living room, wielding his SIG back and forth before him, using a two-handed grip.

The rest of them were upstairs, he decided.

From the foot of the landing, he could see two cultists, Hog Head and Wolf Head, standing under the trapdoor and staring down at him, pistols in their hands. Hog Head fired at Gordon as Gordon ducked behind the wall at the foot of the staircase.

Gordon grimaced in pain. The bullet had connected somewhere in his stomach or lower chest. He wasn't sure. Hell.

The house trembled.

Gordon braced himself against the wall as pieces of the ceiling fell to the floor.

"Quake," cried one of the cultists upstairs.

"Let's beat it," yelled another.

Gordon peeked around the corner of the wall. He fired twice at Wolf Head, who crumpled on the floor. Hog Head returned fire at Gordon but missed. Gordon plugged him twice in the head. Hog Head groaned and somersaulted down the stairs at Gordon's feet, blood percolating through his perforated mask which hung askew.

Gordon wondered if Brady had managed to keep his footing on the pantile roof during the earthquake.

Clutching his wounded, bleeding side, grinding his teeth in pain, Gordon charged up the stairs, keeping his eyes peeled for cultists. He saw the open trapdoor with the ladder under it.

He climbed the ladder to the attic with one hand, his SIG P224 in the other, and peeked through the opening in search of cultists. He didn't see any.

With difficulty, his wounded body aching, he hauled himself into the attic and made a beeline for the open window.

He coughed. Blood oozed out of his mouth. *Shit.* The bullet must have pierced his lung. He would drown in his own blood. He didn't have a moment to lose.

He peered out the window at Brady. "Come here, Brady."

Gordon heard something stir in the attic on his right.

Pig Head was training a pistol on him.

"Drop it," said the female voice behind the mask.

Gordon had no intention of obeying her. They fired at each other simultaneously. Her bullet grazed his shoulder. His bullet struck her chest. Moaning, she dropped to her knees. He fired two more slugs into her mask. She sprawled on the attic floor.

"The girls want to see me fly, Dad."

"There aren't any girls. Come here," said Gordon, coughing up more blood and feeling weak.

"Are you hurt?"

"I'll be OK. Come here before you fall. There could be . . . another aftershock," he gasped.

Brady crept toward Gordon, worried about him.

"You're bleeding," said Brady, nearing him.

"We have to get out of here. More cult members are chasing us."

Gordon helped Brady climb through the window into the attic.

Gordon staggered toward the trapdoor, listening to his wound make a sucking sound, his shirt streaked with bright red blood.

The house trembled again.

Gordon fell to his knees.

"Go down the ladder and go to your mother on the front lawn," he said. "Take the car and get out of here."

"What about you?"

"I'm right behind you. Get going."

Brady hesitated. "I'll help you."

"You can't help me. Get out of this house. Get as far away from it as possible and never come back."

Brady continued to hang fire. "I'll help you."

He tried to help Gordon to his feet. Gordon shoved him away.

"Nobody can help me," said Gordon. "Get going."

Grudgingly Brady scrabbled down the ladder. He stood beside the ladder and looked up through the trapdoor opening, waiting for Gordon.

Gordon crawled to the trapdoor and, grimacing, saw him. "Keep going. Don't wait for me."

Brady darted down the staircase.

Gordon crawled down the ladder, smearing it with blood. He reached the floor and fell to his knees, unable to make it to the staircase landing, blood trickling out of his mouth. Mustering what diminishing strength remained to him, he managed to get to his feet.

He saw Hog Head grab Brady's foot in the living room and trip him. Brady fell face down on the carpet.

"Fucking kid," groaned Hog Head through his blood-streaked mask. "I'm gonna kill you."

Gordon felt lightheaded. His knees buckling, he collapsed.

Screwing up his face in agony, Gordon crawled along the floor to the landing, reached over the top step, drew a bead on Hog Head, and blew his head apart with two slugs. Gordon's previous two shots at Hog Head must have only grazed the thug's head, which was obscured by the mask.

Gordon could feel himself losing consciousness, slipping into darkness.

"Dad?" implored Brady, springing to his feet on the living room carpet and staring at him.

Gordon planned to kill Brady to thwart the satanic cult from getting their hands on him. His face sweaty, Gordon trained his piece on Brady. Gordon didn't want Brady to fall into their clutches. He couldn't imagine the horrors they had in store for the kid. He couldn't let them get him.

A pearl of sweat dripped into Gordon's eye, stinging it and forcing him to squint.

Was it really that hopeless for Brady? Couldn't Karen help Brady escape? She was waiting for him outside. Gordon couldn't bring himself to shoot Brady if there was an iota of a chance Brady could escape the cult. But was there an iota of a chance?

Petrified, Brady riveted his eyes on the gun Gordon was aiming at him.

Gordon had no time to think about it. He knew he was going to black out any second. He had to squeeze the trigger now or never.

He couldn't do it. Whether it was from failure of will or from hope that Brady would escape the cult with Karen's help he couldn't say.

Gordon lowered his SIG and waved for Brady to get going.

The last thing Gordon saw was Brady sprinting out the front door.

Chapter 88

Brady scrammed out the front door to his mother.

Karen hugged him. "Are you OK?"

"Yeah. Dad's hurt."

"Where is he?" said Karen, disquiet in her voice.

"On the stairs. He said we have to get out of here and never come back. More pig people are coming after us."

"I'll get him."

"Did you feel the earthquake?"

"What earthquake?"

"The house was shaking like crazy."

"I didn't feel anything. Wait here."

Karen wasn't going to leave Gordon behind. She started to run to the front door when, for the first time, she spotted Armitage's dead body lying on the front lawn with his throat cut and one eye gouged out. She gasped at the grisly sight.

"Hog Head did it," said Brady, his voice quavering with fear.

"Don't look," said Karen, turning Brady away from the cadaver.

Leaving him she rushed to the front door. When she reached it and looked inside, the house fell to shaking violently. Parts of the ceiling crumbled and fell to the floor.

"Another earthquake," said Brady, running to her.

"It's not a quake. It's this house. It's cursed and falling apart. It's not safe."

She needed to find Gordon and leave before the house collapsed with him inside it.

"Gordon," she cried into the living room, her voice urgent.

He didn't answer.

Another section of the ceiling collapsed and fell on the living room carpet. Clouds of plaster dust erupted from the rug and spread through the room.

"He got shot," said Brady.

Karen couldn't leave Gordon, but she dreaded entering the house. The demon was lurking inside. Maybe it was causing the house to disintegrate. The demon could be waiting to control her if she entered the house.

Against her better judgment, Karen belted across the living room to the stairway and searched the landing for Gordon. He was lying motionless on the top riser, staring unseeing ahead of him, his mouth agape, his hand stretched out in front of him, his palm vertical, like he was gesturing for her to stay away.

A huge section of the ceiling cracked and caved in, thundering to the floor and missing her by inches. Plaster dust blossomed upward around her.

She turned and scrammed for the front door. The house by this time was shaking the best part of three feet up and down. She lost her balance thanks to the violent juddering of the floor and fell on the carpet. Above her she saw another chunk of the ceiling getting ready to fall. She sprang to her feet and ran for her life over the debris on the floor, coughing on the thick clouds of plaster dust suffusing the living room.

She tripped over the threshold and tumbled into the front yard at Brady's feet.

Coughing on the plaster dust that coated her body, she got to her feet and tried to brush the dust off.

The house was collapsing.

A terra-cotta tile from the roof fell near Brady and broke into pieces on the grass.

"The girls are still on the roof, Mom," he said, looking up.

Karen scoped out the roof. She didn't see any girls on it. She didn't want to see any. She just wanted to get as far away as possible from this house of demons. Brady was right about one thing. The pig people would arrive any second. They would figure out Gordon had driven her to their house to rescue Brady.

Karen hunkered down and stared Brady in the eye. "We have to go."

"All right, Mom. You *are* my mom."

She smiled at him and tousled his hair.

She stood up and gazed at the crumbling house. "It's so riddled with corruption it's falling apart."

She and Brady had to be long gone before the cultists arrived.

The front yard wasn't shaking, but she could see the house shuddering and imploding. It wasn't any earthquake that was leveling the house. It was the demon. Deirdre's restless spirit that could not find peace beyond the grave because of the ghastly crimes she had committed against her children, crimes that she could never atone for because of the demon possessing her. The demon had been in the process of possessing Karen and would have forced her to kill Brady like Deirdre had killed her two daughters if Karen had stayed in that cursed house any longer. The demon had already forced her to issue death threats against Brady. The next step would have been for her to carry them out.

She grabbed Brady's arm and hightailed it to the rental car.

As they piled into the car, a deafening crash sounded.

The splintering house imploded, fueled with the hate and guilt felt by Deirdre's demon, hate and guilt too strong for her spirit to endure and keep on surviving. In the act of killing herself once again, this time for good, she destroyed the house and all the evil connected to it, and perhaps redeemed herself in small measure by taking with her to the grave the corpses of some of the cultists who had plagued her.

"Theresa wants revenge," said Brady in an eerie voice.

"What?" said Karen, not understanding.

In the shotgun seat Brady withdrew his gun from his trouser pocket and shot Karen in the heart.

Through the windshield he peered up at the roof, which was about to collapse, and saw Theresa and Frieda looking down and smiling at him. They disintegrated into a cloud of flies that dispersed.

ABOUT THE AUTHOR

Multi-award-winning author Bryan Cassiday writes horror fiction and thrillers. His postapocalyptic horror thriller *Horde (Zombie Apocalypse: The Chad Halverson Series Book 6)* won both the Independent Press Award for Best Horror Novel 2022 and the American Fiction Award for Best Horror Novel 2021. His Scott Brody thriller *Threads* won the Independent Press Award for Best Thriller Novel 2023 and the American Fiction Award for Best Hard-Boiled Crime Novel 2022. He lives in Southern California.